Mission Accomplished

by

Sophia Ryan

This is a work of fiction. Names, characters, places, and incidents are either the product of the author's imagination or are used fictitiously, and any resemblance to actual persons living or dead, business establishments, events, or locales, is entirely coincidental.

Mission Accomplished

COPYRIGHT © 2022 by Sophia Ryan

Cover Art by *Diana Carlile*

The Wild Rose Press, Inc.
PO Box 708
Adams Basin, NY 14410-0708
Visit us at www.thewildrosepress.com

Publishing History
First Edition, 2022
Trade Paperback ISBN 978-1-5092-4461-4
Digital ISBN 978-1-5092-4462-1

Published in the United States of America

Dedication

To everyone who finds the
courage to keep moving forward.

Acknowledgments

Most readers skip past the acknowledgement in a book, eager to dig into the good stuff. If that's you, thank you. Enjoy! For those of you who have paused here, also thank you. You deserve more than a blank page, so here we go.

I started this book when my husband was alive. Trying to finish it during the three years following his death was like swimming in a razor-blade-filled tar pit. Grief had hijacked my brain, my heart, my characters, my story, and blinded me to a way through. Without the love and support of the patient souls in my life, encouraging me to continue onward, not just with this book but with life, I wouldn't have been writing this acknowledgment. It's to them that I give the bulk of my gratitude.

Next, I am forever grateful for Diana Carlile, the editor and designer at The Wild Rose Press who helped me get this book—and my seven others—out into the world. And for insisting we include the juicy car scene.

Lastly, this acknowledgement wouldn't be complete if I didn't mention the incredible person who served as a model for the hero in Mission Accomplished. To him, I say, Thank you for Everything.

Chapter One

Alicia Stone had a stomach of iron, nerves of steel, and a will of titanium.

The qualities, forged during her ten years as an emergency room nurse, had served her well—personally and professionally.

Up until this moment.

"You're forcing me to take a vacation?" Heart pounding in her eyeballs, Alicia popped up from her chair and stared down Dan DeSoto, her boss, friend, and mentor. The man was damn lucky he sat behind a solid wooden desk.

"Alicia, please calm down." His poor choice of words confirmed that he was under the gross misconception that telling someone to calm down actually worked.

"No way in hell am I going to calm down until I know what's behind your outrageous idea designed to upend my life."

"I'll explain everything when you sit down."

She took a deep breath, then slowly resumed her seat. As she waited for him to explain, she silently counted to ten, tacking on a few choice words she'd love to say aloud but wouldn't.

"I swear, girl. Only you would consider a vacation punishment," he said with a head shake. "No, HR says I can't force you to take vacation. Not without filling out a lot of paperwork, anyway. But what I can do, as your manager and your friend, is to strongly recommend you take some time away to get over your loss."

Your *loss*. Such a weak word to describe the potent force that had flipped her life upside down and inside out and gutted it.

"I *am* over it," she said. It was mostly true.

Dan's bushy gray eyebrows rose into his forehead, signifying his thoughts on her thin statement.

Sure, there were a few aspects she hadn't yet come to terms with. Like finding out that her entire marriage had been a lie. Like finding out her husband had cheated on her. Like finding out she wasn't the person she thought she was.

But it had been seven months since Jon had died. Almost a year. The expiration date for coddling and wallowing and soul-searching was over. What she needed most was to dedicate herself to her work. Move forward. Like she was doing. The melancholy that still clung to her was no problem. She'd brush it off. Eventually.

"I'm at work, every day, doing my job, just like I always did before—"

He held up his hand to halt her lie. "You're at work, but it's not like before."

Nothing was like before. Her skin prickled into goosebumps that shot a chill through her body. "Dan, cut to the chase. Why am I here in your office instead of out there on the floor doing my job, saving patients?"

He screwed up his mouth into a bottom-lip pucker the way he did when he was gathering his thoughts. Then his face went neutral, no emotion to show what he was feeling about the bomb she had seen coming the second he'd asked her to step into his office.

"Over the past few months, I've received complaints about you."

At hearing the words she never believed she'd hear about her work or her behavior, she felt blood rush from her face, leaving it numb. Her muscles bunched under her like a spring to launch her out of her chair again, but she thwarted the unwise action. Instead, she swallowed her emotion and zipped her mind back through *the past few months* to evaluate any behavior that could have triggered a complaint.

She lifted her chin. Nope. If anything, she was even more efficient than she was before her loss, making absolutely sure she followed the rules to a T, with no emotion fueling her actions so her sometimes wayward mind wouldn't skip a step. Dan's information was obviously faulty, but she'd hear him out and then refute every lie.

"What kind of complaints? From whom?" she asked, the demanding tone burning her mouth.

Dan put on his glasses, picked up the folder on his desk, and opened it. "Nurse Stone is repeatedly short-tempered, rude, inflexible, demanding, aggressive, argumentative…"

Her confidence deflated as the litany of criticisms continued. She hadn't noticed any of the behaviors he was listing. But apparently others had and they'd lost patience with the person she'd become. As someone who had always prided herself on being at the top of her game at work, it was a jagged, bitter pill to swallow.

Locking into the demands of her job was what had kept her together—mind, body, and soul—over the past seven months. Yes, she had hardened her outer shell a bit, but who could blame her? Without that shell, she wouldn't have been able to get back to work, back to her life, as quickly as she had. To be honest, without it, she wouldn't have been able to get out of bed in the morning and survive her twelve-hour days still standing.

"Hardass was mentioned several times." Dan closed the file and removed his glasses, the concern he was feeling for her evident in his soft gaze.

She swallowed the plume of panic rising in her throat. "Dan. I'm good at my job."

"No, you're outstanding at your job. You're the best damn ER nurse I have. You've always been a favorite with staff and patients alike. Something changed in you after Jon died, and believe me, I can understand it." His gaze slid to the photo on his desk. "After LeMar passed, I…I wasn't myself." He cleared his throat, and the gaze that returned to hers was edged in grief that her heart recognized. "But I can't allow your behavior to continue. It's bad for morale and for business—and for your own mental health."

"Then give me some specific scenarios where I've failed, and I'll make sure not to repeat them, but don't send me on a vacation."

"You can't slap a smiley-face bandage on this one and call it good, Alicia. The truth is, grief is running your life, and following a flimsy list of do's and don'ts won't fix it. You need to work through your grief— preferably with the help of a professional—and let go of whatever baggage you're still carrying around from Jon's death. Once you've done that, I'm confident the behavior issue will vanish."

"I saw the grief counselor. It didn't help."

"You went once."

"It was a waste of time. I was trying to get over my grief by not focusing on it every second of every day, and all she wanted to do was trap me there and talk about it nonstop. People grieve differently. You know that. She wanted tears and wailing and zombie brains. That's not me, and minus those textbook signs, she was lost as to how to help me other than push little magic pills."

"Which you refused to take."

"I work ER. I can't walk around numb and in a fog. People will die."

Dan pinched the bridge of his nose, then sighed deeply, showing that his frustration level had risen to a dangerous level. Only their friendship and mutual professional respect were saving her from being fired on the spot. "Is it any better that you're acting like a porcupine, shooting your quills at anyone and everyone in your line of sight?"

He paused, not to let her respond, but to let the gravity of the situation sink in. Besides, there was no answer to his question she could give that would help her.

"I noticed the change in you when you first returned, but I know how strong you are and figured you'd work it out. You refused my suggestion to continue to see the counselor, to take the antidepressants, to take some time off, and I see now that I should have insisted. I won't make the same mistake again."

No, Dan, don't. Please.

"I want you to take some well-deserved time off to figure things out and come back to us your usual kind, efficient, flexible self—the woman we know, admire, and count on."

The joke was on him. That woman was gone and wasn't coming back. Being baptized in the acid of grief and betrayal does that to a person, destroys who they were.

Her gaze dropped to the black ECG line inked on her index finger that she'd gotten after she'd graduated and landed her first nursing job. It was a visual reminder of the three most important tasks in her life—keep her patients alive, keep her relationships alive, and keep herself moving forward, regardless of the challenges ahead or behind. The talisman was no longer working. It was just a jagged line that mirrored her jagged life.

Anger swelled in her at the truth laid before her, and that blip gave her energy to rage against it. Her gaze rose to pierce Dan's.

"That's your solution? Send me on a mission to find myself? That's about the lamest thing I've heard you say." She scoffed, an ugly sound that would seal her fate.

Quiet filled the office and squeezed around her, and the look on her boss' face told her she'd leaped over the line…and made his point. Before she could find the right words to apologize and prevent her firing, he spoke.

"Take the rest of December off. Talk to someone. Work out what's going on inside you. Come in after the first of the year, and we'll reevaluate the situation." Signaling the end of the conversation, he stood and strode across the carpet to his door.

Her legs like jelly, her face burning, she stood and

followed him.

Setting his hand on her shoulder, he squeezed gently. "Take care of yourself, Alicia."
****

Dan's words spun in her head and stomach like a spike-wrapped top as she gathered her things from her locker and left the hospital. On the drive home, she thought of all the reasons he was wrong. As she polished off a bottle of wine in the bath, she accepted the fact that it didn't matter what she thought. It only mattered what he thought because he held her job in his hands. As she turned out the lamp to chase sleep around the room, she resigned herself to figuring out how to make whatever changes were necessary to keep the job that was her lifeline.

While she was wallowing in the contemplative mood, she also accepted that she wasn't past Jon's death. Wasn't past what he'd done to her to make the woman she'd been die along with him in that plane crash. So that's where she'd start—trying to forgive him and herself, sever the last remaining elements tethering her to her lie of a past, and become someone else.

It sounded so cliché. So trite. So common. The every-widow mission to learn to be someone else after half of her had been ripped away, but to save her job, her life, she'd take on that mission. She wouldn't just change. She would become someone who was better than before. She would find a way to enable her greatest self to rise from the ashes of her lesser self. And she knew just the place to make it happen.
****

As she approached the *Welcome to Sandia Hills,*

New Mexico sign, Alicia heard Jon's voice telling her to slow down. Heeding the silent warning, she lifted her lead foot from the accelerator of her rented SUV and applied it to the brake, slowing to a twenty-five-mile-an-hour crawl.

She scanned the area up ahead. The Sheriff's Department SUV that often hid behind the trees at the side of the road just past the sign was absent. For a second, she thought about speeding up, but the memory of the pricy speeding ticket she received on her and Jon's first trip out to the cabin kept her to the posted speed limit.

With a population of just over five thousand full-time residents, the comatose burg in the ten thousand six hundred eighty-foot Sandia Mountains about a half hour from her cabin was home to Doc's Quik Shop, the town's only grocery store and where she'd be buying supplies before entering solitary confinement. It would be her last contact with civilization.

Surprisingly, the store's tiny dirt parking lot was crammed with people and vehicles, including two Sheriff's Department SUVs. The few times she'd visited this place, it had never been busy. *Seems like half the population is there today*, she mused as she steered into the last open space. Hopefully, none of the drama going on inside the store would affect her ability to buy supplies. She did *not* want to drive the hour back to Albuquerque through I-40 traffic.

Supplies list at the ready, she climbed out and locked the door with a beep that drew the gazes of the crowd milling about, and at least two dozen pairs of eyes escorted her to the door. A jingling bell over the door announced her arrival to the store's four occupants, their sharp stares pinning her feet to the floor.

To the strains of *Holly Jolly Christmas*, she scanned the otherwise dead silent space. Behind the counter, the cashier—a thin woman with bottled-platinum hair except for a three-inch strip of black roots bisecting the top of her head—perched on a tall stool. At the far side of the store stood a lanky, broad-shouldered man wearing a coffee-brown Stetson and a matching jacket with the word *Sheriff* in blocky yellow letters. At his side was a heavyset deputy garbed similarly. She recognized the grizzled, bearded man huddled near them, sporting a "Walter White for Prez" T-shirt, as Doc, the store's owner.

Although the four sets of eyes demanded she leave, their voices didn't, so she moved to the counter where a demi-tower of plastic grocery baskets was stacked.

"Afternoon," she said to the cashier as she took two baskets.

The cashier, whose name tag read Pixie, muttered a cool, "Hey," and punctuated the word with a muted pop of the bubblegum in her pink-stained mouth.

"Never seen you guys this busy," Alicia added, an invitation for the woman to dial back her suspicion a few notches.

The opportunity to gossip winning out, Pixie practically beamed. "And it's about to get a whole lot busier."

"Oh really? Why's that?"

Pixie's gaze darted toward the men, then back to Alicia, and she leaned in as if to whisper a secret she wasn't supposed to share. "Doc found a body behind the dumpster a half hour ago. Shot execution style in the head and tortured. Sheriff Johnson thinks the dead man is a gang member who turned witness against them. Name of Cowboy, I think they said. The Albuquerque FBI is on their way here to help investigate, even though Sheriff Johnson told them he didn't want their help."

The store phone rang, and as Pixie turned away to answer it, Alicia took the opportunity to get on with her shopping so she could put this chaos in her rearview mirror. Rubbing elbows with local drama wouldn't aid in her magical plan to rise from her ashes.

She wandered the narrow, reasonably stocked aisles, adding items from her list into the baskets. Standing on tiptoe to reach the big bag of coffee on the highest shelf, she almost toppled forward when a large masculine hand grabbed it out of her reach.

"Let me help you with that, young lady," came a low drawl from behind her. The sheriff stood two feet from her, a lazy smile on his rugged face.

Alicia hated to be called *young lady* almost as much as she hated being called *honey* and *sweetie*, but she gritted her teeth to hold back an admonishment. She'd probably never see the sheriff again, so she wouldn't waste time and energy confronting him about his condescending word usage.

"Thanks," she said and waited for him to hand her the coffee, but he didn't.

"You're not from around here," he said.

"What gave me away?" she said.

"Doc's isn't a place people like you just stumble into."

"People like me?"

His catlike hazel eyes crawled down then up her

body so slowly it felt as if she were being frisked. "Strangers."

"You're probably right about that." She tugged on the bag of coffee in his hand until he released it. "But this isn't my first time here, so technically, I'm not a stranger." She added the bag and a second one to her basket and moved down the aisle to add two loaves of bread.

"What brings you here this time?" he said, right behind her. "Right as snowstorm season is about to hit?"

Biting her tongue to remind her to…well, bite her tongue…she forced a small smile into play and faced him. "Sheriff, this interrogation is making me feel like I should have brought my lawyer with me."

The corner of his mouth twitched in a smile that never broke through. "Interrogation? No, ma'am. This here's just a friendly chat."

A friendly chat usually didn't include the person stalking her, crowding her personal space, and settling his palm firmly on the handle of his holstered weapon as a visible reminder of who had the greater physical power. But she'd get nowhere fast if she didn't at least try to quell whatever suspicions he had wrongly formed about her.

"I'm here to spend the Christmas holiday at my cabin. I needed supplies, and I remembered this store from previous visits."

The sheriff made a show of slowly pulling a little black notebook and pen from his uniform shirt pocket. "That the Anaya cabin? Number 11 off Route 5?"

"What makes you think that?" she asked.

"Well, now. It's the only cabin in these parts not

owned by locals."

"The cabin is off Route 5 and it is Number 11, but I don't call it the Anaya cabin."

"What do you call it?" he asked, pen poised.

"Are you asking me my name?"

Their gazes locked in battle. He grinned, but it didn't reach his eyes, where annoyance gleamed, most likely from what he considered her insolence.

"If you don't mind."

"Alicia Stone," she said and pulled her wallet from her purse and handed him her license in an attempt to shorten the conversation.

He gave it the onceover—twice—before making a notation in his book. "You're a long way from Seattle, Alicia Stone," he said. "I hope you're not up here by yourself."

The truth hovered on the tip of her tongue, but something about this man, about this situation, about the flint in his eyes, made the yes melt like a snowflake, a warning that it would be wiser if he thought she was not alone.

"My husband's with me." *In spirit,* she added silently to spin the lie into a truth.

He gave her a squinty-eyed, you're-lying-your-ass-off stare, then craned his neck to peer over the shelves and out the window toward her SUV, likely looking to see whether her husband occupied one of the seats. Seeing no one, of course, he zeroed his gaze back on her, one eyebrow lifted.

"He's at the cabin," she responded before he could ask. "Probably wondering what's taking me so long."

Technically, Jon was at the cabin—in his clothes hanging in the closet and in the dresser drawers, on the couch facing the massive fireplace, at the kitchen table, in their bed. His essence permeated the entire cabin. The thought swelled her heart, lifting it into her throat. Of course he was there. She swallowed hard to contain the sudden and surprising emotion bubbling up.

The lawman's glare raked over her face, pausing on her mouth, as if he had seen the lie puff out in a telling plume of purple and green smoke.

"Why don't you give him a call? I'll let him know what's going on here so he won't worry."

"Surely you remember that there's no cell reception at the cabin."

"I seem to recall that, yes. City folk like you doing without cellphones and internet more than a minute?" He shook his head. "Mighty strange, if you ask me."

"We like being unplugged while we're here. It's part of the attraction. May I have my license back?"

"Admirable, but not smart, under the circumstances," he said, ignoring her request.

"What circumstances are those?"

He nodded toward the front of the store. "Pixie told you about the man killed out back."

"Yes, but that has nothing to do with us."

"The deceased was a member of a local drug trafficking organization. Many of the suspected members reportedly live up in the area near your cabin. They're ruthless criminals who won't think twice about killing anyone who gets in their way. If they suspect you're law enforcement trying to sniff them out, they won't ask questions. They won't take chances. They'll kill you."

On that dramatic note, he handed back her license. She snatched it from him and slid it back into her wallet, which she returned to her purse. Although she knew he was being overly dramatic to scare her, a chill zipped up her spine at the potential danger, but she refused to bite at his transparent attempt to scare her away.

"If their whereabouts are so well known, why doesn't law enforcement swoop in and clear them out?" she asked.

"We're working on it. But it takes time, proof, and manpower, and we're short all three. That alone is reason enough that you and your husband would be better off heading elsewhere for your vacation. I hear Arizona is nice this time of year."

The bastard! Now, she was beyond perturbed at his attempts to make her leave. "I appreciate your concern for our safety, but neither I nor my husband are in law enforcement or into drugs, and we plan to keep to ourselves within our own property boundaries, so there's no need for *anyone* to be interested in us. Now, if you'll excuse me, I'd like to finish my shopping."

She turned away, but he grabbed her arm, stopping her. She glared at his hand, then lifted that glare to his eyes, holding firm in her best you-don't-intimidate-me stare. "Let go of my arm, please."

"Be careful, Mrs. Stone. You're too pretty a lady to end up like that unfortunate fellow outside." A thin vibrating strand of menace rode his low voice.

"Don't worry, Sheriff. Knowing that we won't be able to count on help from the overworked Sheriff's Department will make us all the more cautious during our stay."

After a tense few moments, he released his hold. She turned and clipped down the aisle away from him.

"Merry Christmas, Mrs. Stone," he called out.

"Happy Holidays," she said as she turned the corner.

Eager to be away from the sheriff and his small-town drama, she quickened her pace and was able to finish, unimpeded, her shopping and her departure, but she felt his eyes on her the entire time.

In her ten years as a nurse, she had developed a sixth sense that enabled her to see the invisible writing on certain people's foreheads that said *danger*. On this man, the word was written in block letters as big as those on his jacket. And they were flashing.

Chapter Two

The rugged tires on Alicia's four-wheel-drive SUV made quick work of thirty-five-minute trek up the tortuous and rutted Route 5. At the National Forest sign, she slowed to watch for the one-foot square metal sign with the number eleven on it that signaled the turnoff to her cabin. She almost missed it, the vegetation around the sign having grown since her last visit fourteen months ago. At the last second, she slammed on the brakes, backed up, then turned off the pavement onto the dirt and gravel road that was buttressed by sentinels of spruce and piñon. A quarter mile up and she was there. The squat eight hundred-square-foot log cabin was tucked at the back of a good-sized clearing and butted the edge of a dense wood that climbed straight up the mountain.

She pulled to a stop and turned off the engine. For a moment, she just stared out the windshield, the thick, tinted glass separating her from the onslaught of memories that would soon rush forward to challenge her beliefs about her marriage, her husband, and herself.

The feeling of homecoming that usually spread across her at this point and began unknotting her tangled nerves was absent, which was surprising. She had felt an affinity with the place from the first day she'd seen it ten years ago. Something about it had always soothed her senses and spoke to her in hushed whispers, like a lullaby only she could hear, one that said she was home. She and Jon had bought the property the day they'd seen it and visited every summer in August around her birthday. Except this year. Because Jon had been dead three months by then. And so had she. She came here, banking on the idea that the cabin's alchemy would work this trip when she needed it most.

Overall, the place looked the same as it had during her last visit. It was as if it had been frozen in time to pay homage to the golden moments she'd enjoyed in her pre-apocalyptic life. Would it be the same inside the cabin, where the bulk of those golden moments lived? Or would she find it changed? Find that everything she thought she knew had been a lie?

Only one way to find out.

She stretched her fingers out of their death grip on the steering wheel. Glancing at the black ECG line inked on her index finger, she heeded its advice to *move forward*. Taking a deep breath, she left the safety of the SUV.

She'd never seen the place in winter. It was as beautiful as it was in summer, only different. More solemn. Cozy. Hunkered. As if it was submitting to its inevitable crawl into hibernation under a blanket of air that was heavy with evergreen and winter's icy breath.

Hearing boisterous bird call above her, she gazed up at the faded blue sky, skimming the tops of the piñon, juniper, and aspen for a glimpse of eagles, hawks, or ospreys that used the broken tops to build nests. She spotted a pair of dark-winged birds gossiping in the gently swaying branches that streaked the dotted whipped-cream clouds across the sky.

She closed her eyes and let the low hum of nature's vibration flow over her. It slowed her rushing tide of thoughts and brought awareness to her *self*, to the taste of her breaths coming and going, the organs powering her body, the bones strengthening her, the blood fueling her. The palpable thought washing over her was that being here would help her bury the skeletal remains of thoughts and memories and tendencies that no longer served her and help her re-create her identity.

And save her job.

That audacious mission would require she make some huge changes to who she was. She'd always lived her life as a by-the-book rule follower, someone who measured twice and cut once, who did the math, twice, and who didn't make risky decisions. Because that path was no longer working for her, maybe the answer was to go in the opposite direction—become someone who could forgo the rules in order to fully immerse in experiences.

At a sudden temperature drop and a shadow veiling her face, she opened her eyes. A puffy cloud edged in titanium had blanketed the sun, and the wind had picked up, spurring the loose wisps of curls around her face to twirl in a frenzied dance. She didn't know what answer the sudden weather change had intended, but she was interpreting it as, "you can no more toss aside your rule book than you can fly under your own power like the birds above you." Oddly, the answer didn't bring her comfort.

The breeze slicing through the trees spurred her forward and up the wooden porch steps. Steps that looked weatherworn and in need of a paint job, she noted as she creaked across the cracked boards of the porch.

She pulled open the screen door and was greeted by the ever-present squeak that Jon claimed was the cabin saying welcome back. Ignoring the squeak—and the holes in the screen—she unlocked the wooden door and shoved it open with a dusty bang as a warning to any creatures lurking inside to prepare for eviction.

The closed-up smell of old memories and abandonment wafted out with puffs of dust, curling her nose and tickling her throat. She stepped inside, letting the screen door slam closed behind her. The interior was darker and shabbier than she remembered. The summer sun had always filled it with such light, freshness, and life. Or maybe it had been Jon who'd done that.

After a quick sweep to check for squatters of the nonhuman kind, she threw open the windows to let the light and air resuscitate life back into the cabin.

Every surface, every corner, every item the light and her gaze touched was covered in dust and memories. Jon's *Psyclepath* mug that proclaimed his love of cycling hanging next to her *Nurses Call The Shots* mug. The faded *chile ristra* magnet he'd bought at the airport their first trip here still clinging to the fridge. His favorite books filling the bookshelves lined up next to hers. The rustic Americana decorations tucked here and there. Swiping away dust would be much easier than swiping away memories.

To hold at bay the wave of emotions rising within her from all the memories, she focused on the task at hand. She'd face the emotions. Head on. But for the last three hours of daylight, all she wanted to do was accomplish the tasks on her Day 1 to-do list and get settled before she allowed herself the luxury of having a useless meltdown.

Focused and forward her mantra, she set to work wiping, sweeping, scrubbing, and mopping every inch of her month-long cocoon. Cleaning done, she put away the food and supplies and stored her first aid kit in the bathroom cabinet. As a nurse, she never left home without it. Lastly, she brought in her two suitcases—one packed with clothes, the other with bedding.

Use of vacuum-sealed storage bags and careful packing had enabled her to fit her bedding and extra blankets into one suitcase. She'd wanted to be prepared if the old furnace failed her. She and Jon had always visited in the summer and had never needed it. But here in December, it was prudent to be prepared.

As she made the bed, chills skated across her skin at the irrational thought that Jon was watching her. They had made love in just about every spot in the cabin, but mostly in this bed. She could still pick out their sounds and scents that lingered in the room. In the mattress. In the checkered curtains billowing at the windows like lungs breathing. In. Out. In. Out.

As difficult as making the bed was, cleaning out the dresser and the closet would be worse. It required her to see and touch the clothes Jon had left behind, a piece or two every visit over their ten-year marriage. When she asked why he left them, he'd said it was so that if someone needing shelter broke into the cabin, they'd have warm, dry clothes to wear. She had countered that the only entities breaking in for shelter and using those clothes would be bugs and critters. He'd just laughed.

Today, when faced with having to see and touch those clothes, knowing his hands and eyes were the last to touch them, she wished he'd just packed them like she'd asked him to, or wished she'd just done it herself, which usually was how she'd done things. That had been their way. She'd been the one in the relationship who took charge, made sure things got done, and he was the one who got to surf through life on a rainbow.

Because that's who she still was, she'd take this matter in hand, too. Get it done.

Grabbing a garbage bag, she yanked open the dresser drawers, scooped up the assorted sweatshirts, sweatpants, T-shirts, boxers, and socks, stuffed them into the bag, and cinched the top tightly. Later, she'd sort them into a keep, donate, or trash pile, but now she'd keep them out of sight.

"That wasn't too bad," she said as she wiped down the dresser and put in her clothes. "Grab 'em and bag 'em. Don't spare them more than a fleeting thought or glance."

Grab 'em and bag 'em was a good plan until she stood, a second bag in hand, in front of the open closet and more of Jon's things. Beanies and caps stacked on the shelf. Hoodies and flannel shirts hanging on the rod—the blue plaid flannel shirt, in particular. The thin line of tiffany blue running through the royal and navy plaid had matched his eyes, eyes that had mesmerized her the first time she'd seen him their first day of college. He'd later confess—on their first date—that the second he'd seen her that first day, he'd turned to his best friend and proclaimed that he'd found the girl he was going to marry.

Alicia slid the shirt off the hanger and brought it to

her face. Along with the mustiness that clings to clothes that haven't been worn in a while was the faded scent of wood smoke and Jon's cologne. Hugging the soft shirt to her chest, she closed her eyes and let a sunshine-warm memory sluice through her mind of the last time he'd worn it.

Fourteen months ago, end of August, her thirtieth birthday, their last visit.

The night had been too warm for a fire, but Jon built one in the fireplace, and they'd shared a bottle of wine in its rosy glow. Halfway through the bottle, they'd stripped off each other's clothes, and he'd used that shirt to tie her wrists together above her head and to the coffee table leg. Their raw sex on the floor in front of the fire had filled the cabin with flickering fornicating shadows and unrestrained moans, spurring and validating their passion and love.

Nothing about that dream night and those that followed had foretold the nightmare ending awaiting them.

A potent cocktail of emptiness, loneliness, and anger gutted her, drawing a strangled moan from her mouth. A sudden and intense pressure squeezed her lungs. Her heart thundered in her ears. Her throat tightened, and she gasped for breath. Emotions and the dizzying sensation of spinning out of control were fast consuming her trembling body.

The nurse in her recognized the panic attack gripping her, but that knowledge didn't change the fact that it felt like a heart attack that was mere beats from ripping away her life.

Air. She needed air.

She dropped the shirt and raced from the room,

from the cabin, and into the yard. Bent over, hands on her knees, she drew in deep breaths of the chilled twilight air to cool her raging panic.

A noise behind her interrupted the self-indulgent freak-out. Alarmed, she jerked upright and spun toward it.

A large tawny dog stood a few yards from her. He didn't look threatening, but as an ER nurse, she had treated too many dog-bite wounds delivered by beloved family pets to completely believe this one presented no danger. She glanced around to see whether his owner was nearby.

Seeing no one, she crouched and held out her hand to the animal. "Well, hello. Where did you come from?"

The dog ran to her and jumped on her, paws on her shoulders, licking her face so enthusiastically she nearly fell over. Laughing, she turned her head to stop the wet assault and stood.

"You're certainly a friendly pup," she said, scratching behind his ears.

The dog panted.

"You thirsty?"

His tongue lolled out of his mouth, an action she took as a yes.

"I'll bring you some water, but then you should get home before it gets dark."

When she went inside for the water, he nosed his way in through the screen door and followed her into the kitchen. He sat on his haunches, watching her every move.

"I don't remember inviting you in." She set the bowl in front of him.

Dipping his snout close to the bowl, he examined the water but didn't drink. Instead, he padded to the fridge, sat in front of it, and looked back at her.

"Oh, so you're hungry?"

The dog jumped up, stood on his hind legs like he was dancing, and woofed his affirmative response.

She laughed at his antics. "Lucky for you, I was about to start dinner. You can have the steak bone, but then you're outta here. Your owner probably has dinner waiting for you at home." She knelt. "But first, let's check to see whether you're carrying any creepy crawlies."

A close inspection found no unwelcome boarders. It also revealed that he was well cared for. His short coat was clean, shiny, and unmatted, and no ribs showed. Likely someone's pet.

He stayed by her side as she prepared dinner and followed her to the table when the food was ready, charming her into sharing her steak and steamed vegetables. While she did dishes, he enjoyed a gnaw on the bone she'd promised him, and he settled on the couch next to her as she read. Like it was their routine.

A couple of hours later, eyes, mind, and body heavy with exhaustion, she rose from the couch and stretched.

"Okay, fella," she said to the dog who hadn't left her side since he arrived. "I enjoyed your company, but it's time for you to go. I'm off to bed." She urged him off the couch, with the intent to shoo him out the door, but he had a different idea. He trotted into the bedroom, curled up on the braided rug beside the bed, his head resting on Jon's flannel shirt that she'd forgotten to pick up, and looked at her through pleading blue eyes.

He was a big dog. She couldn't deadlift him, and she didn't want to potentially hurt him by dragging him out of the cabin. Letting him stay was a mistake, but what the hell. She needed sleep and wasn't up for a fight.

"You can stay the night, but tomorrow you're going home," she said in her firmest voice.

Considering the matter settled, the dog released a contented sigh and closed his eyes.

After a hot shower to wash off the day's grime and the residue from her emotion overload, Alicia rechecked the doors and windows to make sure they were locked, then turned out the lights. She had just crawled into bed and turned off her lamp when her guest growled, jumped up, and with a barrage of barking raced to the front door.

Flipping on the lamp, she followed him. She turned on the porch light and peeked out in time to see a critter scurry into the darkness. Once the creature vanished, the dog calmed. After sending her gaze on a final slow crawl across the front yard, she turned off the light, rechecked the doors and windows, and carried with her to the bedroom a heavy sense of uneasiness.

Heading straight for the closet, she pulled down the locked box that held Jon's pistol, a nearly full box of bullets, a gun-cleaning kit, and the gun manual and set it on the rug. Sitting beside the dog, she followed the manual to unload the gun, clean it, reload it, and set the safety.

She had shot the weapon before but not often enough to feel comfortable doing so. Over the next couple of days, she'd take it out for target practice to make sure she remembered the basics.

Just in case.

The tingles scurrying up her spine and over her shoulders suggested there might be a case, and unless her aim and reflexes were very good, this loaded pistol wouldn't stop whatever might be coming for her.

****

An hour before dawn, Alicia gave up the bed to the memories that had tossed and turned her all night. After washing up and dressing, she went to the kitchen to make coffee and fix breakfast. The scents of cooking soon drew her overnight guest into the kitchen, and he plopped down at her feet.

"Go outside and do your business before you eat," she said and opened the doors. "I don't like messes."

He bounded into the woods so fast she was sure he'd headed for home, but minutes later, he was scratching on the door and grumbling for his share of breakfast. The way he ate, her supplies wouldn't last the month. She'd have to make another trip to Doc's. And just in case he decided to stay or to continue his visits, she'd also buy a bag of dog food.

She appreciated his presence as she started on the tasks filling her Day 2 to-do list. Task No. 1 was to hike up the steep path behind her cabin to locate the spot where cell service was strong enough to make calls. She grabbed a kitchen trash bag and cut it into long, narrow strips, then stuffed them along with a bottle of water into her backpack. She pulled on her boots, hat, and jacket, and grabbed her phone.

"Let's go, Panza," she said to her companion, deciding to call him by the name that befitted him, Sancho Panza being Don Quixote's devoted sidekick who accompanied him on his quest and guided him out of madness.

She and her *guide* pushed up the pine-needle carpeted path, the flashlight on her phone showing the way through the predawn light. This speck of the world was quiet, the fishhook moon sleeping in the slate sky, but the sun was minutes from rising and taking command of the day.

She held her phone aloft as she climbed, watching for the bars to appear. Finally, in a relatively open area where tree cover was less dense, a couple of bars danced upward. She tied a plastic strip around a trunk on each side of the path to mark the beginning of the spot.

As she ascended, so too did the bars, indicating a stronger signal, and all along the way, she tied more strips to trees to mark the trail. She'd remove the ties at the end of her visit so it didn't endanger the wildlife, but for now, she'd leave the breadcrumbs in place in case she had to find the spot quickly.

At the spot where the signal was strongest, she tied a final two strips, then she shrugged off her backpack, sat, and turned on her phone. A plethora of texts, emails, and phone messages awaited—from friends, co-workers, her dad, Jon's sister—each filled with expressions of concern.

Taken as a whole, the missives suggested that everyone in her circle thought she was up here falling apart on the mountain. The half-truth she'd told them was that she was taking time off from work during Christmas and coming here to pack up the cabin to sell. Apparently, her skills as a liar left a lot to be desired. Or maybe their concerns stemmed more from her decision to run off across the country to an isolated mountain cabin in winter by herself less than a year after the love of her life died and stay for a month. And what city girl in that environment wouldn't be contemplating suicide?

Uh, me.

Maybe it was insane to leave her familiar environment for an isolated one where she had no one to talk to and nothing to do but remember and feel and immerse herself in examining her old path and planning a new one. Yes, it was painful. And nerve-wracking. But she wasn't suicidal. Far from it. She had high hopes for seeds of change to germinate during this trip that would lead to a lush harvest of life-changing possibilities.

She knew who she didn't want to be and would use that knowledge to inform her decisions about who she *did* want to be. Whoever that turned out to be, one thing was very certain. She would make it back alive and whole and sane. There was no other option.

After sending quick texts saying—*Thanks, I'm doing great!*—she turned off the phone and slipped it into her backpack. Being in this place would allow her time and space to evaluate *what had been* and weigh each element for value and verity. It would help her let go of the baggage that had changed her so radically it had threatened her job. Clarity—like the cabin itself— was too far away to see, but the focus would come and, with it, answers that would help her decide *what was to come*.

The crack of two gunshots, seconds apart, ripped a hole in the stillness. Fairly close, by the sound of it. Hunting wasn't allowed in this area, and hunters didn't hunt in near darkness. Unless they were poaching. Or hunting two-legged prey.

Panza had scrambled to all fours at the sound, nose up to sniff the air. A cold sliver of warning pierced the spot between Alicia's shoulder blades, the feeling that usually heralded a patient's attack. At its most basic, the sign simply warned of danger.

An urgency to get back to the cabin rushed over her, and she stood, slinging her backpack over her shoulder. She and Panza headed home just as the sun burst over the mountain, its beams zigzagging between the trees and down the path toward the cabin.

Chapter Three

A soft noise jerked FBI Special Agent Nick Navarro up out of a hazy sleep. The charcoal gray light filtering in through the cracked window said it was an hour or so before dawn.

He heard the sound again, and this time identified it as soft rapping on his door.

Tightly gripping the gun that almost never left his hand, he rolled to his feet. He opened the door a crack and filled it with the business end of his gun.

"What?" he growled at the threat.

"Man, it's me. Let me in."

At the nervous low voice of his informant, Kei Askook, aka, Kook, Nick opened the door. As soon as the gap was wide enough for his skinny body to slither through, Kook slipped into the tiny travel trailer, his eyes wide with what looked like fear. "Man, you gotta get out of here. Now."

"Why?"

"Henry's got some of the leaders all spun up about you. They're planning to search your trailer and question you after breakfast."

Henry Duggar had been a pain in Nick's ass since day one, always questioning him, trying to trip him up, and talking shit about him. Well, not about him…about Rey Cruz, Nick's alias while undercover with the Los Matos gang. Duggar had finally said the right words to make the right people pay attention.

"How do you know?" Nick said.

"I overheard the guards talking just now when I went to get coffee." Kook's grip on the plastic cup in his hand tightened so much the lid popped open. "If it goes down and you're here, I can't help you, man. They'll kill me. I got a wife and kids…"

Nick squeezed Kook's shoulder to keep him from spinning out. "You need to get your family out. Now. This is the only warning I can give you. I'll be back. And I won't be alone."

Kook nodded, and Nick guided him toward the door.

The man stopped and turned back. "I almost forgot." He dug into his pocket, pulled out a key and a scrap of paper, and handed them to Nick.

"What's this?"

"The key to the POS truck. It works okay unless you turn it off then try to start it again right away. You gotta let it sit four or five minutes. On the paper is the new code to the gate."

"Thanks, man." Nick offered his hand to the criminal who might have saved his life.

Kook shook it. "Get out quick and get as far away as fast as you can. They won't stop 'til they find you. You know what they did to Cowboy."

Nick nodded. He'd captured the brutal torture and slaughter on his phone, and the images were burned into his brain.

As Kook rushed out of the trailer toward his own several yards away, Nick swept his gaze across the Los Matos compound. Nothing stirred. No sign of the guards. But he'd found, with this gang, that routines changed in a heartbeat and for no apparent reason.

Not wanting to waste another second of Kook's warning, he pulled the army-green duffel bag out of its hiding place under the floor. He'd leave everything else—a few clothes and toiletries—behind. His only mission now was to get the duffel containing the evidence he'd collected over the past five months, three weeks, and two days and get it to his team. Evidence that would put the members of the drug trafficking and terror organization away for the rest of their miserable lives.

He shut the door and made a beeline for the gate, sweeping the darkness with his searching gaze and keeping his ears cocked for the smallest of sounds that indicated he had company. Sweat dotted his forehead despite the chill in the air, his muscles clenched, and his heart pounded like surf in his ears, signs confirming that his senses were fully engaged. He'd need them all to get out of here alive.

The fishhook moon did little to light his way across the cold ground, but he didn't need the light. He knew where he was going, had practiced this maneuver so many times he could do it blind.

Thirty feet more.

Twenty.

The towering metal gate loomed before him, the light on the lock panel a solid green. He punched in the code, and the mechanism opened with a beep. He rolled the gate open, then ran to the vehicle lot a few yards away to locate the POS truck.

As he rounded the tailgate, he sensed a presence behind him. He spun around just as one of the guards, Harvey Duggar—Henry's brother—walked out of the semidarkness.

"Yo, Cruz. Where you sneaking off to this early?" Harvey asked.

In rapid fire, Nick clicked off his options. *Knock him out. Choke him out. Shoot him. A gunshot will gain attention. A choke out will take too long.*

Nick's heart shifted in his chest the second the guard stepped closer and eyed the duffel.

"What's in the bag?" the man said.

Option one it is.

As if sensing some vague danger, Harvey raised his gun. "Put down the—"

Before Harvey had finished his sentence, Nick swung the duffel in a tight arch and hit him upside the head, propelling him sideways and knocking him hard to the ground, gun flying out of his hand.

Nick yanked open the truck door and slung the duffel inside. A shot sounded from behind him, the bullet's ping against the truck door giving proof that Harvey wasn't out. Nick raised his weapon as he spun around and shot, giving the man a third eye.

Definitely out now.

He jumped into the truck, fired up the engine, then roared through the gate and headed down the winding mountain road that would take him into town. To his team. Once the evidence was safe, he'd deal with his remorse at taking another life, but now he needed all his attention on completing his mission.

Behind him, an alarm sounded in the compound. Likely they'd heard the shot, discovered the open gate, and found Harvey's body. When they also realized Rey Cruz was gone, they'd be after him. And like Kook said, if they caught him, they'd kill him. And take the evidence. A glance at the duffel in the seat next to him was a reminder that defeat wasn't an option. He stretched out a hand to pull it closer, and a sharp stab in his side ripped the breath from his lungs.

He flipped on the interior light. Blood blanketed his side at his waist and hip and down his thigh. A lift of his T-shirt showed a seeping hole in his side.

Son-of-a-bitch. Harvey had shot him. The *pinche* who couldn't hit a target two feet away.

Panic started to uncoil inside Nick's gut, but he fisted it down. Panic would get him killed. Calm logic and strict adherence to his training would get him through this.

He braked hard, turning the tires into the side of the mountain so it wouldn't roll, and climbed out. He shrugged out of his jacket and shirt, roped the shirt, wrapped it around the wound over his T-shirt, and tied it tight, then pulled his jacket back on and slid into the truck. He shifted into gear, and the engine sputtered and died, refusing to fire to life even after several tries.

"Fuck!" he yelled and evaluated his next step. It for damn sure wasn't to wait four or five minutes for the truck to cooperate.

The truck would roll most of the way into town on momentum alone. Only, the slope ended too far from where he needed to be, which meant he'd be caught or bleed out before he got to his team or they to him. Also, his bleeding would only get worse. He could pass out behind the wheel, end up killing himself or someone else. Driving was out. So was walking. It was a good thirty minutes down by vehicle. He'd die before he got there.

He focused his gaze beyond the dirty and cracked

windshield and scoured the surroundings. The truck lights showed nothing but trees and more trees and… A glint of metal a few yards away caught his eye. A sign with the number eleven on it.

A sliver of hope sparked through him. As part of his research before starting this assignment, he'd located a place not far from the gang's compound where he could get away if needed, a safe house of sorts. The cabin at the end of the quarter-mile dirt road was it. The available intel indicated that the owners were from out of state and visited once a year in the summer. He'd checked it out months ago just to find it but hadn't been back since.

Covering his tracks and holing up in that cabin until help arrived was his best and maybe only hope for survival. Even with the life bleeding out of him, he could walk there in less than five minutes. He'd call his team, then clean himself up and hope for the best.

Nick climbed out and grabbed the duffel, setting it at the side of the road. He flipped off the truck lights and turned the steering wheel to point the wheels toward the mountain cliff, then pushed. Gravity propelled the truck forward and raced it toward the edge. He watched it go over and heard it crash through the trees to the ravine below. He picked up the duffel and headed down the dirt road to the cabin just as dawn filtered through all but the thickest parts of the woods.

Halfway to the cabin, he dropped the bag that now seemed to weigh a ton and stole a precious moment to lean against a tree and fill his lungs with a deep enough breath of frigid air to keep going. The pain in his side had amplified and was radiating through his body. And fuck, he was freezing.

If he lost much more blood, he'd be dead. If the gang found him, he'd be dead. Hell, he'd probably be dead no matter what happened next. But he wasn't giving up. When he was dead, he'd give up. Right now, he had a job to do—get the evidence to safety and call his team. If he managed that, it didn't matter what happened to him. Ignoring the pain in his side, he grabbed the bag, pushed off against the tree, and headed onward.

Minutes later, he halted at the edge of the clearing where the cabin stood. The silver SUV parked in front wore local plates. The owners, departing from their normal routine? Or the gang, expanding territory? He should have checked it again before now.

From the safety of the trees, he analyzed the area, watching for movement, listening for any sound, alert to anything that indicated a threat. Except for birdsong and two squirrels racing each other across the clearing to the cover of the woods, it was still and quiet.

The snake of danger that usually slithered up his spine when he was walking into a trap was largely absent. With his body not fully functional, he didn't trust the absence of that warning, but it didn't matter. He was going for it. It was his only option.

Pressing his hand to his injury to protect it as well as he could, he ran crouched over to the squat woodshed that sat catty-corner to and several yards from the cabin. Every step was like a knife stab to his body, but he made it and went inside. Thick logs climbed more than halfway to the ceiling, and behind him, on the wall, hung a dull axe.

He moved a few of the logs and set the duffel in the open space, then piled the logs on top to hide it. The actions nearly yanked his legs out from under him, and he braced a hand against the wall to steady himself. After taking a moment to breathe through the nausea and light-headedness, he forced himself upright, fished his phone from his pocket, and stepped outside to call his team.

No cell service. Man, this wasn't his day.

New plan. Take the SUV, hopefully without having to shoot anybody else, and get close enough to town to call his team and tell them where he'd stashed the duffel. He couldn't risk taking it with him and having the gang find him.

He checked his gun. Full magazine, minus the one he'd used on Harvey.

Leaving the shed, gun at the ready, he crept toward the cabin. His legs were already feeling rubbery, and a chill blanketed him, but his mind willed his body to ignore the weakness. One foot on the step and a big yellow dog raced around the corner of the cabin. Right behind him was a woman—late twenties, slim build, five-four, long red hair, faded blue jeans, purple ski jacket, brown hiking boots, dark purple backpack slung over her shoulders.

Nick backed up a few steps and faced the duo head on, setting his wobbling legs to firm just as the woman came to a full stop.

The dog, who looked the bigger threat, didn't even bark. Instead, he pranced over to Nick like they were best buds and licked the hand that held the gun. Reminding him that he held a gun. He raised it toward the woman.

"Give me the keys to the SUV."

The woman's questioning gaze had been scouring

his body in the seconds since they'd come face-to-face. Now that gaze settled tight on his eyes.

"I could do that," she said, "but with that wound, you wouldn't get more than a half mile down the mountain before you passed out and drove off the road, killing yourself and anyone unlucky enough to be on the road with you."

"Then, you drive. My gun will help you navigate."

"You're still going to pass out, and when you do, I'll have no choice but to get the sheriff involved. There's no hospital or urgent care facility for miles, and I don't want to have to explain why I have a dead body in my vehicle."

Well, shit. The local sheriff was the gang's head man and the one alerting them when search or arrest warrants were issued for members. Or so said the evidence he'd collected. That the woman was up here, in the middle of Matos territory, hadn't freaked out like any normal person would when seeing blood oozing from a body, and knew the sheriff pointed to the possibility that she was one of them.

Nick was out of ideas, his brain using all its energy to focus on not passing out. "Spare me the doom and gloom and just give me the fucking keys."

"There're inside. How about we go in and get them. And, if you like, I'll take a quick look at that wound." She took a step toward him.

He brought the gun up again and shook his head in a clear warning not to come any closer.

She stopped and raised her hands, palms facing him, in the universal sign of, *I'm not a threat*, which more often than not was a ruse, Nick had discovered.

"I'm Alicia, by the way. And you are…"

"Not interested in chatting."

"I don't blame you. I imagine it's hard to talk right now, with blood seeping from that wound in your side. But believe it or not, this is your lucky day." As if she'd interpreted his doubtful look, she added, "I'm a nurse. I can bandage your wounds so you can be on your way. Safely."

A nurse? Okay, but it still didn't mean he could trust her. "Why would you help me?"

Her gaze dropped to his wound before again meeting his eyes. "You're hurt. Pretty badly, too, if that blood soaking your clothes is any indication."

"And you're honor bound to uphold your Hippocratic oath?"

"That's only for doctors."

"Nurses don't get one?"

"Of course we do."

"Wanna tell me before I bleed to death?"

"Nurses pledge to treat whoever's in need and to abstain from deleterious and mischievous behavior."

If he weren't minutes from dying, he would have appreciated the wry tone and could have given her a grin and not a grimace. He faltered, the gun lowering.

She stepped forward.

"Stay back," he said.

She didn't listen. That alone was reason enough to shoot her. He told himself to shoot her. But something—maybe the honest concern on her face— stopped him. And then it was too late. She was at his side, sliding her arm around him and staring up at him with eyes the color of green sage.

"Let's get you inside," she said, her voice commanding, like it wasn't a request.

In the ultimate betrayal, his body allowed her to guide him up the steps and into the cabin. With his luck, a posse of gang members waited for him inside to bring a quick end to his suffering.

After the woman kicked the door closed behind them with one booted foot, Nick mapped in detail the visible interior. Kitchen, living room, two doors off the living room, likely a bedroom and bathroom. The three-person dinette pushed against the window in the kitchen. The coatrack, next to the door, on which hung a Seahawks key ring with a key, probably to the cabin, and a key fob to her SUV. He'd pocket the fob and get the hell out of here as soon as he could.

Other than the dog, it appeared she was alone. Nothing he saw indicated that she was with the gang, but the lone fact that she was here was suspicious.

She guided him toward the couch, but he redirected. "No. The table."

"It would be better for you to lie down," she said.

He left her side, staggered to a chair, and plopped into it.

"The table it is." She joined him and slipped out of her coat, hat, and backpack, setting them out of the way. She touched his arm. "I'll be right back."

He grabbed her hand. "Where are you going?"

"My first aid kit's in the bathroom," she said.

Her hand tight in his, he noticed the thin black ECG line tattoo that ran along her index finger. If she had one tattoo, she likely had others. And if she had the Matos tattoo that all members wore to show allegiance—a knife dripping blood impaling the side of a skull—he'd know his next step.

"Show me your tattoos," he said.

The look on her face said those were the last words she expected from his mouth, and the scoff that followed it suggested he was an idiot for even asking.

"I'm not showing you my tattoos."

She tried to jerk her hand away, but he held firm and raised his gun. "I insist."

She raised her chin in defiance. "I insist more."

"Now, goddammit," he growled.

"We're wasting precious time on this nonsense," she said, her voice firm and insistent. "You're bleeding to death."

"Show me, or I'll fucking strip you down and find them myself." The words gritted out through his teeth, hopefully showing her that he was in no mood for defiance.

"You're in no condition to do that," she said. "Especially if I'm fighting you. One good jab of my fist into your wound would be enough to take you down."

"You're not the type to inflict harm."

"You want to bet your life on it?"

"You want to bet that your fists are more lethal than my bullets?" he whispered.

He didn't move, and except for her pulse hammering wildly in her lovely throat, she didn't move either. But the air between them was pulsing, almost alive. Every breath he took fed the ice-cold lightning storm raging through his veins.

"I don't believe you'll shoot me," she whispered back, in almost a dare, her eyes pinned to his.

She was right. He wouldn't. Unless he had to. But it would be safer for him if she believed he would shoot. He didn't want to scare this woman, but it was better that than her fighting him. He needed to control this situation, or it could have dire circumstances for both of them. His only option was to ramp up his asshole persona. The time-tested tactic for throwing opponents off their game—if even for a moment— might stun her into compliance and enable him to avoid more drastic measures.

His sharp gaze locked into hers, he rose from the chair. Taking a second to steady himself, he stepped into her space, his bigger body dwarfing hers, and he shuffled her backward until her back kissed the counter. He kept coming until their bodies met, chest to chest, thigh to thigh, core to core. He was so close he could hear her fluttery breath, inhale her flowery scent, feel her soft breasts surrender against his hard chest and his skin absorbing her body's warmth.

He rubbed the tip of his gun over the jagged black line on her hand. "What does this one mean to you?"

Her throat bobbed in a hard swallow. She was scared. He had heard it in her voice and saw it in her eyes. But he admired that she kept her gaze locked on his, her spine rigid, refusing to cower. She was one tough woman, whoever she was.

"That my most important job is to keep my patients alive, keep their hearts beating," she said. More evidence that she was a nurse.

"Next," he said.

She stood still, glaring at him, her lips ziplocked.

Fine. She had chosen this path, not him. "Turn around," he said.

"Why?"

He spun her around to face the counter. Her hands braced on the edge.

He tried to pull up the back of her shirt with one

hand, but that thick storm of fiery hair blocked him. "Hold your hair up."

When she didn't, he pressed against her backside and bit the top of her shoulder where it met her neck. "Do it." Her body trembled against his.

"You know," she said, gathering her hair in her hands, "This kind of caveman barbarity doesn't make me want to help save your life. You could think about being a little nicer."

Her words were feisty, but there was a tremor to them that said her fear was stronger than she pretended. Its presence both pricked and relieved his conscience.

No tattoos, gang or otherwise, on her back or neck, he discovered when he lifted her T-shirt. But the sweet curves carved into her silky skin carried a dusting of rose-gold freckles, and up her torso floated several thin, parachute-like seeds of a dandelion that originated from underneath the low band of her jeans. He tucked a finger into the denim band and pulled it down an inch. Before she twisted away, he saw a puffball sitting low on her hip, ripe with seeds ready to release, some having just left.

"And that one?" he said.

"A reminder to spread healing love into the world."

"Any more tattoos?"

"No."

Her slight pause and exaggeration of the word told him she was lying, but the adrenaline rushing through his veins that had been helping him stand and search her body was on empty.

Releasing her shirt, he stepped back and swayed, his stomach plunging into his feet. He just managed to get back into the chair without falling and swallowed a few times to keep from throwing up.

"Can I go get the medical kit now, or would you rather I stand here and watch you bleed to death?"

The woman had bite. That was for sure. He waved the gun toward the bathroom, and off she went.

He kept his gaze focused on the path she'd taken and instantly realized his mistake. She could have a gun in there, and he had let her go get it. Fuck. His incompetence over the past half hour had been appalling. His tombstone would read, *Here lies Special Agent Nick Navarro, done in by a series of fuckups.*

Holding his weapon as steady as he could, he pointed it toward the bathroom. If she came out, gun blazing, he'd get in at least one lethal shot and there'd be two of them dying in this cabin before nightfall.

A shaky sigh of relief exited his lips when she returned armed only with a large rectangular box in her hands. Setting it on the table, she opened it and pulled out assorted medical supplies, then turned to him and put her hands to the front of his jacket. "Let's get this off you."

She removed his jacket, gently but rapidly, and laid it beside him. Applying quick fingers to the blood-soaked flannel shirt knotted around his wound, she untied it, and it joined his jacket, then she grabbed the scissors from the box.

He caught her by the wrist. The spurt of energy it used up made his head swim. He was nauseated and having trouble keeping his eyes focused. Chills hugged his body.

"I'm cutting your T-shirt off," she said. "Pulling it over your head will be too painful."

Not having the strength to oppose her, he released

her. Let her stab him in his fucking black heart and get it over with.

The thing that bothered him most about dying wasn't the dying part. His old friend, Death, had shadowed him for nearly two decades, first in high school with his love of extreme sports, then during his stint in the Marines, and now with the FBI. No, the worst thing about dying today from an idiot gang member's bullet was knowing he'd failed—failed his mission, his team, the public he'd sworn to protect.

Wouldn't his old man just love that, knowing that what he'd suspected all along was true, being able to say, I told you so? The thought pissed him off so much it gave him a burst of energy to stay alive. Just for spite.

Chapter Four

Fear electrified the blood flowing in Alicia's veins, but she ignored it. Calm logic and strict adherence to her training would get her through this ordeal alive.

She'd patch the man up and send him on his way. If he refused to leave, she'd get away as soon as she could—he'd pass out sooner or later—and go find the sheriff. But first things first.

Scissors in hand, she cut his blood-soaked T-shirt down the middle, neck to hem, front and back, then pulled it off his shoulder on his uninjured side and peeled it away from his bloody side.

He gritted his teeth against the pain the movement caused, but a small groan made its way out through his tight lips. The sound squeezed her heart in empathy. She knew it had to feel like his skin was being lifted away with the sticky scrap. Despite all his bravado and bluster, his face was pale and clammy, his teeth and eyes clenching as if he tried to control the pain and shivers surging through him.

She'd never been shot, but she'd treated enough patients who had to know the pain was all-consuming until the meds kicked in. The pain reliever in her kit was limited to a nearly full bottle of extra-strength ibuprofen and a half-full bottle of a powerful opioid that Jon had been prescribed two years ago when he'd had surgery on his wrist. The narcotic had made him nauseated, hence the half-filled bottle. The narcotic would be more effective than the ibuprofen for her patient, but it would be unethical to offer it. Hopefully, the ibuprofen and the antibiotic ointment enhanced with a numbing agent would be enough to dull his pain.

Panza stood watch as she unpacked the needed items from her kit and put water on to heat. She was surprised the canine hadn't come unhinged at the sight of this stranger. But just because he hadn't attacked didn't mean the man presented no danger. Not for a second did she allow herself to believe he wasn't trouble. He was. With a capital T. Regardless, as a nurse, she was obligated to treat him. He might still die, but if he did, it damn sure wouldn't be because she failed to do her job.

Pushing aside all thoughts unrelated to the task at hand, she assessed his bloody torso and wounds. Clear entrance and exit wounds on his right side about an inch in were bleeding out. Blood staining his skin from above his bellybutton down to his groin and beyond indicated significant blood loss.

A few more minutes out there and he'd have died.

A few more minutes in here without treatment and he would die.

Working fast, she opened two quick-clot hemostatic pads and snapped on a pair of gloves. Taking a second to glance at the tattoo on her finger, she moved closer to him, her nostrils flaring at the scent of the metal bite of his blood. Her stomach pitched, but she swallowed to contain the nausea. She placed the pads on his wounds—one on the front, the other on the back—and pressed hard, leaning into his body with most of her weight.

His breath dragged through his gritted teeth, his body jerked and tensed, and his hand gripped the table edge. "Damn, woman," he said. "What the hell kind of nurse are you? Tying to fucking kill me with as much pain as possible."

"Stop being such a baby and hold still, or I'll let you bleed to death."

"And break your oath?"

She smiled that he remembered their earlier conversation. Nothing wrong with his mind. "Dead men tell no tales."

"That's comforting," he said.

She kept the pressure strong and hoped he was a fast clotter. She wasn't sure how long either one of them could hold out. It took a lot of muscle power to stop bleeding wounds. And by the pallor of his face, he didn't have much life left in him.

After a few minutes, her arms and his body trembling, a clot formed around the holes in his side. She'd stopped the bleeding, his own body aiding in squeezing the hole together and stopping the flow, but a glance at his face said it might not be enough to save him. He was fading fast and looked a few heartbeats away from accepting his reservation to a shiny morgue table.

She removed the saturated pads and added them to the growing pile of bloody items filling the trash can. "You're a fast clotter," she said to engage and encourage him.

"One of my many talents." Even pitted with pain, his wit came through, revealing his strong will.

"Right now, it's a really good one to have." She pulled off her gloves and brought the warmed water and handful of cloths to the table, setting them next to the saline from her kit.

"That bad, huh?" he asked, his eyes locked on hers.

In her ten years as a nurse, she had become skilled at identifying the range of emotions patients revealed through their eyes. The emotion revealed in the intense gaze that gripped hers was fear—one of the oldest and most primal.

To be honest, she was right there with him, feeling the fear but unwilling to give in to it. *Strong emotions steal one's ability to think clearly and render actions and decisions made under their influence ineffective.* That was a lesson she'd learned early in her career. His quick suppression of the emotion suggested that somewhere along the line he'd learned the same lesson.

"No, because this is your lucky day," she said.

"Gonna have to disagree with you on that assessment, sweetheart. How bad?"

"Without the aid of medical imaging, I can't be absolutely sure of my diagnosis, but from visual inspection alone, it looks fairly superficial, likely with no serious internal damage. But I need to clean your wounds and inspect your body for signs that indicate the bullet broke up and took dangerous turns."

"Which would require more medical attention than you can provide," he said with a knowing tone that suggested he was no stranger to receiving medical treatment.

"Yes. But like I said, it doesn't appear that's the case. Were you shot with a handgun?"

His eyes narrowed and bore into her. "Why would you think that?"

"Your entry and exit wounds are fairly small.

Bullets from other types of guns can leave gaping exit wounds the size of an orange. Your wounds are bad, but nowhere near as bad as they could have been had a different weapon been used."

"Cool. Slap on a couple of bandages and I'll get the hell outta here."

His blasé tone belied the strain in his eyes and the tightness around his mouth that told a different story.

"I'll get to that, but first, undo your jeans and push them and your underwear down."

"As luscious as you are, sweetness, I'm not in the mood for sex."

Luscious. That word hadn't been on Dan's list. "I need you to move your jeans out of the way so I can clean your wounds and the surrounding areas. The bullet went through your jacket and your shirts, dragging in God knows what when it went through you. If infection sets in, you'll die. Instead of giving me a hard time, how about you help me save your life."

Her reasoning was sound, her tone authoritarian, so the logical course would be for him to do as she asked, but he just starred at her, and in those melted midnight eyes, she could see the thought process spinning in his mind. She understood his hesitation. He had bullet holes in him, and his shirt was off. With his pants down, too, it left him completely vulnerable, even with that big gun of his, and obliterated his sense of control. And control seemed to be very important to this man. Even so, she wasn't budging on her need to control this scenario. This was her turf, and she'd have it her way.

At his continued silence, she ramped up her request to a challenge. "Pull them down, or I'll do it for you."

A bronze light flickered in his hooded eyes, and

one corner of his mouth turned up in a faint grin. "Okay," he said, his voice rough and low. "Do it for me."

She was no stranger to patients slinging suggestive comments, and she'd learned to let them bounce off. But somehow, this man's suggestive tone and that spark in his eyes struck her deep, causing her pulse to ping-pong at the side of her throat and her body to suffuse with heat. In an attempt to get a grip on her professionalism and the task at hand, she shot him a laser-focused glare. "Stand up."

After a moment, he struggled to his feet, eyes on her, hands holding on to the table for support.

Keeping her gaze locked on her hands, which had started tingling the second she touched his fly, she yanked open the button and wrangled down the zipper over his sizable bulge. His hand settled lightly on her head at her first touch of his fly, making the action of exposing him feel intimate and routine.

Focus! She shouted the order in her head and shoved his jeans down his hips, a little rougher than she should have, considering his injury. Blood had seeped through the denim, leaving his low-slung gray cotton boxer briefs awash in crimson. She scooched them down, too, just past the edge of his dark bush.

"A little quicker and rougher than I expected, but I appreciate your enthusiasm," he said.

Damn his stupid little sexy sliver of a grin making her body pulse and tingle and go lush. "You can sit. When was your last tetanus shot?"

"Couple years," he said as he lowered himself back down.

"Do you have any medical conditions?"

"No."

"Are you allergic to any medications?"

"No."

She set the bottle of ibuprofen in front of him. "Take four."

He made no move to get it. Instead, he eyed the items in her kit.

"I'll apply an antibiotic ointment to your wound that'll help fight infection, but the ibuprofen will help curb your pain. You're going to need it. Having your wounds cleaned isn't just going to hurt, it's going to feel like a grizzly bear clawing its way out of hibernation inside you."

"Thanks for that graphic and imaginative description of the pain I'm about to experience," he said. "Thank God you're not one of those sweet, caring nurses who wastes time trying to soften the blow for their patients. You know, so as to not cause them more pain."

The man's comments took her mind back to Dan's about her abrasive manner. Even before Jon's death, she'd been direct with her patients, never wanting to lie to them. But she admittedly remembered using a softer delivery.

"I'm not a pediatric nurse. I'm an ER nurse," she said. "I believe adult patients deserve the truth about their condition and their care."

She turned away and went to the refrigerator for a bottle of water to help him swallow down the pills. She cracked open the lid and turned back to give him the bottle. The narcotic vial was open in front of him, and he was popping a pill into his mouth. He grabbed the bottle of water from her hand, gulping deep.

"Let's hope you're not allergic to oxy. If you are and have an allergic reaction out here, miles from a care center, it could be life-threatening."

"Thanks for the warning, but the big O and I are old friends."

Snapping on a fresh pair of gloves, she got to work, starting at the front, irrigating the wound. His body tensed, and he hissed in a sharp breath but stayed put. Then she ran the warm, wet washcloth across his side, his stomach, his hip, and lower to remove as much blood as possible. The water, the cloth, and her gloves grew crimson, and she changed them several times before the area was sufficiently clean.

As she repeated the procedure on the back wound, she noticed a tattoo on the back of his neck of a blood-dripping knife shoved through a skull, the words, *Los Matos*, in script beneath it. Not that she was an expert, but it looked like a gang tattoo. Was it what he'd been searching for on her? Proof that she was or wasn't a gang member?

Terrific. She should have just given him the damn SUV.

After spreading antibiotic ointment on both wounds, she covered them with sterile gauze and a thick pad. She secured them in place with a long strip of gauze, followed by medical tape, then wrapped an elastic bandage around his torso to hold the bulk tight and in place. Her bedside manner might have slipped, but her technical skills were still top notch.

****

As Nick watched his Florence Nightingale—Alicia—treat him, her hands moving fast and efficiently but gently, trying hard not to cause him pain, he realized three things. One, she had done this before. Two, it was doubtful he could have managed a bandaging of this complexity by himself. Three, he was damn lucky he'd ended up at her cabin.

It would be a shitty way to repay her kindness, but as soon as she was done, he'd take her SUV and head down the mountain to his team. The bleeding had stopped, and he was well bandaged. Being a few liters down, he felt like death on a slab but should be able to make it to town…or close enough to make a call.

Alicia secured the tail end of the bandage, then stood. "That'll do it," she proclaimed and removed her gloves as proof. "If you take it easy, it'll hold until you can seek more thorough medical attention."

Before she'd finished speaking, he was on his feet. He paid for the quick move by having to grip the table to steady himself. Taking a deep breath, he forced himself to an upright position and pulled up his jeans.

"Thanks." Gun in one hand, jacket in the other, he headed toward the door and grabbed her key fob from the coatrack on the way.

The dog blocked his way, as if he were trying to keep him from making a huge mistake.

As Nick shifted around him and opened the door, a wave of vertigo plowed into him, nearly kicking his legs out from under him. Head spinning, heart racing, stomach churning, he grabbed the doorframe to steady himself, the jacket and fob falling to the floor. *Must be the pain meds kicking in. Maybe two had been a bad idea.*

"You should rest," she said.

Her voice sounded muffled, as if his ears were packed with cotton, but he heard her words. Yes, rest would be best. It might settle the swirling vertigo and nausea, the pounding in his head, and the sheet of aches wrapped around his body. But his mission was more important than rest. More important than anything. Only, he couldn't make his feet move.

Suddenly, she was at his side, arm around him.

His gaze found hers and gripped it like a life preserver. "I need to get out of here. Now."

"I understand, but driving in your condition will be suicide," she said. "Lie down for a bit, clear your head. Surely a few minutes more won't matter."

He let her lead him across the room toward the couch. She tried to settle him onto it slowly and carefully, but neither his muscles nor hers could hold his weight. His body, feeling like a bag of wet cement, fell heavy onto the couch, dragging her down with him, on top of him. Pitchforks of pain shot through him, releasing a loud groan and giving him enough of a burst of energy to grab her hair at the back of her head. He pulled her close and saw the fear in her eyes.

"Don't tell anyone I'm here," he growled.

"Uh…"

"Promise me!" He fought to hold on to consciousness long enough to hear her promise, but his mind and body were giving up. He could feel it. "Please. Alicia."

"I promise," she said finally, giving him what he needed.

Just in case these were his last seconds on earth, he pulled her into a hard kiss then plunged into the dark pit that opened beneath him. He let it swallow him and his pain whole, and he dragged with him into that oblivion her scent, her green eyes and the taste of her lips.

Chapter Five

The scent of torn flesh, fear, and iron hung so thick in the air Alicia could feel it and taste it. It filled the small space with unease and tanked her adrenaline levels, leaving her body depleted.

He was a gang member. She was ninety-nine percent sure of it. One that had done something bad enough to get shot over. Whether lawman or criminal had done the damage was immaterial. A man like him, with wounds and a gun like that, dragged behind him bags of trouble. Trouble that wouldn't give up until it found him. Which meant it would find her.

The safer-for-her choice would have been to let him take her SUV when he'd first asked for it. It would have solved the problem. With his death. But she couldn't in good conscience have allowed that. The desperation in his eyes and tone when he'd pleaded with her, growled her name… It had struck deep and was what had convinced her that here was where he needed to be until he was healed enough to go.

The decision was made, so it was up to her to protect herself. And she could. She had a gun.

Her eyes cut to his weapon.

And so did he. It had remained clenched in his hand from the moment he'd appeared, as if it were a part of him, an extension of his arm. She'd hide it so he couldn't use it against her. And she'd use his or hers or both against him if she had to.

She tried to pry the weapon from his grip, but even out cold, he held it tight. A harder tug separated it from him. He was not a man who gave up easily. After putting the weapon out of sight on the top shelf of her closet, tucked into one of Jon's beanies, she knelt at his side to begin a thorough inspection of his body. Panza remained close by in case she needed a second opinion.

His breathing wasn't terribly labored—his bare chest rose and fell with deep, even breaths—which further supported her belief that he hadn't suffered internal damage. She didn't have the instruments to perform surgery, so she needed to know whether she should hike up the mountain to the hotspot to call an ambulance, despite her promise not to tell anyone about him. If his condition took a turn for the worse, she'd have no choice. Saving his life was more important than keeping her promise.

After removing his boots and socks, she stripped off his bloody jeans and boxer briefs and let her touch and gaze skim every inch of him. The slow, thorough inspection across masculine dips and planes, under his arms, between his legs, revealed no other fresh wounds but a scattering of healed ones that proved he'd shown up for the challenges life had lobbed at him. That said he was no stranger to danger.

What made him doubly dangerous to her was that he oozed sexiness, from the souvenirs of his wild life to his heart-pumping, fantasy-inducing physique. It was a crime for anyone to be as attractive as he was. In fact, he should come with a warning label tattooed on his chest. *Caution: May cause female genitalia to combust in lust.* That bold kiss he'd stolen before he'd passed out had certainly done the job. Her lips—and other body parts—still tingled like she'd applied the cut end of a habanero to them like gloss.

Her fingers traced the semper fi tattoo set in script low on his hip. Latin for always faithful, semper fidelis was the motto of the US Marine Corps. His long hair and scruff were too nonregulation for military. Ex-military maybe? The tattoo ran counter to the prominent gang tattoo on his back. Maybe being a good guy hadn't paid well enough. Or maybe he'd pledged fidelity to the gang. A couple of tribals snaked down his arms from his shoulders, completing the dangerous bad-boy look.

His tattoos turned her thoughts to his insistence on seeing hers and how he'd yanked her shirt up to check out her back and had run his fingers over her dandelion tattoo. That action said he was the kind of man who took what he wanted without asking. The kind of man who thought he deserved to have everything he wanted, when he wanted it. Her insides still simmered over the look in his fevered eyes that, for a moment, had suggested he wanted her.

Speaking of wanting…

The nurse in her insisted she skim past what was behind his boxer briefs—if he were still wearing them, that is—but the woman in her ignored that recommendation and instead allowed her gaze to take a leisurely and appreciative stroll over the masterpiece and contemplate whether he was any good with it. Thinking about him using that equipment triggered an intense squeezing sensation in her core. The foreign feeling was a shock to her system. Guess she'd been wrong about her libido being buried along with Jon.

Covering the man with a blanket and leaving him to sleep, she grabbed his jeans, underwear, socks, and jacket. His phone and her key fob fell out of the jacket pocket. She grabbed them and carried everything to the kitchen table. Even if his phone wasn't locked, there was no service at the cabin, so that was of no help. Setting it aside, she checked his jeans pockets, which turned up a bit of change, a lighter, a pocketknife, and an expensive-looking leather wallet.

Inside the wallet were several bills in various denominations and a California state driver's license. The license photo was him, with combed-back shoulder-length dark hair, no smile on that full, wide kissable mouth, and deep chocolate eyes that forewarned of his dominant personality. The license was issued to a Rey Cruz and showed a Los Angeles address and a birthdate that made him twenty-eight as of July 18. *July 18. A Cancer.*

A former nursing student on rotation in the ER had told her that of all the zodiac signs, Cancer was the sign most likely to be a killer. He'd also claimed that the information came directly from FBI statistics, which rated Cancers twelve out of twelve on the danger level. Alicia found it highly unlikely that the FBI included astrology in its profiling efforts, but if that "fact" were even a little true, she was in for a rough ride with Rey Cruz.

After storing his possessions in a kitchen drawer, she threw the scraps of his T-shirt and the bloodstained items she'd used to clean his wounds into the metal trash barrel outside and set it afire so the smell wouldn't attract animals or stink up the cabin. Then, she ran soapy water in the kitchen sink and plunged in his bloody clothes. After they'd soaked, she would wash and dry them in the compact stacked unit in the kitchen. He'd need them when he was able to leave.

She also removed some of Jon's sweats, shirts, and socks from the bags and put them on to wash. If Rey ended up staying a day or two to recover, he'd need something more comfortable to wear than the jeans he showed up in. And finally, she took another blanket from the closet and worked it under him so his bare skin wasn't against the couch surface.

****

Throughout the day and into the night, she sat at Rey's side, either in the rocker or on the floor beside him to soothe his forehead with a cool cloth, hold his thrashing body, and comfort him with low whispers and soft caresses. All the while, Panza lay in vigil by her side. Time slowed, the seconds lengthening. It gave her ample opportunity to study her patient, get to know his face, and evaluate the kind of man he might be.

The straight slash of his thick dark eyebrows that turned toward each other when he was angry, or hurting, gave him a perpetual serious look. The wide fullness of his mouth promised he knew how to kiss, and the slight jag in his nose said he could take a punch. His shoulders stretched across the full width of the couch, and the sculpted muscles in his arms, chest, and legs made it clear he lived a physical life and used his body as a tool. Or a weapon. Even his shoulder-length hair—thick, dark, and slicked back from his forehead— was sexy in a wild way that made her heart trip all over itself.

Each all-male component put together in its right place with the others created an enticing image of strength, confidence, and capability. The full package made the woman in her want to curl up next to him and let the warrior in him keep her safe and satisfied.

Jon had been the opposite of this man in nearly every way, from his golden good looks to his lean physique from years of cycling. Her patient was taller than Jon by at least three inches and seemed more suited to rugged activities. Jon had the look of fun and safety, which had always appealed to her, while the man on her couch had danger tattooed all over his fuck-me body.

An image of the long, thick rod that lay between his legs, resting against his hefty sacks, materialized in her mind's eye, and for one naughty, unethical moment, she contemplated lifting the blanket and enjoying another peek at the miracle that had her all-woman parts coming alive as if they'd been probed with a lightning bolt.

"Fuck!" The outburst from the man startled her, and she jerked back, like a warning from above against crossing the line. A string of Spanish words followed, sprinkled liberally with the word *fuck*.

A closer glance said his pulse was racing but that he still slept.

She dipped the cloth in the bowl of cool water she'd placed on the table, wrung it out, and dabbed his heated skin.

"Rest easy, Rey. Whatever your secrets are, I'll protect them like my own."

Almost as if he'd heard her whispered voice, he reached out and grabbed her hand, holding tight as if it was the only thing that would save him.

The need and strength in that grip, especially in his

weakened, vulnerable state, stirred feelings of sympathy and reaffirmed her decision to do everything in her power to keep him away from the edge of death, keep him safe.

She held his hand and whispered words of comfort to soothe him, calm him, settle him, let him know he wasn't alone.

It was a while before he slept quietly.

Only then did he release her hand.

Only then did she sleep. Or try to.

Having a stranger, a gang member, in her house, inches from where she sat beside him, had made her too anxious to sleep much. As the first rays of dawn's light streamed in, she rose.

Rey was still sleeping, so she didn't disturb him to check his wounds. After showering, she made breakfast for her and Panza, then reviewed her Day 3 tasks. With Rey to look after, she chose a task that required little thought and could easily be halted. Boxing her and Jon's books fit the bill.

Although she had planned to drop each book into the box without looking at it, she found herself leafing through each one, stopping on passages Jon had marked with a star, underlining, or comment. For as long as she'd known him, it had been his way—writing his opinion about the passage in the margins or some observation or connection to something in his life, or some phrasing that had resonated with him. When she'd asked about it, he said that marking the text was his way of entering it, mingling with it. Reading Jon's books had felt like eavesdropping on a conversation between him and the book, author, or character.

All his books in the box, she started on hers, setting

aside an unread romance, psychological thriller, and classic to occupy her during her visit before stacking the rest of her books atop Jon's. Her fingers paused on the slim tome of sensual poetry he used to read to her. She paged through it to her favorite poem. Three photos fell out. The ones they'd taken with the old instant camera they found at a yard sale during their last visit.

Breath caught in her throat at seeing Jon's smile and eyes beaming from the first image. The blue flannel shirt was tied low around his hips, and his toned muscles glistened. One hand fisted a long-handled axe while his other arm struck a flexed-bicep muscleman pose.

She smiled at the memory of that day, how she'd mentioned wanting to build a fire in the fireplace. Seconds after the wish left her lips, Jon marched outside. A few split logs were on the porch, but he insisted that she deserved fresh-cut fuel for her fire. Grabbing the axe and a few logs from the woodshed, he went to work.

His display of outdoor aptitude and the late summer sun conspired to strip the shirt from his form. She'd captured the moment with the camera, then rewarded him with a kiss, a caress, and a promise to properly express her appreciation and admiration after he'd started her fire.

The memory the image conjured was almost as real as the moment had been. She could feel his heat, smell the scent of his exertion, taste his salty lips, hear his guttural *hwah* as he struck axe to wood. She could even recall the torrid bout of carnality that had sparked from that scenario. But the memory failed to trigger the desire that had exploded through her back then. Today, it produced no pearled nipples, no fullness blooming low in her core, no moisture flooding her pussy, no rapid heartbeats or bated breaths, no hungry need clawing for satisfaction.

Truth was, she hadn't felt even a tug of desire since Jon had pulled the rug out from under her.

Well, until yesterday.

Her gaze cut to the couch and caressed the man lying there.

She didn't know what was more troubling about Rey Cruz—that he was a gang member or that his presence had so easily and quickly resurrected her libido. It didn't matter. Her body's response was nothing more than its seven-month sexual drought and his body's perfect-for-her blend of pheromones. Chemistry and circumstance. Holding tight to that belief would keep her desire in check.

The next photo was of her standing in front of the flickering flames of the fireplace, wearing nothing but a satisfied grin and Jon's blue flannel shirt. The buttons were undone, revealing the curve of her bare breasts, stomach, and the shadowy vee between her tanned legs that was still damp with his sweat, spit, and semen.

They'd just made love, and she'd slipped into his shirt to go to the kitchen for another bottle of wine. He'd teased her about it, asking why she needed to get dressed to walk a few feet to get wine. She'd told him she liked to wear it because it smelled like him. He'd laughed, saying that after what they'd just done, every part of her smelled like him. That he'd snapped a photo of the moment was his way of saying it was memorable to him.

In the last photo, the two of them stood together in

front of the cabin, arms around each other, her hand on his chest at his heart as if claiming it. He held the big, boxy camera out in front of them for the selfie, and the resulting image had captured them from the waist up, with only the tip-top of his head cut off.

Judging solely by the joy on their faces in the pictures, their life had been nirvana. That illusion had shattered the day Jon flipped her world upside down.

The man in the pictures, who she'd loved for all her adult life and thought she knew better than herself, was gone, and because of that, the woman in the pictures also was gone.

Memories spun here at the cabin were the toughest adversary she'd faced since her life changed, because here, they all had been labeled sublime. Her job, while here, was to rip off those labels and force herself to see their true identity.

"Were they all lies, Jon?" Her whispered voice sounded like thunder in the silent room.

Panza, thinking she was talking to him, left his spot at Rey's side and trotted over to her. He licked her hand. She reached out to pet him, but he turned and raced to the door, growling. Shoving the lies back into the book, she dropped it atop the others in the box and rose to see what had captured Panza's attention.

A Sheriff's Department vehicle had parked alongside her SUV, and a tall, lanky man wearing a brown Stetson and matching jacket strode toward the cabin, his palm on the handle of his sidearm.

Sheriff Johnson.

Her heart plummeted and roasted in the acid of her stomach. Borrowing Rey's favorite word, she said it aloud. "Fuck."

Chapter Six

Alicia stepped onto the porch, a growling Panza at her side, and closed the door behind her. She didn't want the sheriff to see Rey and insist on answers she didn't want to give.

"Good morning, Mrs. Stone."

"Sheriff Johnson," she said.

At the man's slow approach, Panza barked, forcing Alicia to drop to one knee and put an arm around him to thwart a possible attack. Luckily, the dog's aggressiveness also halted the sheriff.

"You didn't have a dog with you when you were at the store," he said.

She contemplated lying and saying Panza had stayed home with Jon, but if the sheriff recognized the dog, he'd know she was lying. Lies would pique his interest even more. And that was the last thing she wanted.

"He just showed up," she said.

"If he's a bother to you and Mr. Stone, I can take him off your hands."

"No, we enjoy having him here."

"Is your Mister around? I'd like to meet him."

"He's hiking," she said.

"Alone?"

"He's an experienced hiker, and I had stuff to do here."

The sheriff sent his gaze on a slow crawl across the property, as if he were expecting someone to pop out from behind the trees at any moment and wanted to see the second it happened. As if finally convinced they really were alone, he returned his gaze to hers.

"Sheriff, why are you—" Before she could finish her question, he spoke over her.

"There was a report of gunshots in this area early yesterday morning before dawn. Thought I should check on you and your husband."

"Thanks for your concern, but as you can see, we're fine."

The sheriff zipped his coat a little higher against the wind that had kicked up and made her wish she had put on her own coat before coming out. The temperature had dropped several degrees since she first arrived, and the thick gray clouds rolling in made it feel colder.

"Well, I see you and the dog. I have yet to see this husband of yours. For all I know, you've offed him and hidden the body somewhere. Or maybe he was never here to begin with."

She chuckled to show how ridiculous she found his statements. "I see you suffer from the malady that affects most members of law enforcement, Sheriff."

"What's that?"

"You see problems where there are none. We simply wanted to get away from the city and enjoy a relaxing time in these beautiful mountains. That's it."

He stared at her so intently for such a long few seconds, she was beginning to doubt how long she could hold her poker face. Then he spoke, and she let herself take a breath.

"If you insist on staying," he said, "you should know that snow is expected up here in the next day or two—several feet likely—and power often goes off during big storms."

"There's plenty of wood in the shed if we need it," she countered.

He glanced at the meager pile of wood stacked on the side of the porch opposite from the bench. "Using it for heat and cooking, it'll go fast."

"We'll be fine."

His rough chuckle scraped across her skin. "You don't scare easily, do you, Mrs. Stone."

"Is that the reason for your visit? To scare me?"

"No, ma'am. Just a friendly visit to warn you about the potential dangers you face up here."

"Well, you've accomplished your mission and can now check it off your list," she said, trying to keep her tone light.

He reached into his shirt pocket and pulled out a business card, then stretched forward to hand it to her. Panza bristled but her hand on him stopped an attack.

"Call my office when you need help," the sheriff said and turned, then stopped and turned back. "Oh, that's right. You can't call. No cell service up here. Right?" With a wry grin, he touched his finger to his hat in farewell and headed to his SUV.

"Uh, Sheriff?"

He stopped again and turned to her.

"You didn't say what the gang's name was."

"Los Matos."

Rey had a Los Matos tattoo on his back. No doubt about it. She was harboring a gang member.

Despite her dislike and mistrust of the sheriff, she

contemplated telling him about Rey. It would be the safer choice. For her. But not for Rey. In fact, her gut was telling her that the sheriff would not keep him safe. So instead of saying, "Sheriff, there's a wounded Los Matos gang member on my couch and you need to get him off my property immediately," she said, "Thanks. We appreciate the information."

"I'm here to protect and serve, Mrs. Stone."

Endanger and annoy was more accurate, she mused as he continued to his vehicle. Even after he'd driven out of sight, the skin-crawling feeling he'd inspired remained. She would follow his advice, though, and split more wood. It was smart to be prepared. But first, she'd put on her coat, hat, and gloves. The air felt and smelled like snow.

****

Nick awoke, a blanket of pain covering his body head to toe but targeted most intensely in his side. He pried open his heavy eyelids to a squint and moved his hand to the epicenter of his ache. His fingers touched on a thick bandage that went all the way around his torso. He lifted the blanket with thumb and forefinger and peered down the length of his body.

Naked all the way to his goddamn toes.

Where were his clothes? More important, where was his gun?

He let his gaze crawl around his accommodations. A padded wooden rocker standing sentinel at the side of the couch. A massive rock wall fireplace. Log walls with a few cheesy decorations. Wooden floors with a scattering of multicolored, oval braided rugs. Four windows with checkered curtains pulled closed all but a crack, through which filtered muted light.

It had been minutes into dawn when he'd gotten here. It now looked like late morning. Shit, he'd been out for hours. He had to get out of here. He attempted to sit up, but pain clobbered him, and he dropped his head back onto the pillow.

Barking and then voices coming from outside snapped him alert and had him craning his neck toward the door. The first voice was a woman's, probably the woman with the blaze of red hair who had bandaged him. Alicia. The second voice, a man's, sounded familiar but he couldn't pinpoint it. Nick listened keenly but couldn't catch what they were saying. He needed to get closer. Needed to know who was out there and what they were saying. His life depended on it.

Gritting his teeth against the pain, he rolled into a sitting position, the muscles in his stomach screaming in protest. He shifted his legs, one at a time, over the side of the couch, then gripped the armrest and pushed himself to standing. It felt as if the bones in his body had melted and leaked out with his blood.

You're on your feet. That was the hardest part. You can do this. Don't be a wuss.

Pressing his hand to his bandaged side to support the wound, he shuffled toward the door, leaned heavily against the wall, and peeked out through the curtain.

His heart dropped into his stomach, making his wounds pulse. It was the sheriff with Alicia. She had ratted him out.

Adrenaline shuffled his feet into the kitchen. He grabbed a knife and positioned himself so that he'd be behind the door when it opened, giving him a short-lived advantage. If she brought the sheriff in, he'd be dead, but he wouldn't make it easy for him.

Minutes later, the sheriff got into his SUV and backed out. Alicia didn't open the door until he had driven out of sight, then the dog came in first, her behind him.

"What did you tell him?" Nick demanded, kicking the door closed.

The dog positioned himself between them, growling low. Alicia's gaze cut to the knife, then back to Nick's eyes. "I'll tell you whatever you want to know, but not at knifepoint."

The air between them was electric as they stared at each other, each waiting to see what the other would do, who would give in first. After a beat of contemplating whether he could trust her, he set the knife on the coatrack. Out of his hand but within easy reach. He heard her soft sigh. The dog stopped growling but stayed put.

"You're bleeding again," she said.

A glance down confirmed that blood was seeping through the bandage, but he paid it no mind. "Why was he here?"

"To let me know that a snowstorm is coming, and that I need more wood."

Johnson suspects something. Or Alicia told him I'm here, and he's gone for backup.

"Bullshit. You're lying," he said and staggered forward. His knees chose that moment to buckle. He was falling, and there was nothing he could do to stop it. He hit the floor, the jolt sending pain vibrating through every inch of his body.

"Fuck!" he growled long and loud, in pain and anger.

Panza bounded toward him, crept close, whining, and licked his cringing face.

Alicia held back.

Not that he blamed her. There were many reasons for her to be afraid in this moment—her isolation with him, no cell service, him pointing a knife at her—and he watched them zoom fast and furious in her mind's eye. But seeing him lying on the floor, helpless, bleeding, in pain, physically unable to get up, must have pushed aside her fear and let her training take over because she rushed to the bathroom, grabbed the first aid kit, and returned to him. She unwound the bloody bandage and positioned herself over him. Placing clean pads over the bloody ones, she applied firm, direct pressure to stop the flow.

"Did you tell him I was here?" The shaky words slid through his clenched teeth.

"No."

"Why not?"

"For some stupid reason, I promised you I wouldn't."

He reached out and cupped her head, gripping her hair, and she tensed, probably wondering what he was going to do to her now.

"You saved my life," he said and released her, letting his hand fall limply onto the floor. "Again."

"And you're making me regret it by pulling stunts like that," she said and focused on stopping the bleeding.

Minutes later, the flow subsided, and she had him rebandaged.

"Let's get you back to the couch." She leaned close and wrapped his arm around her neck. "Hold on to me.

I'll help you sit, then stand."

She eased him upright, then to his feet with little help from him. He almost toppled her when he stood, but she held firm and absorbed his weight. He tried not to lean on her, but his muscles weren't working. She guided him toward the couch.

"Bathroom, first," he said, and she changed direction. "Why am I naked?"

"Don't worry about it."

Nick had no hang-ups about his body, but wobbling naked across the floor, hanging on to Alicia, was fucking embarrassing. It got worse when she stayed in the bathroom with him and stood beside him, watching him pee.

"Do you want to hold my dick and aim it for me, too?" he grumbled.

"Nice of you to offer, but no. I'm checking to see whether there's blood in your urine."

"You could have just asked," he said and flushed the toilet.

She squirted hand sanitizer on her hands, then his. "Next time."

The trip back to the couch seemed longer than the trip to the bathroom, but he made it—with her help— and all but collapsed onto the couch, his body exhausted.

"Do you feel up to eating something?" she asked and covered him with the blanket, tucking it around his suddenly shivering body.

"How long was I out?" he asked.

"All of yesterday and part of today."

"What?" That long! Hazy memories flitted across his eyes like a movie clip. Of her leaning over him, pressing a wet cloth to his forehead and brushing it across his skin, of her sitting beside him and soothing him with soft unintelligible words and sounds. "Did I say anything?"

"You mean, other than your penchant for liberally peppering your sentences with the word *fuck*?" she said, her grin suggesting that he had let something slip. Shit. As if she could see that the thought troubled him, she chuckled and laid her hand on his chest. "Don't worry. Keeping patients' secrets confidential is section three of the sacred nurses' pledge."

Her teasing attempt to calm him didn't dissipate the tension clenching his muscles. He grabbed her hand, held tight, and her smile faded.

"Did I say anything?" he repeated, making the words low and sharp so she knew he meant business. He had to be sure.

"Nothing of interest to me. Most of it was in Spanish, so I didn't understand it. Now, will you release my hand before you break it?"

He hadn't realized how tightly he was gripping her hand, but at her request, he released it and ignored the urge to apologize for his brutish behavior.

She stood. "I'll bring you more pain meds and water."

"And another blanket," were the last words he said before he crashed again.

Chapter Seven

Nick woke with a pressure weighing on his chest, the scent of flowers in his nose, and a hand on his dick.

He blinked to force himself awake enough to see what the hell was going on. Stuck in that hazy moment between awake and asleep, he couldn't be sure whether what he was seeing was true, but damned if it didn't make him smile.

Alicia sat on the floor, one arm slung low across his hips, her head using his chest as a pillow, her mass of hair cascading around him, and her hand at the base of his very large, very awake erection.

Having her this close, and so intimately positioned, spurred a battalion of thoughts that further hardened his morning wood. He settled his hand lightly on her head. The curls were soft beneath his palm, and he had a sudden urge to grip them in his hand and pull her head up into a deep kiss. Instead, he moved his hand away. She had tended his wound, cared for him, sat vigil by him for hours to make sure he lived, and hadn't ratted him out to the sheriff. She deserved better than awakening to his morning wood up her nose.

Keeping his body still, he thought of every nonsexual thing he could to recede the surge of blood erecting his cock. It was working until she stirred with a soft groan and pressed her palm harder against him to help her rise. With all of his effort destroyed, the only thing left to do was enjoy the hell out of the unexpected gift. But before he could, she bolted upright and snapped her hand back from his morning pecker like it was sheathed in barbed wire. Her gaze zipped to his face, likely to check whether he was awake and had witnessed her copping a feel.

Had he been a gentleman, he would have pretended to be asleep to save her the embarrassment instead of looking at her like a hungry *lobo*. But hell, it had been a long time since he'd woken with a beautiful, sweet-scented woman's head on his chest, her hand on his cock. He was damn happy about it, and it was wasted effort to pretend otherwise. A soft chuckle slid from his throat before he could stop it, which made her face go redder.

He might not be a gentleman, but neither was he a complete asshole, so he staunched his desire to say something suggestive and instead went with, "Good morning, *farolita*."

Why he'd tacked the Spanish word for *little fire* onto the end of his low greeting was a mystery. True, it had been his first impression of her, with her spicy tongue, all that thick red hair, snapping green eyes, and petite kick-ass body with feminine dips and swells in all the right spots that lit up his insides. He'd never had naughty nurse fantasies before, but he had one now.

Sitting up taller, she stiffened her spine, darted her tongue across her lips, and let her gaze zip from him to that tattoo on her finger. Then, in no-nonsense motions, she folded back the covers from his chest, low enough to reveal his bandage.

"A good laugh and a long sleep are often the best cures for what ails you." The dredges of sleep were still wrapped around her, making her voice husky and sexy. "You've had both. Let's hope all that mirth didn't rip open your wounds again."

As she went about the task, he watched her face, mapping the shape, sight, and texture of it. A soft sprinkling of freckles saddled a slim nose that tilted up slightly at the tip. The soft curve of her cheeks were flushed. The lush fan of dark auburn lashes matched her brows. Plump lips looked as if they'd just been kissed hard and long and thirsted for more.

He licked his lips and swore he could taste her there, as if they'd kissed before. A memory slid into view. He had kissed her. Right before he passed out the day he arrived. He'd like to do it again, now that he was no longer at the edge of death and could enjoy it. He inhaled a slow breath, drawing in her distinct scent that acted as an accelerant to his desire and an extinguisher to his pain.

"No blood seeping through," she said, her voice drawing him out of his fantasy. "Your color is better, and you look less…agitated. All good signs."

After ensuring the bandage was secure, she again met his eyes. It felt as if she were looking at him, not as a man but as a patient. Her calm, clear voice backed that assessment. The only remaining clue she was still flustered by being busted copping a feel was the fading flush to her cheeks.

"One to ten, how much pain are you in?" she asked. "One being none, ten being excruciating."

She was staring at him, waiting for a response, so he zoned in on his wounds and on his body to determine what he was feeling. The pain was less severe than when he'd arrived, but still—

"One to ten?" she repeated to hurry his response.

"Are you this demanding with all your patients?" he asked.

She laughed, a husky, sexy sound that brushed across his skin like a caress. "Only the ones I like." She put the covers back into place over his chest and stood. "How about some breakfast? Something *soft*." He didn't miss the inference in her word or wry grin.

He grabbed her hand before she could go but immediately released it when she tensed. "How long was I out this time?"

"Most of yesterday. Excessive sleep is not uncommon in trauma like yours and aids in healing, but I swear it's like you haven't slept for years."

She didn't know how spot on she was with that statement. He never slept more than three or four hours a night when on assignment. Too dangerous to try for more. Sleeping was just as dangerous here in this cabin, with holes in his side, jelly for muscles, mush for brains, no way to reach his team, and stuck with this stranger who could kill him—or get him killed. But for some reason, he had felt comfortable enough to slip into sleep.

"Now that you're awake and a little more alert, is there someone I can call for you?" she asked. "A spouse? Or a friend?"

The only people he needed her to call was his team, but if she was part of the gang, asking her to call them would sign his death warrant. He'd just have to suffer through this on his own and hope for the—

Full realization of what she'd said knifed through him at the memory of trying to use his phone when he first got here. Was the little witch trying to trick him into saying something incriminating?

"Bring me my phone, and I'll do it," he said.

"Well, there's no service here at the cabin, but—"

"Then how are you going to call someone for me?"

"If you had let me finish my sentence, you'd have learned that further up the mountain there's a spot where service is available. I could hike up and call someone for you, let them know you're all right. They must be worried because you didn't come home."

His initial belief was that no cell service at the cabin meant she couldn't rat him out. Now knowing that she could sneak out at any time and call the sheriff—or someone in the gang—refilled him with unease.

"No," he said, firmly so that she would drop it.

"I'll get the oatmeal going then." She stood.

Oatmeal. Sure. Why not start the day with slimy beige goo. Not having enough of an appetite to ask for something else, he didn't argue. "Fine."

"I think what you meant was, thanks," she said.

After a long pause, he gave her what she'd asked for. "Thanks."

Then she smiled, giving him what he needed and hadn't even known it.

****

Alicia's eyes bore into his like lasers, and the studied look on her face said she wanted answers to the questions spinning in her head. Hopefully, she'd let him get through breakfast in peace before starting the inquisition. He ate slowly, just in case.

"So who shot you?" she asked from the rocker at his side, her ever-present four-legged protector occupying the space between them.

So much for his hopes for a delay. He spooned the sweet tan mush, which surprisingly didn't taste like glue, into his mouth because it gave him time to come up with an answer. He kept his gaze on his bowl as he responded so he didn't have to look her in the eyes and lie to her. The situation demanded he lie, and he had no trouble with that, but for some reason, lying to *her* made him feel like shit. "Never saw the shooter."

"What were you doing up here?"

"Hiking." Not the most brilliant answer, but it was better than the truth. Her knowing the truth would be bad for both of them, even if she really was a nurse. The blob of oatmeal in his mouth wasn't any easier to swallow than the previous one. Lies added a bitter spice to any meal.

"Do you always wear a gun while hiking?"

"Yes."

"Why?"

"Protection."

"Against?"

"Wildlife."

"Let's try an easier question," she said with a wink.

Spoken like a woman who could smell bullshit miles away and wasn't shy about calling the bullshitter out on it. An admirable skill, one that he himself proudly possessed, but it wouldn't help her avoid the frustration of not getting the truth.

"What's—"

"Speaking of my gun," he cut in, "where is it?"

"It's safe. You'll get it back when you leave here. What's your name?"

He quickly scanned the ramifications of her knowing his assumed name.

"I ask for no other reason than it would be nice to call you by your name," she said when he didn't respond.

"Rey." He spooned in another bite of oatmeal.

"Got a last name to go with that?"

"Not important."

"Do you live in this area…Rey?" The way she said his name suggested she doubted its validity. He'd love to question her about why she was convinced that wasn't his name.

"No."

"Hmm. That's odd."

He couldn't help himself from asking. "What's odd about it?"

"That you'd come up here to hike."

"You think it's odd I'd hike in the mountains? Not much fun hiking in my driveway at home."

"This area is private property, so that's why it's odd. Where's home?"

"Why? You thinking of moving?"

"Where's your vehicle?" she said, ignoring his question. "Surely you didn't hike all the way here from…your home?"

Nothing wrong with her interrogation skills. He took a breath and released it slowly, ensuring a bogus look of pain twisted his face as he did. "As much as I'm enjoying our conversation, my side's hurting. Think I'll sleep awhile." When she looked like she was about to argue, he held out his empty bowl. "If you don't mind."

After a pause, she took the bowl.

"Breakfast was…soft." At the last second, he tacked on her favorite word. "Thanks."

Then he turned his head away from her, toward the

back of the couch, and closed his eyes, hoping it would shut down further questions and prevent him from having to be an even bigger asshole.

Fortunately, she didn't press but took the bowl into the kitchen. The dog, however, set his paw onto Nick's arm and stared at him, as if chastising him for being difficult. And a liar.

"Come on, Panza," Alicia said to the dog. "Let's go outside and let Rey sleep."

He couldn't have planned that better if he'd tried. With Alicia and her guard dog outside, he could search for his gun.

"What are you going to do outside?" he asked to get an idea how much time he had.

She headed to the door, where she pulled on her boots. "Split wood in case the furnace goes out. Apparently, power up here often goes out during storms, and a big one is headed this way."

"Who told you that? Your buddy, the sheriff?" He hadn't meant for his tone to come out so antagonistic, but at seeing her reaction—one of disgust—he realized he could use that to his advantage and maybe gain some valuable information.

"First of all, he's not my buddy," she said and pulled on her hat. "I don't even know him. And second, regardless of whether he's being truthful about the power and the storm, it's prudent to be prepared."

How well she knew the sheriff was still to be determined. But she didn't like the man. That much was clear.

"Always be prepared," he said with a wink. "I bet that's the tattoo you wouldn't show me."

The peachy stain blooming on her cheeks

confirmed his suspicions that she was hiding at least one more tattoo. It sent his gaze on a slow crawl over her body to try to identify all the soft, hidden spots it could be.

"That quality you're ridiculing is the very one that saved your life," she said and slipped into her coat, zipped it, then pulled on her gloves.

He chuckled at her response. "Sorry I can't help you chop wood," he called out as she opened the door.

"Oh, yeah, me too. Enjoy your nap."

"Something about your tone tells me you don't really mean that."

The shutting door cut off the last of his statement and his laugh.

****

Damn the man!

He could make fun of her all he wanted, but he'd be on his knees, bending over to kiss her feet if the storm did hit and cut the power. Then she'd remind him, every hour, *I told you so.*

It wasn't just his teasing. Or even his flirty teasing. She was used to that behavior from her patients and had never before had trouble ignoring or deflecting it. It was his seeming ability to know just what to say to press her buttons and get the fire inside her roaring. His gaze crawling over her body, methodically searching for hidden ink, had made the tattoo she hadn't shown him pulse with need, saying *I'm here, Rey. Find me. Touch me. Devour me.*

Needing to cool her steamy thoughts and her burning face, she pulled in a deep gulp of the frozen air and turned her face upward to catch the falling snowflakes on her skin.

Snow had begun falling a short time ago, fat flakes that clumped even before they hit the ground in a pile, and the temperature had dropped significantly. It was looking very white Christmassy, but the dreaminess of it would die fast if the power and the furnace went out.

Pushing aside her useless frustrations about Rey, she focused on her goal—split enough wood to get them through the coming storm and any other that hit before she left at the first of the year.

She headed to the woodshed and grabbed the axe from the wall. The tool probably needed sharpening, but she didn't know whether a whetstone was on the property or, if so, how to use it, and no internet meant she couldn't research it. The axe's current level of sharpness would have to suffice. She pulled out a few thick logs, choosing the lighter ones that already had a crack in them for easier chopping.

Although she had no concrete idea how much wood she'd need if the power went out and stayed out for the duration of her visit, as part of her research before coming here, she'd read that an eight hundred square foot insulated cabin like hers might need about two cords a season—a cord being about a four feet by four feet by eight feet stack. Her stack on the porch was a decorative one foot by one foot by two feet, but more logs were in the shed, and she wouldn't be here an entire season. The current amount probably was sufficient, but she didn't want to be splitting more in the middle of a snowstorm if the furnace conked out.

Calling up the memory of how Jon had done this task, she got started. It wasn't as difficult as she'd imagined, and after she got going, a rhythm kicked in and slabs of wood calved off fairly easily. It felt good challenging her body like this, although she might need pain reliever and extra time in the hot shower tonight.

As wood piled up around her, she put them on the porch along with the kindling. When her stack reached three feet by three feet by five feet, she called it quits.

She put away the axe and the gloves and went inside the cabin to troubleshoot any problems with the fireplace and her undeveloped fire-building skills while the power and heat were on, so she didn't have to do it when they were off and she was freezing.

The measured rise and fall of Rey's naked chest and his soft snoring confirmed he was sleeping. She pulled the blanket up over him to keep him warm and tucked it around his feet, which were ice cold. She made a mental note to pull out some socks from the bag for him to wear.

Having swept the ash and debris from the fireplace the first day she'd arrived, she opened the flue, then lay the wood in the grate. Setting a match to it, the logs caught fire easily, the flames licking up the edges.

"So far, so good," she whispered to Panza as warmth suffused the room. She watched to make sure smoke wasn't going to be an issue, then added more wood to keep the fire going.

When two o'clock came and Rey was still sleeping, she warmed up the soup from the night before and ate with Panza.

Washed dishes.

Read.

Watched the sun set from the porch.

Showered and got ready for bed.

Fixed herself a cup of chamomile tea.

Enjoyed the ambience of the fire and the softly

falling snow.

It was a great distraction…for all of a few hours.

With no conversation to engage in, no TV to watch, no internet to get lost in, no emergencies to resolve, and her patient sleeping like a Rip Van Winkle descendant, memories of her life with Jon in this cabin and in Seattle gathered like ghosts around her and crawled into her lap. Refusing to let them infect her, she headed outside, Panza at her side, to bring in more wood to keep by the fireplace.

****

Nick's plan had been only to pretend to sleep to avoid his host's questions and to find his gun, which he'd found right away on the top shelf of her closet, inside one of the beanies. He left the gun there but pushed it to the back of the shelf behind the other hats. But the next thing he knew, he was waking up, with a roaring thirst and a pounding headache. He needed water and more pain reliever. And he needed them now.

"Hey," he called out, his scratchy voice hoarse and dry, his head pounding.

Alicia didn't respond, and the dog, which usually rushed to his side the second he awoke, also didn't make an appearance.

He eased into a seated position and glanced around the room. A fire was burning in the fireplace, and he smelled the lingering aroma of food. But he didn't see anyone and didn't hear any noise from the bedroom or bathroom. He craned his neck toward the door. Snowflakes floated in the darkness behind the windows. She wouldn't be out in that.

Anger and vulnerability rushed over him. Had she left? Slipped out to call the sheriff?

"Alicia," he called, the word thundering in his head. The panic in his voice pissed him off. Pissed him off that he was weak and having to rely on someone for his well-being.

The door opened and the dog—what did Alicia call him…Panza?—stampeded across the floor, slid to a halt beside the couch, and shook himself, slinging snow all over him and everything in a six-foot radius. He then sniffed him, as if asking how he was feeling.

And then she was there—Alicia, *farolita*—with an armful of wood.

"Where were you?" he said, pain driving each word from his mouth in a sharp stab.

"Well, hello to you, too," she said and set the wood near the fireplace, instead of coming to see about him.

She added a couple of pieces to the fire, instead of coming to him.

She pulled off her gloves and stuffed them into her coat pocket, pulled off her coat and hat, and hung them on the coatrack, instead of coming to him.

It irritated him that he depended on her right now and she was sporting such a cavalier attitude for his health.

"Glad you're awake. It's time to check your bandage," she called out as she washed and dried her hands at the kitchen sink. Then she joined him, sat beside him, and eased the blanket down past his hips.

She smelled like the outdoors, like snow and piñon. Like Christmases of his childhood. A sparkly net of fragile snowflakes danced in the golden-red halo of her hair. It made her look like a demon angel, one whose eyes and smile could lure even the most devout into hell without protest.

She fiddled with the bandage, pulling back the wrap, all of which irritated him because even a breath on it hurt like his guts were being scooped out with one of the logs she'd brought in. He hadn't had his pain meds in a while.

With her normal efficiency, she had everything checked and back in place in minutes, including the blanket tucked up over his chest. She laid her palm against his forehead, the side of his face at his temple, then under his chin at the side of his throat.

"You're a bit feverish, and your pulse is erratic, but your wounds look pretty good—no redness, swelling, or pus, just normal discharge." She patted her palm against his chest at his heart. "I think you're going to live. How about something to eat?"

"Water," he said and grabbed her hand, held it lightly. "I thought you left."

He wasn't sure why he'd chosen to share that thought with her, but he had, and the smile she beamed his way was his reward for his honesty. It rushed warmth through him and probably spiked his temperature to a level that would have alarmed her had she stuffed a thermometer in one of his orifices.

"I won't leave you," she said in that sincere, serene voice she had. She squeezed his hand. "I promise."

Even though he wasn't the trusting type, the look she gave him made him want to believe every word she'd said.

"And I promise I won't kill you," he said in the same whispered tone, just to keep her on the edge if she weren't telling the truth.

Her smile didn't falter at his weak threat. In fact, her eyes danced. Then she laughed. It was like she could see through his bullshit threats and found them humorous.

"Okay, tough guy," she said and let go. "I'll bring you some water, but I want you to eat something before you take more pain pills. They can be hell on an empty stomach." She went into the kitchen and returned with a bottle of water.

"You were sleeping when lunch was ready, so I didn't wake you," she said, watching as he guzzled the water.

It felt like he hadn't had water in days. The cool liquid sizzled in his throat on the way down.

"It's leftover soup and cornbread."

Food of any kind sounded gourmet to his grumbling stomach. "Fine," he said. "Thanks," he added because the word seemed to make her happy.

The sounds and scents of domesticity filtering to him from the kitchen buffered his pain a bit. The feeling of being cared for was something he hadn't felt in a long time. Except in the rare instance he had no other option, he didn't let himself be taken care of. He was a man. A decorated FBI special agent. A combat-hardened former US Marine. The lesson he'd learned long ago was that allowing himself to be vulnerable with anyone led to disastrous endings.

Alicia's friendly and caring demeanor—and her melodic voice coming from the kitchen as she chattered about the beautiful snow—made him realize he'd need to fight hard to remember that lesson while he was stuck here with her.

Although he didn't fully trust her, a buried-deep chunk of him—growing with every encounter they had—said he could. And in his delirium, it also was telling him the most outlandish lies, like how good it would feel to crack open his chest, slice open his heart, and lay out his clusterfuck of secrets and sins for her inspection. The biggest lie of all? That she would stare into the mountain of muck and say, *You're a good man, Nick Navarro. You do good for the world. I love that about you, and I love you just the way you are.*

"It's official, Navarro," he mumbled. "You're unfit for duty. You've allowed this *brujita-curandera* to wrap a spell around your brain and make you forget who you are. You're fucking doomed if you don't stop it now."

Chapter Eight

Hearing Rey call out for her in that pained, panicked voice revealed the vulnerability he was feeling and reminded her that, despite his swagger, he was still in a vulnerable state physically. His injury was relatively superficial, but his condition could change in an instant if it got infected. With no antibiotics in her box of modern magic, they'd both be in trouble.

The soup ready, she ladled it into a mug and set it and the last wedge of warmed cornbread on a tray with a spoon and a napkin. She carried it to him and set it on the coffee table.

"Let me help you sit up so you don't dribble hot soup into your bellybutton," she said.

"Speaking of bellybuttons, where are my clothes?" he asked as she helped him sit up and scoot back against the pillow she propped behind him.

"It's easier to check your wounds, change your bandage, and sponge-bathe you if I don't have to move your clothes out of the way every time."

A grin lit his face. "You're giving me sponge baths?"

"To keep your wounds clean, your fever down, and prevent you from making the place smell like a bag of old corn chips."

"Do me a favor, *farolita*?" he said.

"What's that?"

"The next time you give me a sponge bath, wake me up first."

She lifted one eyebrow. "Why?"

"I'd enjoy it more if I was awake," he said.

"That comment proved to me that you're well enough to sponge yourself." She picked up the tray and settled it legs down on either side of him, careful not to let it brush his wound. "Are you comfortable?"

"I'd be more comfortable with my clothes on."

She marveled at his single-minded focus to get his clothes back on. "Eat first, then we'll discuss it," she said and settled into the rocker beside him.

Panza claimed his spot between the couch and the rocker and watched Rey, on alert for any indication he'd like to share his food.

Rey crumbled the cornbread into the soup. At a soft woof from Panza, Rey picked out a piece and gave it to him.

The small act of kindness touched her heart. "You gotta watch that one," she said. "He'll end up eating it all."

As Rey ate, she watched him, deciding that he was the most beautiful man she'd ever seen, even without the haircut, shave, and shower he so badly needed. The more time she spent with him, the more curious she became about him, the more she wanted to know who he really was. So despite knowing it annoyed him, she would keep asking him questions.

Yes, she wanted answers, but she also just wanted to hear his whisky voice and feel it rumble across her body like a velvet-sheathed bolt of thunder. She wanted his coffee-colored eyes on her, caressing her skin and caffeinating her sleepy libido with every stare. And she wanted more. Her face burned as her mind listed every delicious element included in the *more.*

She was not acting like herself, and she didn't understand it in the slightest. If she believed in magic, she'd blame it on a spell this man had twisted around her head and heart and ovaries. But because she didn't believe in magic, she'd say it was nothing more than that he was a sexy, handsome man who knew how to recharge a woman's dead libido, and she was a woman who was in sore need of a jump.

****

Nick was no stranger to being ogled by women, but Alicia's ogling wasn't about admiring his body or face. She ogled with the intensity of a hunter seeking her prey—truth. He recognized the look in her eyes that said she was generating new questions to fire at him.

"If you feel up to something more substantial than soup tomorrow night, I thought I'd make roasted chicken and vegetables," she said. "Do you eat meat?"

Finally, a question he could answer truthfully. "I eat everything."

"Everything? Really?" she said, raising a perfectly shaped eyebrow, an action he'd learned meant she thought he was lying. "Most people have at least one food they refuse to eat. For me, that's liver."

"Most food can be tasty if prepared right," he countered and took another bite of soup. "Even liver."

"Sounds like something a gourmet chef would say."

He kept eating.

"So you're a chef?"

He practically snorted at the ridiculousness of the idea. "No, I'm not a chef. I like to eat good food, so

I've learned some basics."

"What's your favorite thing to make?"

"I don't know…steak, I guess." Actually, it was a steak dish he'd created that included garlic, green chile, cilantro, tomatoes, and corn, but she didn't need to know that. Only a few select people knew about his culinary skills. Hell, maybe he *was* a bit of a chef. Maybe he should keep his big mouth shut.

"Let me guess. Your favorite thing to eat also is steak."

"One of my favorites."

"What's your top favorite?"

He wiped his mouth with the napkin. "For dessert, how about you let me get in a question?"

"Cheese enchiladas," she said before he could ask a question.

"What about it?" he asked.

"It's my favorite food," she said, her words lifting his lips into a grin, because it was his favorite, too.

He wanted to ask whether she liked red, green, or Christmas, but if she said Christmas… That would be one more thing they shared, and he didn't want to share commonalities with this woman, or with anyone, especially while he was working a case.

Not that sharing his chile preference on enchiladas would be life-threatening. He just didn't want to start down the path of sharing personal information, especially with a beautiful woman who could make a man forget which head to think with.

He'd seen it happen with other undercover agents. Every time they shared a truth with a "special" person, it was easier to share the next time and the next time, and suddenly they were spilling secrets with every breath, and the mission was compromised, or they were dead. Or both.

"Christmas style," she said. "You know, with red and green chile. And I like to drizzle honey over it. I had that my first trip out here to New Mexico, and it replaced sushi as my favorite food."

A flutter in his heart expanded his smile. "That wasn't my question."

"What's your question?"

"What are you doing up here alone?" he said.

Her eyes flickered, and her full lips tightened, signs that she would likely give a lie instead of a truth.

"I'm not alone. Panza's here. And now, so are you."

Clever response that told the truth but didn't really answer the question. He'd go in another way. "Why the name Panza?"

"You know… Sancho Panza, Don Quixote's sidekick and ever-faithful companion."

"So if he's Panza, that makes you…" He circled his finger in the air near his ear.

She chuckled. "The crazy one, yes, I know." She reached out and scratched the dog's ears. "He showed up out of the blue when I got here a few days ago, and he stayed, almost like he knew I needed a guide. And he loves to eat. Don't you, boy."

Panza woofed again but toward Nick, asking for another bite.

Nick gave the last bite of cornbread to the dog and set the spoon into the empty mug.

"A guide for what?"

"To bring me out of my madness, of course," she said with a grin.

Her response brought up more questions. "Why are you depending on a stray dog to bring you out of madness instead of the man who put that ring on your finger?"

The question stripped the smile from her face.

"The answer to that question isn't relevant to your care," she said.

"Neither were the questions you were asking me. Let me guess… You guys had a fight and you ran off. Did he forget your birthday or anniversary? Cheat on you?"

"He died."

The anguish washing over her face and the grief riding her lacy voice made him feel like shit for taunting her and made him wish he'd kept his mouth shut. His first thought was to reach out to her, to comfort her, but he checked the impulse. Her drama was none of his business, and the last thing he wanted was to be drawn into it. Besides, letting sympathy drive his interactions with the enemy was never a good idea. But he wasn't a complete asshole either.

"What happened?" he said, his tone hopefully imparting the sympathy he felt.

"I'd rather not talk about it." She lifted the tray from his lap and took it into the kitchen, the dog on her heels.

Nick maneuvered around enough so he could see her. She washed and rinsed the dishes, then pulled out a chair from the table, sat with her back to him, and opened her book.

He wasn't surprised that all it had taken to halt her curiosity was for him to amp up his asshole. It always worked on women who refused to tolerate bullshit men.

But what surprised him most was the guilt piercing his chest about acting that way with her, especially since she'd been good to him.

She hadn't spoken in at least five minutes. Or turned a page. Either she was a slow reader or only pretending to read. Most likely, she just wanted to be away from him. And it pissed him off that all he wanted right now was her—her presence, her voice, her touch, her scent, her smile—back here with him.

If the mountain wouldn't come to Mohammad…

But first he had to pee.

The pull on his side was terrific, but he struggled to his feet. Hand supporting his wound, he took a shuffling step toward the bathroom.

She left her chair and rushed to him. "What are you doing?" She put her arm around him and tried to settle him back onto the couch, but he stood firm.

"Going to the bathroom."

"You should have told me."

"I can make it on my own."

"Put your arm around me, and I'll help you get there," she said and put her arm around him, intent on guiding him to the bathroom.

He didn't move. "If you want to help me, you can get me my clothes."

"Bathroom first."

Because he really needed to pee, he gave up and let her guide him to the bathroom. He wished she had at least given him his underwear. Wobbling naked on shaky legs, his dick on full display and jigging like a puppet, was a little too much vulnerability, especially now that he was more alert and his reaction to her touches would be obvious.

When they made it to the bathroom door, he shooed her away. "I can pee on my own."

"If you fall—" she started.

"I won't," he said and shut the door.

He relieved himself, flushed, and managed the few steps to the sink where he washed his hands and face and even finger-brushed his teeth and his hair.

Exiting the bathroom, he saw her back at the dinette, her steady gaze taking in his slow progress.

"No blood," he said.

"Good," she responded. "I put a pair of clean underwear on the couch for you. That's all you're getting for now."

"Thanks." He headed to the couch, slowly sat, and picked up the boxer briefs. Knowing she was watching him, he called out, "I could use some help putting these on, Nurse Alicia."

"You peed by yourself," she said. "I'm pretty sure you can pull up your undies by yourself."

"That was a lot of movement for one day. It practically wore me out."

"Why don't you just forget about the underwear then."

"Ahh, the truth comes out," he said and slid his feet one at a time into the boxers.

"What truth is that?"

"You like keeping me naked."

She scoffed. "What I like is easy access to your wounds."

He grinned at the unflappable tone in her voice. "Whatever you say, *farolita*," he said, putting a teasing spin on his tone.

He was drained and sitting at about a six on the

pain scale, but lying on the couch twenty-four/seven wouldn't help him regain his strength and mobility. Besides, their light sparring had energized him. He eased himself upright, and as he rose, he pulled up the boxers—slowly to give her a final view of his ass. His hand pressed to his wound, he shuffled his way to the table.

"You should be lying down," she said.

He liked to think that the flush on her cheeks confirmed she'd seen the peep show. It lifted his mouth into a cocky grin.

"If I'm well enough to dress myself, I'm well enough to sit at the table. Besides, as much as I appreciate that couch, lying on it for days has opened up a new set of wounds on my ass." His gaze locked onto hers. "I'm sure you noticed."

"Better have a doctor check your ego as soon as you leave here. It appears enlarged."

He laughed. "I've never had any complaints about its size."

"People lie," she said, keeping her gaze on her book.

"What are you lying about, *farolita*?" he said.

"You first, Rey."

The grin still on his face, he turned the chair beside her sideways to make it easier to sit without bumping into the table on the way down, then slowly and carefully settled himself into it, wincing at the effort. The bending pulled, and the weight of gravity tugging on his side set up a heaviness in that area that compressed his pain, layer upon layer. But he'd die in this chair before he admitted he couldn't tough out a few minutes of sitting upright.

"I'll tell you if you share that coffee with me," he said, motioning to the coffee cup near her.

"I'll make you a cup of echinacea tea with honey," she said and put her book down. "It has medicinal properties that'll strengthen your immune system and help you heal."

"I'm more of a coffee guy." He reached out, scooped his hand around her cup, and slid it in front of him.

Her eyes went wide in surprise for a second, and her hand shifted like it was going to snatch the cup back, but she didn't.

"I should warn you. I like my coffee strong and bitter," she said.

It was how he liked his, too. One sip of the dark brew sent caffeine bursting through his bloodstream like fireworks, making his mind, eyes, and heart thump in sync.

"Man, you weren't lying," he said, holding back a cough. "This stuff'll eat through your stomach."

"It's what gets me through my 12-hour shifts at work."

He took another few sips and studied her as she did her best to pretend to read.

"About earlier and the question about your husband… I was out of line," he said, his pseudo-apology drawing her gaze.

"Yes, you were. But I guess I've been pretty nosy myself."

He held up her cup in a toast. "Here's to curiosity. May we both learn to curb it before it kills one of us."

"Are you implying that I'm going to kill you? Or that you're going to kill me?" she asked.

His gaze scrolled slowly down her body, then back up and held her gaze. "You don't look the part, so…" He raised one eyebrow to finish the sentence.

She cocked her head. "What does a killer look like?"

"Why don't you tell me?" he said with a grin and cocked back in the chair, taking another sip of coffee, eager to hear her answer.

Her gaze scrolled slowly down his body, then up, like he had with her, then zoomed in on his long hair and facial scruff as if suggesting he was it.

He didn't blame her for her assessment. The sponge baths she'd given him were the closest thing to a shower he'd had in days. And the reflection in the mirror staring back at him while he washed up minutes ago resembled the scumbags he'd busted over the years. It was part of the reason he was so good at undercover work. He looked and played the part well. But he couldn't help but feel disappointed that she, like most people, would make that judgment solely on appearance and limited data.

"Hard to say," she said finally. "Until we invent a way to see inside someone's soul to where the truth is, we'll have to go on a person's words and actions."

He knew where she was going with that statement, but he asked anyway. "Like?"

"Like…showing up at a remote cabin on foot with a lethal weapon, life-threatening injury, and a lame story about getting shot while hiking."

"We're back to where we were before we apologized—being too nosy."

"Can you see why I would be?" she asked.

Yes, he could. His own curiosity meter had flipped

to high the second he stumbled onto this property that should have been vacant and saw her and the dog. And the needle hadn't budged much despite her being a little more forthcoming than he'd been.

"Can you see why *I* would be?" he countered.

"No, I can't. There's absolutely nothing suspicious about me or my behavior."

"Not from where I sit."

Her eyebrows rose. "Like what?"

"A beautiful woman all alone in a remote cabin in the middle of winter with no husband, boyfriend, family, or friends with her."

"Oh dear," she said in an exaggerated drawl, eyes open wide, fingers to her lips. "I had no idea women weren't allowed to travel to this state without an escort."

The sarcasm in her voice raked across his skin, opening cracks to the magma of impatience that smoldered beneath the surface. "Why are you here, Alicia?"

"That's none of your business, Rey." Her tone mirrored his.

Liquid anger erupted in his chest at her refusal to answer his question. The long months with the gang had cut the brakes on his effort to control the undesirable emotion, and it often hit him at the slightest provocation. "Just answer the fucking question."

Anger reddened her cheeks and flashed in her eyes, and he felt the pierce of her glare to his core. But instead of the face slap he thought would follow, she surged to her feet and stormed to the coatrack, grabbed the key fob to her SUV, then marched back to him and tossed it onto the table. It slid to a stop in front of him.

"At great personal risk, I brought you into my home and saved your life. The least you can do to show your appreciation is not to bully me. If you can't…"

Her tone was calm and direct, but the look on her face, in her eyes, and her short breaths making her chest fall and rise rapidly, told him she was beyond pissed. But he also smelled her fear. Fear of him. The knowledge settled his anger. He didn't want to hurt her. Wouldn't hurt her. Unless he had no other option.

"It won't happen again," he said, his anger reined in and his voice calm again. And he meant it. He wouldn't allow himself to lose his temper with her again.

"If it does, you'll have to leave, whether you're healed or not," she said. "I don't tolerate that behavior from anyone, even patients who aren't at their best."

The woman had courage, a strong will, and loads of spirit, qualities he admired.

"Understood," he said, then nudged her chair with his foot, the action and his gaze asking her to sit. After a moment, she did, her eyes glued to his, as if she expected another attack and was mentally and physically gearing up to fulfill her promise to kick his ass out.

"I'm not going to hurt you, Alicia," he said with as much sincerity as he could muster.

To convince her, he leaned forward, lifted his hand to her face, and brushed auburn strands of hair back from her face with his fingertips and tucked it behind her ear like he'd seen her do to self-soothe.

It was a bad move. At the first touch of her warmth and softness, feelings of raw need swirled thick and hot through him, like rivers of molten honey. Before he knew it, they were slinking up his dick in long, curling tendrils that were stroking him to hardness.

In a *very* bad move, he let his hand slide to the back of her skull and tangled his fingers in her hair. "I won't harm a hair on this lovely head," he said in a husky whisper.

The luminous green eyes locked on his were syphoning his already low reserves of strength. If he didn't disconnect from her soon, she'd pull him down into whatever maelstrom of emotion and deceit was swirling beneath them, and he could kiss his ass goodbye.

Swallowing the lump of lust in his throat didn't dissipate it. And because his blood was fueling the wrong head, he couldn't stop himself from piling on the stupid. He drew her closer, leaning in farther than pain should have allowed, inching his mouth closer to hers.

A tremor of a sigh slid from her mouth to his, inviting him to come all the way in, and he did, eager to take her plush lips and taste her sweet mouth.

Millimeters from his goal, she leaned back, away from him. A chuckle trickled from her lips, which stung more than a tongue-lashing or a slap would have.

"No more coffee for you." She grabbed the mug and dumped its contents into the sink.

"Why's that?" he asked, annoyed to discover that his chest was burning in disappointment.

"Obviously the caffeine has cut off the blood supply to your brain." She washed the mug and set it in the drainer.

"Because I said I won't hurt you?" he asked, eyebrows furrowed at her poking fun at him.

She dried her hands with the towel, hung it up, and

turned back to him. "Because your mood is all over the place. First you interrogate me, then you threaten to kill me, and a minute later you make a pass at me."

He scoffed, louder and nastier than necessary to negate her statements. "Sweetheart, that wasn't me making a pass at you. That was me being sincere. So you could relax."

She lifted one eyebrow and smirked at him. "I know a pass when I see one. *Sweetheart*."

"Not this time," he insisted and then wondered why he couldn't admit it. He knew it, and she knew it. Why was he denying it?

Because her scoff at his very real attempt had nicked his ego? No, it was more than that. The truth was, she made him feel…things. If that wasn't bad enough, she pretended he didn't stir the same feelings in her. And that just pissed him off.

"Oh, okay. My mistake." She didn't roll her eyes, but her tone was soaked in the emotion that accompanied the dismissive action. She returned to the table, sat, and picked up her book.

After a few long, slow beats, when he could see that maybe he'd nicked *her* ego, he reached out and ran the tips of his fingers along her bare forearm. Feeling goosebumps rise on her soft skin from his touch made him want to touch her in other places, to see what other kinds of reactions it would elicit.

"Must be all the drugs you've given me," he said with a grin.

Her back stiffened against her chair. "Are you saying that the reason you made a pass at me is because I needlessly drugged you?"

Hell, he would have made a pass at her drugged,

drunk, sick, in pain, or stone-cold sober. But he wouldn't tell her that. He'd already shared too much. Instead of lying to her again, he laughed. Let her interpret it however she wanted.

Her eyebrows furrowed, her lips tightened, and she snapped her book closed. She rose from her chair and moved to stand inches from him, right in front of him, between his knees, hands on her hips, arms akimbo.

Shit. He should have gone back to the couch in one piece when he'd had the chance.

"First of all, the pain meds aren't that strong, and second, they're mostly out of your system at the moment." Her voice was low and measured, but he knew that beneath all that calm a firestorm churned.

"That must be why I'm aching all over," he said.

"You're a real piece of work." Shaking her head, she started to walk away from him.

For some asinine reason he didn't understand, he reached out and hooked her around the hips and snatched her close to him, between his spread legs.

To stop herself from falling onto him, she reached out and caught herself on his shoulders. The action triggered a low groan from both of them, and the sound sent lust exploding through his body, cloaking the pain that only moments before had been flaring.

Fanning his hands over her ass and holding tight, he stared up at her, her down at him, and they stood connected, burning in the flash fire that their touches had ignited between them. His heart raced, his breath was choppy, and his cock was as hard as a brick. Unless she was blind, she'd be able to see his condition. What surprised him was that he wanted her to see it and know that it was because of her.

Her eyes on his were sultry and sexy and an open window to the raw desire erupting inside her. Her nipples punched against her shirt like two fresh-from-the-box bullets, and her breath was as ragged as his. She wanted him, too.

In this small moment, they had a big decision to make—slide deeper into the fire or climb out and get far away.

Despite his wound, despite the fact that he was on an undercover assignment, despite the fact that she deserved better than a fast lust-driven fuck, he was ready to go for it if she was. Maybe it was just what the doctor—er, nurse—ordered and would cure what ailed both of them. Because behind that sassy tongue, snapping eyes, and fierce bravado, he could see that she was as wounded and weary as he was. Only her wounds and fatigue were raw and ran core deep.

****

Alicia felt her self-control burning to bits and her long-fallow libido rising from the ashes of the firestorm that was Rey Cruz, and her sex-fogged brain couldn't decide whether to stop it or let it happen.

No man had looked at her with that heightened level of lust in a long time, but she recognized it in Rey, from the heat in his dark chocolate eyes and the slow tongue lick to his full lips, to the big hands possessing her and the torpedo demanding entry into her body.

Jon had once told her in college that she looked like the kind of woman a man wanted to settle down with, not one that a man wanted to fuck, then forget. It was the incident that had incited a surge of rebellion during a night out with her friends and prompted her to get the tattoo she hadn't told Rey about.

Rey was looking at her like he wanted to fuck her—hard and fast and thoroughly—and then, most likely, forget her and move on. Her mind buzzed with one crazed thought. Don't analyze it. Just take all he wants to give and enjoy the hell out of it.

But analyze she did, because that's who she was, and the result that floated up was that sex with a stranger, a criminal, a patient was the absolute wrong decision. She wasn't the kind of woman who let desire drive her actions and decisions. And she wasn't going to race, skip, or stroll down that path now, especially not with this man, who had brought thirty-one flavors of danger into her world the second he stepped onto her porch.

Plus, she was his nurse, he her patient. And there were rules governing that relationship, even in this unusual situation. Intimately touching him, letting him touch her, was pushing the boundary of appropriate, professional nurse/patient behavior. Having sex with him would destroy that boundary—and her career, which was already on shaky ground. It would also distract her from accomplishing her mission here.

Strapping on her strong, capable nurse persona, the one that followed rules and didn't take shit, she eased out of his embrace. The action didn't eliminate the heat between them as she'd hoped. It continued to swirl around them, trying to push her back to him. Even when she stepped back a couple of feet.

"Look, Rey, I know you're not yourself right now, with your wounds and *all the meds I've got you on*, but you need to stop touching me. While you're here, I'm your nurse, not someone you can fondle for fun because you're bored."

His gaze skimmed her alert nipples before gliding back to her flushed face. "I must have misread your signals."

He hadn't misread anything. She had sent signals. Lots of them. Still, this was the right course. "Well, the signal I'm sending now is that I'd rather you not touch me."

"Got it," he said. Rising from the chair, he eased his way back to the couch.

She went into the bathroom to grab the meds from the first aid kit. After taking a minute to breathe and gain full control of her emotions, she joined him.

A look at his pinched eyes and rigid lips showed his irritation. A closer look showed his pain. Likely caused by his venture beyond the couch, including the sparing with her. It reminded her again that he was her patient and helped her shift fully back into professional mode.

She handed him the meds and water, which he downed, then checked his bandage. Through all her ministrations, she felt his gaze on her. It seemed to be calling on her to forget that he was her patient and look at him—and treat him—like a man who needed a more erotic form of tender loving care.

Inspection done, she settled the blanket up to his shoulders. "Get some rest," she said, her voice softer to dull the sharp edges of her earlier lies. *So you can leave me and these erotic fantasies can disperse.* "Tomorrow, we'll get you up and walking, in short intervals. You seem to be strong enough for it."

Getting gunshot patients up and walking once or twice a day was protocol and helped prevent blood clots. In his case, it also might help burn off some of that energy urging him to touch her all the time.

"Do you need anything before I turn in for the night?" she said.

He shook his head.

"Okay. Sleep well. See you in the morning."

She headed to the bathroom to brush her teeth, then to bed to quiet the desire in her body shrieking for satisfaction.

****

Before the pain-quieting effect of the meds kicked in, Nick's mind raced with thoughts of Alicia and the no-touching gauntlet she'd thrown down.

Her body liked his touch. Its reactions said so. But because her mouth had said no, that was the answer he'd have to go with. He'd control his damn self even if it killed him. No man had ever died from the effects of a prolonged, persistent erection and aching balls. At least not that he knew of. He grinned. Maybe he'd ask Nurse Alicia that question in the morning.

But he wouldn't touch her. For reasons she gave, but also because he was on an undercover assignment and she was a distraction that clouded his mind. And a clouded mind could get him killed.

Although it was hardly fair that he couldn't touch her when she touched him all the time—to check and change his bandage, to check his temperature, to give him pills, food, water. A sponge bath. And when her hands weren't touching him, her gaze was. A hungry gaze that begged for his touch. But he'd promised not to touch her, and he'd keep that promise.

Touching her with his words, however, wasn't off limits. He grinned in the dark as he compiled questions to fire at her tomorrow. And he'd back off the asshole bit. Today had showed him that he didn't like to see her upset.

A short time later, pain had unclenched its grip on his body enough for him to drift off to sleep.

Chapter Nine

"Do you like being a nurse?" Nick asked Alicia the next morning as she leaned over him applying antibiotic ointment to his wounds.

"For the most part," she said, her gaze glued to her task. "Lean toward me a bit, please."

He did as she asked. "You're good at it," he said. "Being a nurse, I mean."

"What's your evidence for that statement?" she asked as she wrapped a clean bandage over the fresh pads. Her wry smile suggested she was pleased with his compliment even as her tone downplayed it.

"Your gentle but confident touch. It says you know what you're doing, but you never forget it's a person you're treating, someone with feelings."

After securing the end of the bandage, she settled her gaze on his. "Spoken like a man who has received his fair share of medical care."

He grinned, neither denying nor confirming her statement as he settled back. "What's your evidence for that statement, Nurse Alicia?"

She sat beside him. "The faded souvenirs of old injuries scattered across your body."

"Hmm. Since you've seen all my souvenirs, it's only fair I get to see yours."

"You saw my tattoos. That's all you're getting." Her words were firm, but her eyes sparkled, suggesting she enjoyed their sparring as much as he did.

She shifted like she was going to get up. All he wanted was to keep her here, on the couch, with him. He'd promised not to touch, so he'd stop her with his words. "Do you work in a hospital or a doctor's office?" While she was first treating his wounds, she'd said she was an ER nurse. Would she give the same answer this time?

"I'm an ER nurse."

Hmm. Okay.

"What kind of work do you do?" she asked.

"Oh…odd jobs."

"What kind of odd jobs?"

"This and that," he said. "You must see a lot of gunshot wounds in your job."

"Don't think I didn't notice the change of subject."

He shrugged. "I'm interested in what you do."

"Maybe I'm interested in what you do, too."

"Eh, I'm boring."

A few beats passed as she stared at him. Deciding whether to continue to grill him about his profession? He hoped she'd let it go, because he wasn't giving up anything, and he didn't want to argue either.

"Boring is not a word I'd use to describe you," she said.

Her response both surprised and pleased him. He held her gaze tight, willing her to see inside him, to the real him, so she'd know she was right on with her assessment. He wasn't boring. He wasn't some bum. And he wasn't a criminal.

He let a smile ease across his face. "If you don't mind, I'd like you to keep that opinion of me instead of realizing I'm right."

"Fine," she said with a resigned sigh. "I work in an area of Seattle that sees a lot of crime and violence. Shootings, stabbings, drug overdoses… They're everyday occurrences. Yet even after ten years in nursing, it still shocks me the many ways people find to hurt each other and themselves."

The comment further confirmed that she was from Seattle, which was where the couple who owned this cabin was from. The accumulating body of evidence pointed to her being a nurse, like she claimed, and not a gang member, but as was his way—and standard Bureau procedure—he'd withhold final judgment until he had solid proof.

"It must be tough, always being around traumatic injuries and pain and suffering," he said.

She shrugged. "Sometimes. But I feel like it's the area where my skills are most needed."

"You feel like you're making a difference," he said, filling in the words she didn't say.

"Yes. Well, most of the time." She slid her thumb across her finger tattoo, which seemed like a centering action. "But sometimes…"

She shrugged, but he knew what she meant, because he felt the same way.

"Sometimes it feels like the never-ending wave of suffering is going to drown you," he said.

She nodded. "This deep-seated frustration and sadness will set in sometimes where I feel like what I'm doing is for nothing. I have regulars. I patch them up, but because most of them go right back to the same lifestyle, they get hurt again. Or die. It's heartbreaking."

The sadness in her eyes was sincere, and it spoke to his heart. "You ever think about doing something less heartbreaking?"

"Not really. I mean, when I have a really bad day, I swear I'm going to quit and find a nice, quiet private practice to work, where patients come in to be treated for colds or rashes or need a physical for school or work, instead of coming in with a knife stuck in their heart or at death's door because they've overdosed…again."

"What stops you? From quitting," he said.

"I'd be bored to tears," she said with a soft chuckle.

"Ah… a fellow adrenaline junky."

"No. Well, maybe. I don't know. I like the fast pace and the challenge of not knowing who's going to come through the door, where every situation is different and always demands my full attention and scope of abilities. Being on that edge, fighting against death, is energizing and addictive."

"You're in the business of giving the dying another chance," he said.

She smiled. "I guess so. I want my work to be meaningful. And in the ER, it is."

He knew how she felt. Busting scumbag drug traffickers and homegrown terrorists and getting them off the street to keep decent, law-abiding people safe made him feel like he was doing something important, not just for his city but for humanity as a whole. But seeing offenders get off in the courts or released from jail and go right back to the life that got them busted was frustrating as hell. Yet, like Alicia, he wouldn't change what he did for anything.

It was something Renee had never understood. His ex-fiancé had worked a nine-to-five job and hated that he often worked late and on weekends and holidays. He couldn't get through to her that crime didn't take time off or close up shop at five. She didn't understand his need to go on undercover missions. They fought about it constantly. It was why she eventually would have left him even if he hadn't called off their engagement a year ago when he caught her kissing her boss.

The breakup had been the best solution, for both of them, but man, it had cored him. Her betrayal. His failure to keep her happy. Their inability to let go some of their own needs for the benefit of the relationship. They'd been wrong for each other. On so many levels. Not only because of his career but also because of other things. Like kids. She wanted several. He wanted none.

She had blamed his lack of interest in kids on his profession, said he saw the worst of humanity, which had crafted his myopic opinion that the world wasn't a good place to raise kids. And that was true. But it bothered him that she'd always thought she could change him, as if he somehow wasn't acceptable the way he was.

And his father. Shit. Nick could drown in the disappointment rolling off his father whenever they were within twenty miles of each other. The old man wasn't shy about telling anyone who'd listen how Nick had wasted his life being in the military and then the FBI. No matter how many cases Nick solved, how many scumbags he busted and put behind bars, how many commendations he'd received, it was never good enough for his father, a lawyer and owner of the state's largest and most prestigious law firm. Nick had grown used to the sting of the embedded splinter but could be in his dad's company only in limited amounts.

"Hey, are you all right?" Alicia's voice, and her hand on his, pulled him out of the box where he'd stored old wounds, hurts, and disappointments.

"Yeah," he said finally, though not very convincingly, and slammed shut that lid.

"You looked like you were in pain." She moved her hand away.

How was it that this stranger could decipher his emotions and feelings with a glance? "Yeah, well, I do have two additional holes in my body whose sole purpose is to manufacture pain."

"You're a fast healer," she said. "In short time, this will be just another story you tell to impress your friends."

"Hmm. Since I'm healing so well, think I'll have a shower today."

"It's too soon for that. The area needs to stay dry."

"I'll wrap it with a plastic bag so it doesn't get wet. It worked when I broke my arm."

"I'd give it another day."

"Okay." He raised his arms and placed his clasped hands behind his head. "I'll stick with sponge baths from my lovely and capable nurse." He sniffed his pit and wrinkled his nose. "In fact, I could use one right now. I'm smelling like a bag of old corn chips."

"I wondered what that smell was," she said. "I thought Panza had dragged in a dead squirrel."

He laughed, and the dog at their side grumbled at hearing his name maligned.

Alicia went into the kitchen and came back with a roll of duct tape, a pair of scissors, and a garbage bag, which she split up the sides.

"Up," she said.

Nick eased to his feet, and she wrapped the plastic tightly around his bandaged area, taping it at the top and bottom to block water from getting in. Good thing he didn't have copious hair on his chest and back, or he'd be minutes away from a painful hair removal session.

"How does that feel?" she asked, her hands smoothing down the tape on his skin and the plastic to ensure it was secure.

"Great, other than I can't breathe," he said in a strained voice.

"Better make it a short shower then," she said and headed to the bathroom.

Smiling at her sass and the view of her luscious ass swaying hypnotically in her snug jeans, he followed her to the bathroom. By the time he made his way there, she had started the shower and hung a clean towel over the rod.

"If you get light-headed and feel like you're going to pass out—"

"I'll call out for you to come catch me," he said with a grin.

"Or you could sit down until it passes."

"No offense, Nurse Alicia, but you aren't as attentive to my health as you were as recently as yesterday."

"Yesterday, you weren't asking to shower. Patients who begin to show interest in their hygiene typically are out of the danger zone."

"Damn. I've got to work on keeping my big mouth shut."

She smiled at his joke. "Call out if you really need help."

"You could shower with me to avert all possible danger," he teased. Showering with Alicia would create all kinds of danger, not avert it, and he'd enjoy every bit of it, endure any amount of discomfort, to have her.

"Just be careful, and you'll be fine," she said, then left him.

"Yes, ma'am," he said as she pulled the door to.

The plastic wrapped tight around his mid-section restricted his bending movement, but he managed to wriggle off his boxer briefs and step into the shower.

Task *numero uno*—relieve the pent-up pressure in his balls. Since he'd been with Alicia, he'd had a near-constant hard-on and an ache in his balls that wouldn't quit.

Soaping up his jutting member and using the image of her face, the sweet-sexy scent of her, the feel of her body in his arms as a guiding vision, he stroked with a purpose. In a new Navarro record, he accomplished his mission, the explosion leaving him light-headed and weak-kneed. He hugged the shower wall until the indigo bubbles popping around his head dissipated.

Once he was again able to stand upright, he washed the rest of his body and even washed his hair with Alicia's flower-scented shampoo. Turning off the shower, he wrapped the towel low on his hips to avoid his wounds and stepped from the shower.

He opened the bathroom door to let the steam escape. "Alicia, do you have a comb and toothbrush I could use?"

"In the cabinet," she called from the kitchen.

He found them where she'd indicated and felt human again after he'd brushed his teeth and combed his hair.

"You need a haircut and a shave, Navarro," he said to his reflection. "No wonder she doesn't want to kiss you."

He was about to ditch the towel and get dressed when he realized he had no clothes.

"Alicia?" he called out again.

"Rey," she said at the door, surprising him. In her arms were black sweats, a white T-shirt, and thick socks.

"Well, that's disappointing," he said.

She glanced at the bundle, then back at him. "You've been begging me for clothes for days."

"I'd convinced myself that you had a kinky ulterior motive for keeping me naked and were going to surprise me with it at any moment."

She thrust the pile into his chest, and he trapped them with one hand. "And another fantasy bites the dust," she said and turned to leave.

"By the way—" He caught her hand and ran his thumb over her tattoo. "—that was me teasing you, not making a pass at you." His voice was low and sincere and, hell, sexier than it should be for trying to convince this woman he wasn't making another pass at her.

She licked her lips. "Good to know."

The moist layer riding her lips from her tongue lick inspired him to seek out and catalog every delicious physical change appearing on her body since he'd taken her hand. Her nipples, high and tight, pouting against her T-shirt. Her pulse throbbing at the side of her smooth, lovely throat. Her deep, dilated pupils.

Despite what she claimed, all indications pointed to her wanting him. His closeness. His touch. His kiss. And his mind flamed with the knowledge.

Her gaze dropped to the spot where their hands met, then rose to his eyes. Heat flashed in her cheeks that he was sure had absolutely nothing to do with the humid bathroom.

"And this?" she asked, squeezing his hand, her breathy voice as low as his had been. Another sign that she was affected by his touch. "Is this teasing or a pass?"

"Which do you want it to be?"

She swallowed hard. "Breakfast is ready."

"I'm starving," he said, eyes pinned on hers.

"Rey… We talked about this." Her whispered words steamed with the reminder that she was sticking to her earlier decision. And here he was, breaking his promise.

What the hell was wrong with him? He had always made a point to keep his promises, to respect people's boundaries, especially women's boundaries concerning physical contact. But with her, his libido was calling all the shots, leaving his brain and good sense benched.

Regardless, his struggles to control his libido and his interpretation of what her libido was saying were of no consequence. She had said no touching. And her *no* had to eclipse any yes he thought he felt and saw.

He released her hand. "I'll be right out."

"After you put that away," she said, glancing down, then back to his eyes. Then she left him, closing the door behind her.

He looked down. Grinned. Had she meant the wet towel on the floor or his rigid cock standing at attention? He gripped his rod. "The cock. Definitely the cock."

After hanging up the towel, he grabbed the scissors

he'd seen in the cabinet and cut himself out of the plastic corset. He then took his slow time getting dressed to give his blood pressure, heart rate, and pecker time to calm down.

****

Rey Cruz was more lethal than the weapon he'd come here with, Alicia decided as she leaned against the kitchen counter to get her libido under control after witnessing his fully engorged dick standing at attention between them. It was so close, so tempting, so…big. Her mouth watered just thinking about it.

The man was making her lose touch with who she thought she was. It was obvious she wanted him, and he knew it. Giving free rein to that wanting would set a match to the tinderbox in her core that, once afire, would ignite all of her. And him. And possibly burn the cabin to ashes. That would be plain stupid, and she wasn't stupid. Thank God he had let her go at her feeble reminder. But that image would be burned in her brain forever.

"A hot shower and clean clothes—I feel like a new man," Rey said behind her.

She spun to face him and worked to keep her gaze on his eyes instead of crawling over his body. The sweats hugged him in all the right spots. The T-shirt stretched across his shoulders, caressing muscles likely honed by whatever kind of work he did. Although he needed a shave, his hair was clean and combed back, showing his chiseled and handsome face. He looked as delicious fully dressed as he had fully naked.

As they ate breakfast—both sharing bites of their pancakes, bacon, and eggs with Panza after he'd finished his plain oatmeal breakfast—they shared a light barrage of small talk on safer topics. Breakfast over, he snatched up their dishes and carried them to the sink before she could.

"You don't need to do that," she said, joining him.

"Go away. I'm doing dishes," he teased and ran hot water into the sink.

He had grabbed the dish soap to squirt some into the water, but she took the bottle, she set it on the counter, and turned off the water.

"It's kind of you to offer," she said. "I appreciate it. But I'd rather you saved your energy for a different activity."

He grinned and took her hand in his, rubbing the back with his thumb. "You've got my full attention."

She held back the chuckle inside her at his obvious but mistaken assumption that the activity she was referring to was sexual. "I thought we'd go for a walk."

He blinked in confusion, and his eyebrows furrowed. "A walk? Outside?"

"It'll be good for you to move around and get some fresh air."

He held his arms open and glanced down at his meager clothing. "I'm a little underdressed for a hike through the snow."

"I washed all the clothes my husband left from previous visits and put them on the couch. If you bundle up, you'll stay warm enough. Besides, there's not that much snow. The boots you came here in will be sufficient."

When he didn't move, she added, "Go on. Nurse's orders," and turned to start the dishes, making it clear she wasn't entertaining any discussion on the matter.

Chapter Ten

"Since this is your first excursion out, we'll keep a slow pace and not go far," Alicia said as she and Rey followed Panza into the snow-dusted woods surrounding the cabin.

"No need to baby me. I'm fine." Rey picked up his pace as if to prove his words.

"Oh, I know," she said, looping her arm through his and holding on to slow him. "I'm more worried about me. If you fall again, having to drag you home might kill me. You're what…eight feet tall and made of granite?"

He laughed. "Almost. And you're what…four ten?"

She bumped his arm with her shoulder. "Five four."

"Five four? God, you're huge."

She chuckled at his teasing. "Don't fall."

"So, what do you do for fun in Seattle?" he said, filling a moment of quiet.

"Well, it's a wonderful city—tons of things to do. Have you been there?"

"No."

"Oh. Well, when I'm not working, I like to spend as much time as I can outside."

"Doing what?"

"Running, hiking, skiing… What about you?"

"What about me what?"

"What do you do for fun?"

"Oh, you know."

She stopped and stared at him. "No, I don't know, and your unwillingness to answer even the simplest question about yourself is tiresome and ridiculous."

After a short pause, he answered. "I lift weights and run."

"For fun?"

"Yes. Anything wrong with that?"

"No, not at all. See? Was that so hard?"

"Did that five-word answer open a window into my soul for you?" he asked.

She smiled. "A crack." He resumed walking, and she kept pace beside him, which was a little faster than she liked for him, but she'd let him do what he thought he could do.

"Did you and your husband do all those activities together?" he asked.

At Rey's question, guilt squeezed her heart almost to bursting. "Not often."

"Why?"

Because she had taken his presence in her life for granted and greedily insisted on doing what she liked instead of doing things that he liked. She recognized it now, after the fact. Too bad she hadn't noticed while he was alive and she could have done something about it.

"Our schedules didn't always mesh." It was as much of the truth as she wanted to share.

"Alicia, what happened to your husband?"

"I told you. He died."

"You didn't say how."

"That's because I don't want to talk about it."

He stopped and stared at her, a grin on his face. "Your unwillingness to answer even the simplest question about your life is tiresome and ridiculous."

Hearing her words slung back at her but with teasing made her smile.

"Okay. That's fair," she said. "I'll give you the short version, but then that's all I really want to say about it. Although it's been seven months, it's still painful for me."

"I'm curious about your life, but if it's that painful, I can curb my—"

"The plane he was on crashed," she blurted out. "Everyone on board died."

He took her hand in his. "I'm sorry."

"For my loss or for your prying?"

"Both."

She squeezed his hand in thanks, then let it go.

"Is that why you came here?" he asked. "To come to terms with your loss?"

"Yes, to reflect and decide what's next." And because her boss had put her on forced leave until she had purged her insanity. But Rey definitely didn't need to know that.

"And then I came along and disrupted your plan."

"Not to make light of your injury and what you've gone through, but it's been a good distraction for me. Takes the focus off the difficult tasks I came here to accomplish."

"You're welcome."

Although the conversation ended on a lighter note, talking about Jon dropped a melancholy pall over their walk. To dissipate the unwanted emotions swirling in her blood, she let the sound of their feet crunching on the snowy path fill her mind and push out thoughts of Jon, his death, and the life-changing scenario that resulted in the guilt that weighed on her night and day.

Rey stopped. "Uh…Alicia?"

She stopped too and followed his gaze to the growing circle of blood blossoming through the layers of clothing.

****

The walk back to the cabin seemed to take twice as long because of Alicia's insistence that Nick take a super slow pace. Once there, she helped him out of his boots and extra clothes and back onto the couch. With her usual efficiency, she rebandaged his wounds and gave him more pain relievers, but the excursion, as she called it, left his body a shivering mess. She covered him with the blanket and another one from her bedroom, then lit a fire in the fireplace.

"What's your pain level?" she asked as she sat beside him.

"About a five. Mostly I'm tired."

"I got you up and walking too soon and kept you out too long."

He took her hand to ease the distress in her eyes, in her voice. "I was showing off and walking too fast."

"Guess we both could have done better."

They shared a long look. It was warm and soft, and everything in him wanted to go deeper into it, curl up, and feel nothing but her. That's what would heal him.

"Get some rest," she said, breaking their connection. "I'll make you some hot tea."

He held her hand tight when she would have pulled away. "I don't want tea."

"Do you want something else?" At his grin and the

spark in his eyes, she added, "Something else to drink."

He shook his head. "Just sit with me."

After a beat to consider it, she eased her hand from his, settled into the far end of the couch, and grabbed her paperback from the table.

"We're not going to talk?" he asked.

"If you're talking, you're not resting."

"All right, Nurse Alicia. You win," he said.

"Wow. You gave in quickly. You really are tired," she teased.

"While you're down there, you can rub my feet if you want," he said.

"Thanks, I'll pass."

"If I were taking care of you, I'd rub your feet."

"I'm not rubbing your feet."

"Or you could rub—"

"I'm not rubbing anything else either," she said.

He chuckled. "Can't blame a guy for trying."

His eyes were growing heavy, his voice low and groggy. The meds were kicking in. He was minutes from drifting off, but he kept his gaze on her, wanting her face to be the last thing he saw.

****

After Rey finally succumbed to sleep, Alicia read. Or tried to. Her thoughts turned to the mission she'd come here to work on—packing up her memories and setting a plan for getting on with her life as a new and improved Alicia. Instead of working on that mission, she was taking care of a stray dog who wouldn't leave and a wounded gang member who couldn't.

Her gaze settled on the sexy-as-sin gang member who tempted her at every turn to break all her rules. Tempted her to be someone she wasn't. The more time she spent with him, the more she realized that she didn't mind it that much. Every experience is a lesson, and the things she was learning about herself would be invaluable in helping her move forward into a new life.

Rey was sleeping soundly, so she should get up and tackle the next item on her to-do list. But she stayed beside him. Watched him. Listened to him breathe. Inhaled his scent. Enjoyed the feel of his body next to hers. Those actions led to deep thoughts, like why she felt so content being with this stranger who was feeling less like a stranger every minute she spent with him. And how would it feel to let go of her inhibitions, cross the boundaries of professional and personal good judgment, and let him kiss her, touch her, make her feel again. Like he wanted. Like she needed.

Fantasizing was one thing, doing was another. Once that boundary had collapsed, there could be no going back, no pretending it hadn't happened. She'd have to accept that she was the type of nurse who had sex with a patient. The type of woman who had sex with a stranger. Her pile of regrets was already towering. Adding more wouldn't end well for her, and her ego might not be able to withstand another attack on her bruised psyche. Fantasizing was as far as she'd allow herself to go.

Leaving her patient to sleep, she went to her room, closed the door, stripped off her jeans, and let her fantasies run wild.

****

Alicia jerked awake to the noise of what sounded like a pan clanging to the floor. Long shadows filled her bedroom. A tap to her phone on the nightstand showed a quarter to five. She had fallen asleep!

She jumped out of bed and headed to the living room to check on Rey and then to the kitchen to get dinner going.

He was at the kitchen counter, making a salad.

"I can't believe I fell asleep," she said, joining him.

"You must have needed it," he said.

"What are you doing?"

"Cooking dinner," he said and motioned to the steak he'd set on the counter.

"You should be resting." She went to the sink to wash her hands and tried to move in to take over the salad, but he blocked her.

"I want to cook for you for a change."

"What? You don't like my cooking?" she asked as she dried her hands.

"Yeah, it's terrible," he teased.

"Oh, ha-ha." She popped him on the leg with the kitchen towel.

"Let me cook for you," he said. "To thank you for all you've done for me."

"Are you sure you feel up to it?"

"I feel better every day, thanks to you."

"Okay." She tossed him the towel. "Go for it."

"That didn't take much arm-twisting."

"I rarely turn down the chance to get out of cooking."

"You don't like it?"

She shrugged. "I don't mind it. I'm just not that creative in the kitchen, so it quickly gets repetitive and boring."

"Lucky for you, I am."

"Repetitive and boring?"

A devilish light shined in his eyes, and the devilish

grin tipping the corner of his lips grew as he roped the kitchen towel in his hands. Before she could back up to avoid him, he snapped the towel toward her, popping her on the thigh and drawing a surprised laugh from her. When he tried it again, she caught the towel. He yanked on it, pulling her close, and lightning quick wrapped the towel behind her at the hips and drew her in.

Her hands braced on his chest, and she couldn't turn off her smile.

He looked at her, his gaze going deep. "*Farolita.*"

His low whisper brushed her lips and made them tingle. "You've called me that before. What does it mean?"

"Little fire."

"You know what happens when you get too close to the fire," she said.

"Are you going to burn me?"

"I'm pretty sure I'm the one who's going to get burned." She was already burning from their closeness.

"Let's go up in flames together." He leaned in, signaling his intention in his soft breath on her lips and in his strong arms at her back.

Alarms buzzed in her head, warning her to run from the fire that was about to combust. But she didn't. As if reading that as her silent consent, he brought his mouth down on hers.

Pleasure rippled through her entire body at the first touch of his lips on hers, making her head swim and triggering the sweet and sharp tug of desire she thought had deserted her forever.

His lips were firm and warm, taking and giving equally, but she could feel him working to keep the kiss slow and deliberate, as if he wanted time to explore every spot of the new territory that was her mouth. Like a starving woman too long denied pleasure, she fell into the kiss, reveling in the taste and feel of him, her small hum of pleasure wordlessly begging him for more, urging him to deepen the kiss.

Gathering her closer, his tongue pressed against her lips, inviting her to open to him, and she did so eagerly. Wasting no time, he slid his tongue between her parted lips where hers was waiting. The sensation of his tongue against hers jolted pure need through her. Her hands that had rested at his chest now gripped fists of his T-shirt, trying to bring him even closer to her mouth, to her body.

As if sensing her willingness for more, he fisted one hand in her hair and angled her face for better access to her mouth. Moving the kiss into hot and hungry territory, he claimed her, igniting a need inside her that turned her into an eager participant. She moved her hand up to his head to tangle in his hair and hold his mouth closer to hers. Her lips moved with his. Her tongue danced with his. Her body burned for more of his touch, and he obliged, cupping her breast over her shirt, pressing and kneading her flesh and the tight nipple arching into his palm. His touches heated her blood, swirling desire through her throbbing veins.

His groan, low and throaty, filled her ears, and his hips pressed into hers, making her core clench with want and her hips press back to answer the invitation. Everything inside her wanted to take him to the floor, wrap her legs around him, fill her emptiness with his massive cock, and let him fuck her into oblivion where she felt nothing but orgasmic joy.

His lips left hers, and his eyes burned into hers. "I want you, Alicia," he growled, his voice rough and low and urgent, asking for permission to take the next step they both wanted.

With his cock stabbing hard between her legs, at the very epicenter of her need, the spot where the explosion would ignite if she'd allow it, she had no doubt whatsoever he was telling the truth. She wanted him too, wanted him with a need that possessed every cell.

But the spell had been broken the moment he broke the kiss, the moment he spoke of his desire, the moment she opened her eyes to reality's spotlight shining on them, blinding them. Reason rushed in, a dead calm sucking the wind out of the emotional hurricane he'd swept her up in. Panic rushed through her, reminding her that it would be a mistake to have sex with a criminal and a patient and demanding that she stop this before it went any further. Obeying, she eased out of his arms, away from him, but she couldn't unlock her gaze from the lust flaring high in his.

"I can't do this." The words whispered out on a sigh because she was too damn breathless to speak any louder. All her effort was on slowing her heartbeat to a normal pace and chilling her libido to under a thousand degrees. Rey's labored breath, rapid pulse, and heaving chest suggested he was doing the same. For a moment, neither of them said a word.

"Is it because you'd feel like you're being unfaithful to your husband?" he asked finally.

"No."

"Are you afraid of me?"

It wasn't him she was afraid of. It was her out-of-control desire for him. "No."

"Then why did you stop?"

She did not want to have this conversation, and it ticked her off that he was forcing it. "You mean, other than I didn't want to have sex with you?"

"Don't bullshit me, Alicia. You were into it. If I hadn't said anything, you'd have been under me on the floor, your legs wrapped around my shoulders, screaming as I made you come."

His crudeness found its intended target deep in her belly. "It was a good kiss, and I got caught up in the moment."

"It was a *great* kiss."

Oh hell, yeah, it was a great kiss. The best kiss she'd ever had. "Look, I'll take the blame for this. I should have stopped it immediately, and I didn't. The best thing now is to forget it happened, move on, and agree not go there again."

"So, pretend like it didn't happen, pretend we're not attracted to each other. That's your solution?"

He was being honest and open. He was giving her an opening to be honest, too, to admit she was attracted to him and had given him every reason to think she wanted his kiss and the sex it was rushing toward. It was what an emotionally sound grown woman would do. But she wasn't that woman at the moment. And she wasn't sure she could live with the consequences of taking that course of action. Besides, her saying no should be enough of a reason, dammit.

She turned away from him and washed her hands at the sink. "What can I do to help with dinner?" she asked as she dried them.

"Is that all you're going to say?" He growled the

words.

She hung up the towel. "What would you like me to say?"

"Oh, I don't know. That everything I just said is true. That I'm not imagining you look at me like you want to fuck me into next month."

The heat blooming in her face was the only outward sign he'd get that he was right. "Would that ease your conscience?"

"My conscience is clear, baby. I'm the one telling the truth."

She scoffed. "I doubt you've told me the truth since you got here."

"You haven't exactly been an open book."

"Well, let me drop some truth on you," she said, spearing him with her gaze. "I'm not the kind of woman who jumps into bed with a man she doesn't know or trust. And I'm not the kind of woman who jumps into bed with a man just because he wants it. On top of that, I'm your nurse and you're my patient. There are rules governing that relationship. I adhere to them and to my personal standards, regardless of whether they conflict with what someone else wants. If I didn't, I could lose my job and my self-respect. Is that clear enough for you?"

"I get it. I admire that about you. But why can't you just admit you're attracted to me?"

"Why can't you just let it go?"

Panza pushed his way between them and barked, first at one, then the other, as if telling them to knock it off. The interruption cut their tie and allowed her to switch gears.

"I'll make the salad and potatoes if you prepare the

steak," she said.

"Fine," he said, and in silence, they got to work.

As they worked together to cook dinner, the tension lessened, almost to pre-explosion levels. And after dinner, they did kitchen duty together, her washing, him rinsing. The simple act—standing at the sink side by side, arms brushing, fingers touching at the dish handoff—was ripe with easy intimacy. The moment was almost as passionate as his lips devouring hers. Almost. No, not really, but it was good.

His admission seemed to have braided them together, not so much their bodies, but something else, something deeper. They were connecting in a visceral way, and it felt so much more than the nurse/patient bond they shared. Or so claimed her heart, which had commandeered the situational analysis task away from her brain. Her brain, on the other hand, was sitting in the corner, tied up, loudly calling bullshit and reminding her that this new level of intimacy was a *result of* the nurse/patient bond and should be stopped. Stat.

****

Alicia gathered the pieces of the game she and Rey had been playing since they'd finished dinner and dishes.

"I don't remember this game being so boring," she said as she put them in the box and put the box in the coffee table drawer. "Guess I need to buy new ones."

"It's not the game, Alicia. It's you."

"Excuse me? Are you saying I'm boring?"

"I'm saying that a different kind of game might better satisfy your entertainment needs."

He was back to their predinner conversation and

she was *not* taking his bait.

"What I need is a good night's sleep," she said and stood.

"You're going to bed now? It's barely seven thirty."

"Do you need more pills, water, or another blanket before I go?" she asked, being careful to offer only those items she was willing to give.

"No, but there's something else I want."

"Oh?" She could hardly wait to hear.

His sex-filled gaze and sexy half smile made it clear what that something was. She'd hear him out, let him say it. Then she'd calmly refuse and go to her room. Alone. And suffering with a hunger she wouldn't be able to satisfy.

"A bedtime story."

So not what she thought he'd say. "I…don't know any."

"You've been a nurse for how many years? Ten?"

"Yeah. So?"

"So, you must have hundreds of stories."

"HIPAA rules require I keep patient details confidential."

"I'm not asking for names, social security numbers, and location of identifying moles. Just tell me about your most outrageous cases. The cliffs notes version."

"Too many to choose from."

"Top five then."

"I'll tell you one, then I'm going to bed."

"Just one?"

"That's the deal."

He sighed. "You, my sweet nurse, are a hardass."

Coming from his mouth, the name lacked the sting

it had coming from Dan's. Context was everything. "I'll forgive that nasty comment if you share your blanket with me. I swear it's just above freezing in here."

"Taking your patient's blanket? You're a *ruthless* hardass." He bent his legs to make room for her.

Pulling back the corner of the top blanket, she settled against the couch and covered up. She chose a particularly gruesome story, one that might shut down his desire for more.

"I'd been in the ER for a couple of years and thought I'd seen everything," she said. "Then a middle-aged man came in with a mutilated penis from trying to circumcise himself with an electric saw because his young, new wife complained about the foreskin."

"Ow, shit!" His whole body recoiled. "You started with that one on purpose, didn't you?"

Her grin answered him.

"God, you're a wicked woman," he said and laughed. "Tell me one that won't give me nightmares."

She chuckled. "Okay. My first day of clinicals in the ER, an elderly man came in complaining of chest pains. I was trying to verify his patient history, but he kept saying he couldn't hear me and asked me to come closer. I stepped closer and started to repeat my questions. He stopped me, apologized, and said he still couldn't hear me and that I needed to talk directly into his *good* ear. When I leaned in to repeat my questions into his *good* ear, he reached out and grabbed my boobs."

Rey laughed, a booming sound that bloomed joy inside her heart and triggered her own laugh.

"What did you do?" he asked.

"I jumped back out of his reach. It took everything

in me not to slap him, but I did look him in the eyes and make it very clear that if he did that again, I'd make sure he went home a eunuch. The grin on his face said he was insufferably proud of himself and extremely pleased with his ill-gotten grab. Turns out, he was a regular who was notorious for that behavior and no one bothered to tell the new girl."

"Did he ever grab you again?"

She shook her head. "He'd copped his last feel."

"You mean…"

"He died during heart surgery a couple hours later."

"You sent him to his grave with a smile in his heart."

"From that point forward, I was hypervigilant for that behavior and got really good at identifying and avoiding gropers."

"I'm not excusing that behavior, but I understand the desire to touch something so tempting and delicious," he said, his gaze grazing over the breast he had touched earlier. As if her breast felt the caress of his gaze, it tightened into a form that would fit his hand.

"He was ninety-six!" she said.

"Ah, *farolita*… A man who has touched, tasted, and loved the feminine form never loses his craving for it. Even when he ages. Even when he stands in judgment at death's door."

The poetic words added another piece of the puzzle that was Rey Cruz. Were their situation different, she would eagerly enjoy exploring that aspect of him.

"Do you have a favorite patient?" he said.

"You, of course," she said in a teasing tone.

"I knew it," he said, and she grinned at the smugly

satisfied smile on his face.

"Your second favorite patient," he said. "Tell me that story."

"We agreed to one, and I've told you two."

"Your voice comforts me, *farolita*."

"You mean puts you to sleep?"

He grinned. "One more?"

"One more, and then sleep. I mean it."

****

Over the next hour and a half, Alicia's voice and stories kept a contented smile on Nick's lips and acted like a warm blanket over his body. The warmth and smile remained even after she left him and went to bed.

He wondered whether she was in her bed thinking about their kiss like he was. His instincts said yes. He could still feel her, smell her, taste her. And he wanted more.

He had been with enough women in his thirty-four years to know when a woman wanted him, even if she didn't say it outright. Alicia wanted him. He knew that for a fact. It was evident in her eyes, in her touch, in her voice, in her body's delectable scent that was a siren's call to his unexpectedly hyperactive libido. Especially in the way she responded to his kiss.

His decision to tell her he wanted her hadn't worked out the way he'd planned. He'd hoped that his saying it first would encourage her to come clean and admit she wanted him too so maybe they could do something about it. Or maybe they couldn't, but at least one lie between them could dissipate. But if they did have sex, what then?

It wasn't a case of empty boasting to say he was an expert at giving a woman an unforgettable fuck and a happy ending. However, it was equally true that he was no good at giving a woman a happily-ever-after ending.

He owed Alicia his life. To pay her back, he should do the right thing and get the hell out of her life now before they did the thing they really wanted, which was to fuck like a pair of insatiable wolves.

Although the days of sleep, good food, and spicy bedside manner had done wonders to heal his wounds, he wasn't healed enough. He knew that, but still he'd leave. The sooner the better. For both of them. Because if he didn't, he'd end up ditching every bit of good sense, good training, and good morals he possessed to quench the fire flaming between the two of them.

And if he made love to her, he'd have to keep her. Right now, he was in no position to even keep a fake plant. His world had no room for a permanent woman in his life, especially a woman like Alicia, who deserved and would demand the best from the man in her life. He'd already proven he couldn't deliver those goods. He wouldn't hurt her by pretending he could and then failing.

It was settled. In the morning, he'd take her SUV and drive to town to do what he should have done days ago—complete his mission.

When he looked back on this time with her, he knew he'd regret not taking the risk and trying for more with her. But he also knew that when she looked back on this time with him, she'd be grateful she didn't cross the line and that he'd left before she did.

Chapter Eleven

Alicia woke up shivering in the thick frigid silence filling her bedroom. No buzz of electricity. No warm air blowing from the heater vent. Her flannel pajamas and the blanket and quilt pulled to her nose did little to block the cold air from slicing through her.

Climbing out of bed, she wrapped the quilt around herself and shuffled to the window to push back the curtains. Fat flakes flocked in ice lashed the windowpane in a diagonal slant and blended with the low-hung steel gray sky. Snow more than a foot deep and growing piled on the ground and on the heavily bowed limbs of the trees surrounding the cabin. It looked like a gigantic snow globe had enveloped the cabin during the night and been given a vigorous shake.

She crossed the room to the light switch and flipped it on. Nothing.

Slivers of concern stood shoulder to shoulder with the battalion of goosebumps prickling her skin until she reminded herself that there was no need for worry. She and Rey had the fireplace for heating and cooking, and plenty of wood, food, water, and—

God! Rey had only the two blankets on the couch and the clothes he'd worn to bed. She shot from the room to check on him and start the fire.

A blanket around his shoulders, Rey knelt at the fireplace, building a fire in the grate. He looked up when she came in.

"Guess your buddy, the sheriff, was telling the truth. The power's out," he said in a cloud of breath, and she swore she heard his teeth chattering.

"I noticed," she responded and joined him at the fireplace. "Here, let me do that."

"I got it, but would you make coffee? The hotter the better. I saw a metal coffee pot in the cabinet."

"You mean that quaint piece of Americana decor?"

He grinned up at her. "Your coffee will kill anything growing on it."

"Yeah, okay. But first, I'm putting on more clothes. I'm freezing."

When she came back into the room, Rey had pulled on the freshly washed hoodie and sweats he'd worn on their trek outside.

"Here are more clothes if you need it," she said and dropped a pile of Jon's sweats, T-shirts, socks, and hoodies on the couch, then headed to the kitchen.

During breakfast, Rey was uncharacteristically quiet and looked like he was thinking hard about something. Their kiss? Was he regretting it? She had tried all night long to regret it but failed.

"Hey, you," she said, nudging his leg with her foot. "You okay?"

His gaze left the fire and found hers. "Yeah. Why?"

"You didn't make fun of my coffee or cooking this morning," she said with a grin…that he didn't return.

"Alicia…I had planned to leave today, but with the storm… Guess you're stuck with me a little longer."

A chill seized her heart at his news and stripped her smile. "It would have been foolish to leave. You're not healed yet."

Although that was true, it also was true that he was well enough to drive out of here without passing out behind the wheel or to ride out with her driving him. The storm had made both of those options out of the question, and no way would he make it out of here on foot. No. Rey wasn't going anywhere until the storm passed.

"Healed or not, the storm has made leaving out of the question," he said, giving voice to her thoughts.

"Is that what's bothering you? That you can't leave?"

"I appreciate all you've done for me, but there's something I need to do. And before you ask, I can't tell you what it is. The point is, I can't get it done by staying in this cabin. I should have left as soon as I could walk. Now it could be days before it's clear enough for me to leave."

"Weeks even," she said.

He nodded as if he'd considered that. "Think you're up for it?"

"Up for it?"

"Weeks cooped up with me."

Spending weeks with Rey in this cozy cabin that every moment grew cozier might wear down her resolve to the nub. But she was up for it.

"I've handled the challenge pretty well so far," she said. "What makes you think that'll change?"

"I'm a much bigger challenge when I'm well. Just saying."

"Well, just saying, I've been taking it easy on you during your recovery."

He laughed. "I find that hard to believe, but thanks

for the warning." He downed the last of his coffee and set the cup on the table. "Well—" He slapped his hands on his knees. "—if we're facing weeks of bad weather, we're going to need more wood." He stood.

She stood, too. "You're right, but I got it."

"Alicia—"

"Rey, I split most of the wood that's in here and on the porch. I'm practically a seasoned lumberjack now."

Before he could launch into his argument, she launched countermeasures. "And I have proper blizzard-weather clothing, you don't."

To end the conversation, she went to the coatrack where her boots, hat, gloves, and jacket waited.

Rey joined her and was putting on his jacket.

"No," she said, removing his jacket from the one arm he'd stuffed into the sleeve. She returned it to the coatrack and turned back to him for an explanation.

"I don't feel right letting you go out in that"—he nodded with his chin to the outside—"while I stay inside roasting my chestnuts in front of the fire."

"First of all," she said and yanked on her boots, "you're not *letting* me do anything. I'm doing this because I don't relish the idea of freezing to death." She grabbed her beanie from the coatrack and pulled it on. "Second, our walk yesterday started you bleeding again. Imagine what an hour of swinging an axe would do. And third, even if you didn't have a still-vulnerable wound to contend with, I'd be doing it because I'm a capable woman who doesn't like to be told what she can and can't do."

"Fine." He held up his hands in surrender. "You win."

"I love to win." Grinning, she pulled on her gloves.

Before she could grab her coat, he took it off the hook and held it open for her.

"You just can't help yourself, can you?" she said.

"What do you mean?"

She slid in her arms. "Getting my coat, holding it open for me, although I'm more than capable of—"

He turned her toward him and zipped her up to her chin. "I think what you meant to say is, thank you."

She laughed. "Thank you."

"I'll have another pot of hot coffee waiting for you when you finish," he said. "If that's acceptable."

"It's perfect," she said and waddled over to the door.

He beat her to it and opened it for her.

Piercing cold and blowing snow shot straight through the screen door and her clothes, making her gasp. She yanked her beanie down farther on her head. "Make a lot of coffee. I might need to bathe in it to thaw out."

His soft chuckle added the final layer of warmth she needed to step out onto the porch and into the blizzard.

It was the coldest she'd ever been in her life, but she warmed up when she got into a rhythm and was further energized by the growing pile of wood around her, which she stacked on the porch. Periodically, she saw Rey outside, despite her warning, taking firewood from the porch and carrying it into the cabin. He was bending too much, carrying too much, and moving faster than he should. But seeing him doing something to help her also warmed her.

There was no hiding it anymore. She enjoyed his company. He made her feel alive in a way she hadn't felt in a long time. Despite that, she would not fall for him. And definitely wouldn't kiss him again. Oh God, that kiss. She'd never forget the desire in his kiss-infused voice when he'd groaned her name and said he wanted her. Her body burned with the need to hear it again.

Although she fully recognized that the scenario playing out in her mind was nothing more that the Nightingale Syndrome, that ancient beast that preyed on nurses, that didn't stop the fantasizing. She'd recently read a quote that said that giving in was the only true cure for temptation. At the time, she'd thought it was rubbish marketing. But now…

"Lunch is ready, *farolita*. Come on in."

The sight of Rey and the sound of his voice shook her from her musings. Suddenly, she was starving and hoping another kiss was on the dessert menu.

"Be right there," she said with a wave.

She added the pieces she'd split to the stack on the porch and covered it with a tarp she'd found in the woodshed to keep the elements off. Then she trudged through the snow to the shed to return the axe and the log she hadn't split. She hung the axe on the wall and set the log on top of the pile. The log caused an avalanche. Just in time, she jumped out of the way to avoid having them fall on her. She had lifted a log to stack it back into place when she saw a green duffel with splotches of what looked like blood on it. She grabbed it—using two hands, it was that heavy—and set it at her feet. She unzipped it and pushed it open. Her heart sank.

Guns and ammo. Drugs. A laptop. A few notebooks.

This had to be Rey's. It likely was what had gotten him shot. The gang, or the law, would be after him to retrieve it. His charm, sweetness, kisses, and touches had slowly smoothed over the fact that he was a criminal. This bag of goodies proved it beyond a doubt. She could no longer pretend he was not who he was. And now she was snowed in with him and with no way to call the law or to escape.

Her options were to confront him or put the bag back and pretend she hadn't seen it. The safer choice would be to pretend like she hadn't seen it.

She picked up the duffle and carried it into the cabin.

Rey turned as she came in. The warm and welcoming smile on his face dissolved when he saw what she had in her hands.

"What have you got there?" he asked.

"Why don't you tell me?" she said and set it on the floor.

"Looks like a bag."

"Is it yours?"

"Why would you think that?"

"Are you saying it's not?"

Long seconds passed, with neither of them speaking in words but eyes locked, breathing in sync, hearts pounding as one. Finally, he strode over to her, grabbed the bag, and stormed outside.

She followed him as he trudged through the blinding snow to the shed. "What have you gotten me into?" she yelled to be heard over the storm.

"Go back inside, Alicia," he yelled, too.

They'd reached the woodshed and went inside, and she shut the door on the storm.

"I have a right to know," she said as he started moving some of the logs aside.

She pushed in front of him to get his attention. "Tell me who you are and what you're doing with that bag."

He grabbed her by her upper arms and moved her aside. "The bag and what's in it are none of your business. Don't fucking touch it again. Don't even speak of it. Do you understand?" He released her, turned back to grab the duffel, and put it back where she'd found it.

"This isn't who you are," she said and was surprised to feel her eyes growing misty with disappointment and anger.

Ignoring her, he continued stacking logs in front of and over the duffel, then left the shed and headed back into the cabin, slamming the door behind him, effectively shutting her out.

Closing the shed door, she stood in the yard, eyes on the cabin, feeling lost and frozen inside. The people he'd stolen the bag from wouldn't stop until they found him, taken the bag, and killed him. They'd likely kill her too for no other reason than she was with him and a witness who couldn't be left alive.

Liking her chances on the slick and snow-packed mountain road over being in the cabin with a gang member who had a target on his back, she went inside the cabin, grabbed her key fob from the coatrack, then went outside again, headed to the SUV.

Rey ran out after her and grabbed her arm. "What are you doing?"

"I'm getting away from a gang member who's going to get me killed or kill me himself."

"You'll kill yourself if you get into that vehicle and try to go anywhere in this blizzard."

She shook him off and climbed into the vehicle. He jumped in the other side.

"Get out," she said.

"No."

"Fine. Stay. I'll take you directly to the sheriff, and he'll put you in jail, where you belong." She hit the vehicle's start button, but nothing happened. She kept trying. "Why won't this damn thing start?"

"It's below freezing out here. Temps that low have a negative effect on the battery and oil viscosity," he said, his voice trembling.

She turned to look at him sitting in the seat next to hers. With nothing to keep him warm but a thin T-shirt, a hoodie, and sweats, his whole body was shivering, his teeth chattering. He had snow in his hair, on his shoulders, on his clothes. He needed to get inside the cabin before hypothermia set in. His ice-cold stare said he wasn't going in without her.

No matter what else he was, he was, first and foremost, her patient.

Accepting that the vehicle wasn't going to start, she climbed out and headed back to the cabin, Rey following her.

As she pulled off her outerwear, she noticed the changes in the room he'd made for her comfort. He'd shifted the furniture to accommodate the mattress from her bed in front of the fireplace and piled it with every blanket in the cabin, and the fire was blazing, pushing heat into the room.

"Take off your boots," she said. He tried to bend over to unlace the boots, but he was shaking so bad he couldn't get hold of them. She knelt to do it herself. The laces were stiff with cold, but she got them undone and pulled off his boots.

She led him over to the fire, put a blanket around him, and settled him on the mattress in front of the fire, then went to the bathroom for a towel. She toweled him dry—his hair, his face. Then, because he was still shivering, she knelt behind him, cradling her front against his back, arms around him, and held him, letting the heat of her body infiltrate his.

She should have called the sheriff right away when he showed up. Ignored what her heart was telling her. The old her would have made the right choice and been content with it, not second-guessing it like she was now. He'd needed her help, but he'd gotten her into trouble. She'd allowed it. This was why she followed the rules. If she followed the rules, the answer was there in black and white. But following the rules too closely was what had sent her on this journey. So far, all she'd done this trip was make mistakes.

Even after Rey's shivering had slowed, she stayed behind him, warming his body.

"I like what you've done with the room," she said.

"Here in front of the fireplace is the warmest spot in the cabin," he said after a few seconds. " 'Til further notice, it's the designated living room, dining room, kitchen, and bedroom."

Bedroom. The word flicked the tip of her clit.

They'd be sleeping together every night.

Snuggling beside each other every day.

Close.

Close enough to warm her body with his heat, like now. Close enough to breathe his air, like now. Close enough to sync with the rhythmic pulse of his heartbeat, like now. Close enough to become addicted to the brush of his skin against hers, like now.

The warmth from her, the blanket, the fire had smoothed out his shivers. If she stayed here any longer, it would be obvious that it was because she wanted to, not because she needed to.

"What's in the pot?" she said, loosening her hold on him and shifting to the fire where the pot was. Even with multiple layers of clothing, she was chilled without the heat from his body and wondered whether he was, too.

"Vegetable beef stew using last night's leftover steak."

"Smells great. Are you ready to eat?"

"Sure."

She filled a mug with stew and handed it to him.

"Thanks," he said.

She served herself, settled beside him on their bed, and laid a blanket over the both of them. She took a bite of the beefy, brothy, hot stew he had made for them. It was just what she needed.

"It's delicious," she said, keeping her eyes on the stew. "Thanks for…" Then she looked at him. "Are we in danger?"

She could see the yes in his eyes. And so much more. A shivering sadness, wrapped in pain, that felt as frigid as the wildness raging outside the cabin. She wanted to know what caused it but knew he wouldn't tell her. Then he blinked and it was gone, and she knew. A man like him had no business being in her cabin, her life, her mind, or her heart. But he was in all four. Front and center.

"The people who shot you…they're coming for you and the bag, aren't they?"

He nodded. "Probably. As soon as the storm breaks, I'll leave. You should, too."

"I think I've earned the right to know who you are, who tried to kill you and why, and why they're coming after you."

His only response was to take a bite of stew.

His reaction pissed her off, but she realized that she didn't have a right to get angry about his behavior. He'd been secretive from the second he showed up in her life, and that had changed only slightly in the days that followed. For her to expect anything different now was foolish. Still, she'd hoped he'd be honest about something so life-threatening.

"Are you going to kill me?"

He dropped his spoon into the empty mug. "Fuck, Alicia. You know the answer to that."

"Before I saw that bag, before I saw proof of what you are, I would have said you wouldn't do anything to harm me."

"And now?" he said.

She didn't respond.

He settled his hand on her head. "*Farolita*," he whispered, the tone suggesting he was disappointed in the message threaded in her silence.

At the gentleness of his touch, and the hurt and sincerity in his eyes, she could almost still believe that he wouldn't harm her. She could almost still believe that he was a good man despite what the bag said, despite what his gunshot wound said, despite what this entire situation said.

"What I know is that you'll do whatever you have

to do to protect yourself and what's in that bag."

"Yes, I will. But that doesn't include hurting you. And I'll do everything in my power to protect you from anyone who tries to hurt you. I promise you that."

He seemed sincere, but she had been fooled before. Jon also had made promises that he'd broken. If Jon, her husband, the man who had loved her with every fiber of his being, could lie to her, then this man in front of her, whom she didn't know and didn't love, would have no qualms about lying to save his ass.

What the hell kind of loser had she become that she'd let herself be so easily fooled by another good-looking, charming man? The old her would never have allowed the wounded stranger in to wreak such havoc on her life. She'd have done the right thing and let the law handle the situation. But Jon's death had taken a bigger chunk of her than she'd realized. And now she was going to die before she had a chance to fix her hot mess of a life.

****

With Alicia looking at him like the bastard he was, Nick tried to ignore the voice spewing from the depths of his soul, screaming at him to tell her the truth. The truth might ease some of her fears.

But he'd already made enough foolish mistakes. Telling her he was FBI would be a death sentence if she was with the gang. Although he was ninety-nine percent sure she wasn't, that slim margin could be his undoing. He had an obligation to his mission and to follow the rules.

As soon as he could leave, he would. If he didn't, he would only end up hurting her, emotionally, or getting her hurt, physically. Like he'd hurt and disappointed every woman who'd ever made the mistake of caring about him.

While he was stuck here, he'd do his best to alleviate Alicia's fears and ensure she felt safe with him, but he wouldn't tell her the truth.

Chapter Twelve

Every time Alicia looked out over the next few days, the storm had dumped more snow. She and Rey were officially snowed in.

They couldn't get out, which meant others couldn't get in. And everything they needed to survive was in this cabin. For now, they were safe. And with every passing hour, it became increasingly intimate.

They had filled the long hours since the storm hit sitting or lying beside each other under piles of blankets and layers of clothing, sharing their heat, talking, and playing games in the flicker of the flames. The best part of her day was sleeping next to him at night and awakening in the morning to his arms around her, his body curled around her, as if protecting her from the danger that lingered outside like the dense fog that crawled in to smother Puget Sound. On those mornings, she lay as still as possible, barely breathing, so he wouldn't wake up and move away.

Together in their bed, she felt secure and comfortable, and Rey's calmer demeaner suggested he felt the same. Their forced confinement seemed to have enabled him to let his mask slip so he could behave more like the man he really was, as if the combative alpha warrior who'd showed up bleeding on her porch, ready to strip her down to check her tattoos, had been a role he'd been playing to protect himself until he knew he could trust her.

He was still secretive, but he also was talking more, answering more of her questions, sharing more of himself. Not all. Not fully. But some. It made her work harder to chip away at the role and the mask and uncover the man who lay beneath. She wanted to know him.

As much as she hated to admit it, her standards were melting a little more every hour like candle wax under a flame. By the time the storm passed, they'd be nothing more than a puddle of unrecognizable goo. And if it didn't get her killed, it would at least break her heart.

She rolled onto her side, facing Rey, her head supported on her hand, and drank in the sight of him on his back, one arm behind his head as a pillow, reading a spy thriller he'd dug out of her box of books. As if he could feel her stare, hear her thoughts, he grinned.

"I know that look," he said with a mock rebuke.

"What look?" she asked, punctuating the question with an innocent smile.

He turned to meet her gaze. "The look that says you're loading up more questions to fire at me."

"You're beginning to know me too well," she said.

****

Alicia was right. Nick was beginning to know her. Very well. The more time he spent snowed in with her, the harder it was to hold the real him back. He wanted her to know him, and he wanted to know her. He couldn't remember falling for a woman so quick and so hard. He liked everything about her. Not just that thick hair of hers that invited him to dig in and use it as a handgrip to pull her closer and hold her there so every breath he drew would be filled with her scent and taste.

Or her fiery green eyes that followed him into sleep every night and caffeinated him every morning.

Or those full lips that begged for a thorough kissing that would curl more than her cute little painted toes.

Or her sexy body that kept his buzzing twenty-four/seven.

It was the calm and caring tenor of her voice. Her loving and giving spirit. Her wit and sense of humor. Her feisty and curious manner that turned his blood into rivers of gas on fire. It had tethered him to her, making him greedy and always seeking more of her.

Then there was the fact that she couldn't seem to get enough of him. The woman seemed genuinely interested in what he thought and felt and liked and wanted and dreamed. That kind of attention was addictive. And seductive. And dangerous. But he couldn't stop himself from giving her what she wanted. At least some of what she wanted. He still had some measure of control. Hadn't completely abandoned the undercover agent's unwritten code of not falling for the enemy. Well, he no longer believed she was the enemy, but he had other reasons to remain cautious. Namely, protecting his heart from the woman who already had the fingertips of both hands dug in deep. Removing them would leave a mark that would never heal.

He tossed his book onto the table and rolled onto his side to face her. The soft glow on her face settled an extra layer of warmth on his skin, almost eliminating the need for blankets or the fire. "What do you want to know?"

"Tell me about your family."

"Ask a specific question, and I might give you a

specific answer."

"Do you have a large family?"

To avoid revealing his true identity, he'd been sticking mostly to information from his assumed alias profile to answer her questions, leaving out the more colorful parts that would have her hauling out her gun from the closet to protect herself.

"Five siblings. Parents died when I was four. Car accident." His profile detailed that Rey Cruz's parents were killed in the car accident that resulted from the cops chasing them after a drug bust. "My father's mother took care of us kids after that."

Sadness filled her eyes. "That must have been devastating for you to lose both parents at the same time."

She was offering true sympathy for a fake situation, and it made him feel like shit. He'd come to absolutely despise lying to her.

"I grew up not knowing any other way."

"What's your best memory of them?" she said.

Cruz's parents—and family—were drug dealers and users, thieves, and a total waste of space. Nick would pull from his own memories to answer her question.

"My mom made the best bizcochitos, and my dad was a diehard Cowboys fan." Giving her the truth eased his heart and put a smile on his face.

"I love bizcochitos," she said. "But I'm a proud twelfth man."

"Seahawks, huh," he said. "I'm not sure we can be friends."

Her soft laugh lit up her eyes and skin and made his heart flip. God, he wanted to eat that mouth.

"Which sibling are you closest to?" she continued.

The profile said all his siblings but one were dead or in jail. "Elena, my baby sister. We're the youngest kids, so we bonded over birth order against the older ones."

In reality, he was the oldest child, the only son, and equally close to his two sisters, who spoiled him as much as his mother did.

"Wow. I really called that one wrong," she said.

"Called what wrong?"

"I had you pegged as a first-born."

"Oh? Why's that?"

She shrugged. "A lot of things."

"Like?"

"Like you're definitely a leader-of-the-pack kind of guy. You like to take charge. Control the situation. And you're, uh…no offence…a little bossy."

"*You're* calling *me* bossy?" he said, pointing first at her, then himself.

She laughed.

He took her hand and lightly bit her finger with the tattoo on it, suggesting that the nurse in her was bossy, too.

"Anything else?" He linked their fingers, and she didn't pull away. Joy melted over him like hot fudge on ice cream.

"I see you as the protector in the family."

"You've got all kinds of crazy ideas about me in that beautiful brain of yours." He brushed a shock of hair from her face and looped it behind her delicate ear to give him a full view of her smile.

"The role fits you. Plus, from what I understand, those born under the sign of Cancer are big on protecting loved ones at all costs."

At her words, a warning light began blinking furiously at the corner of his vision. Rey Cruz was a Cancer, but how did she know that? Suspicion slithered up his spine.

"How do you know I'm a Cancer?" he asked and let his hand slide away from hers.

"Well, your birthday is July 18, so that's Cancer. You didn't know your sign?"

"What I mean is, how do *you* know it?"

"I emptied your pockets the day you arrived so I could wash your jeans, and I saw your wallet. I wanted to know who I was harboring, so I looked at your license. After all, you had just showed up with bullet wounds in your side and a really big gun."

"You looked through my wallet?" He tried to keep the annoyance from his voice, but the look on her face said he hadn't succeeded.

It didn't bother him that she had looked at his stuff. It bothered him that she'd seen his license but pretended she didn't know his name or where he lived, like she was testing him, trying to catch him in a lie. Now, he was back to wondering whether she could be trusted. To preserve their growing closeness, he'd put his suspicion on the shelf but within easy reach, and he'd be more cautious going forward.

"I didn't take anything," she said as if she thought his reaction was about invasion of privacy. "It's all in the kitchen drawer by the fridge." A tone of defensiveness colored her voice.

"I wasn't suggesting you had," he said. "Thanks for keeping it safe."

"Sure." The tone in the clipped word was still

strained.

"My turn," he said when she went quiet. "Tell me about your family."

Her brief pause before answering suggested that she wasn't ready to jump back into conversation, or that she, like him, was speaking from a script and needed time to get things straight in her mind. Or maybe she wasn't close to her family and the topic was a bitter one.

"My parents met in the Peace Corps after medical school. About a year in, they cut their trip short so I could be born in the US. Up until I started first grade, we lived all over the world. I'm an only child."

Her tone was flat, like she was just going through the motions of answering the question.

"Are you guys close?" he asked.

A wistful smile that told a story of its own slightly lifted the corners of her lips. "They're that couple who wants only each other. I'm living proof that popular contraception methods aren't one hundred percent reliable. They raised me, of course, and very well, but I always felt I was keeping them from the life they wanted to live. As soon as I left for college, they sold the house and joined Doctors Without Borders."

"You didn't want to follow in their footsteps and become a doctor?"

A soft exhale and head shake preceded her statement. "No. To their great disappointment."

"Why disappointment?"

"That I didn't show enough ambition to *go all the way*. That despite earning bachelor's degrees in nursing and psychology, a master's degree in nursing, and an emergency nurse practitioner certification, I had settled for second best."

It was an attitude Nick understood well. His legal eagle father was horrified when he—his only son and namesake—left law school a year in to join the military. He didn't speak to him for over a year. He'd also lost a longtime girlfriend who was unhappy about losing a potential lawyer husband and settling for a lowly jarhead.

"If you're happy with what you do, what they think doesn't matter," he said as much for himself as for her.

She nodded. "I'm happy with my career and wouldn't change it."

"Did you miss not having siblings growing up?" he asked a minute later.

"Yeah, I did. I always told myself that if I had kids, I'd have at least two to ensure they never felt the loneliness I sometimes did."

"I'm guessing you didn't have kids?"

"Why would you guess that?" Her tone carried a hint of defensiveness, indicating another touchy subject.

"You would have mentioned them. Mothers always bring up their kids in conversations with everyone."

"Well, you're right. No kids."

"Why not?"

She shrugged. "We talked about it—my husband and I—but it never seemed the right time. We got busy building our careers, then when we finally circled around to the topic about six years in, he said he no longer wanted children."

"So...end of story?"

"My life hasn't been lacking because we didn't have them. I have plenty of friends and interests I enjoy and a demanding job that I love. Do you have children?" she asked, flipping the spotlight on him.

The Rey Cruz profile said he had several kids with several different women. At the gang compound, he'd had no trouble bragging about how far and wide he'd spread his seed. But he couldn't bring himself to share that with Alicia. Somewhere along the line, her opinion of him had started to matter. Once again, he'd pull from his own life to answer her question. "No."

"Why not?"

"I haven't found a woman I want to have kids with." The realization that those words were the God's honest truth ricocheted through him. His pat answer had always been a solid, I don't want kids.

"So, you're not married?" she asked.

"No."

"You came close, though, didn't you?"

His eyes widened slightly, and he was caught off guard by her question. "Why would you think that?"

"The look in your eyes when I mentioned marriage. Your tone of voice. Your pause. Even your breathing changed slightly. As a nurse, I've gotten pretty good at knowing when a patient isn't telling me the truth or has told me only part of it."

"There was someone."

"What happened?"

"The usual."

She was studying his face so intently he felt like he was under a microscope. And damned if it didn't compel him to add more—just for her—hoping the small gift would make her happy. But he'd build parameters around it.

"We discovered we wanted different things out of life," he said.

"Like?"

"Like, I wanted her and she wanted another guy."

"She broke your heart."

At her soft words, he swallowed hard to push the memories back into the box they'd suddenly popped out of like a gruesome jack-in-the-box. Yes, Renee had broken his heart. A year ago this coming February. But the broken pieces, give or take a few, had fused back together.

He attempted a grin that would make Alicia think that the big ugly truth was no big deal, but the effort that went into the attempt belied it. So instead, he shrugged and stared into the fire so she couldn't read more of the truth.

"We broke each other's hearts," he said. "I couldn't be the man she needed so she went to someone else." He couldn't believe he was talking about this, but as a reward, Alicia reached out her hand and scooped up his, linking their fingers like he'd done with her.

"It's still painful for you." The kindness in her words drew his attention back to her, and the sincerity in her face and eyes kept it there. Beyond the compassion, he saw the pain that said she knew how he felt.

"I'm guessing your husband broke your heart, too," he said.

In response, Alicia extracted her hand from his and twisted the ring on her finger that anchored her to her past. A past she didn't want to talk about and had come here to bury.

Chapter Thirteen

Alicia twisted the ring that was one of the last tangible ties to her past. To Jon. To her former self.

"Yes. He did," she said.

"You're still pissed at him."

She wanted to deny it, but she couldn't form the lie, much less let it leave her mouth. She was angry. So angry that it had threatened her ability to do her job.

"Is it that obvious?"

"Yes, but why wouldn't you be?" Rey said. "His death ruined your plans. Changed your life completely. Left you alone to pick up the pieces and start over. In a way, his death took your life."

His assessment was so right on, it hurt. "Sounds like you were pretty angry, too," she said. "Maybe still are? I hear it in your voice."

"I was for a long time, even though, logically, I knew the breakup was for the best," he said.

"And now?"

"The anger I felt toward her, her betrayal, the situation, has been, shall we say, redirected and renamed."

"Let me guess. Guilt toward yourself, for what you see as your failure."

He nodded. "But it's fainter every day."

"I'm still firmly in the anger phase and guilt has joined the party as the loudmouth who dances on the table naked. How did you get past it?"

"The usual stuff."

"Other women?"

"Work," he said.

"Those odd jobs you mentioned?" she said with a wry smile, which he returned.

"Something like that. And shoving the feelings deep into the box I created for them."

"You didn't have a close friend to talk to about it?"

"Yeah, but it got old quick. Made me feel weak. Which made me feel worse."

She nodded. "My friends tried to get me to talk about my feelings, but I didn't want to, so I instead tried to convince them I was fine so they'd stop asking."

Yes, her friends had been her life support through those first long, numb weeks of grief, when the ability to sleep or eat or breathe had all but vanished. But she had quickly grown uncomfortable with the maudlin condolences, pitiful back pats, and sad-eyed looks that had become her world since donning the ill-fitting widow's cloak. Most of all, she grew weary with talking, talking, talking about her feelings.

So she tasked herself with becoming so convincing that she was fine that everyone soon stopped asking how her effort to sweep up the crumbs of her old life was progressing. They assumed she was handling it like she handled every task thrown at her. Focused and forward. And she did nothing to dissuade that slightly erroneous belief. She hadn't realized just how toxic the lie had become until it began affecting her work. She could see that now.

"Sounds like there's more to your story than just

losing a husband," Rey said, bringing her back to her place beside him.

"You're right."

"It's been festering inside you for seven months, like a splinter of wood. Time to dig it out, Alicia, before it infects your entire body."

"Actually, I agree. I'm considering therapy when I go back home. You know, just to say everything out loud to someone neutral, someone who doesn't know me, Jon, or our marriage."

"Say it to me. I won't charge you a dime."

"Think you can handle the tears?"

"Maybe I'll cry with you."

Though she doubted she'd ever see this big, strong alpha man cry, the level of compassion that saying it revealed about him peppered her grief with holes that let in the light.

"Not sure where to start," she said finally.

"Was it a bad marriage?" he said to get her going.

A thousand memories, good and bad, flashed in her mind about her marriage, memories that probably should stay locked inside and never breathe the air of freedom. On the other hand, maybe talking about it was part of her metamorphosis. Say it and release it. One step of many to finding herself again.

She met Rey's eyes, deciding whether to spill her secrets and how much. Once he left, she'd never see him again, so what did it matter.

"No. It was a great marriage. For a while. At least I thought so."

"What changed?"

"A few weeks after our tenth wedding anniversary, this past March, he asked me whether our marriage could survive a little shake-up in our sex life. We'd always been pretty open about experimentation, so I thought he meant masochism or group sex, two things we hadn't tried because they didn't appeal to me."

"But it wasn't either of those?" Rey asked.

She shook her head to strengthen the soft "no" that followed.

"What was it?"

She'd never spoken of it to anyone. How would it sound out there? How would it sound to a stranger who didn't know how kind, loving, and trustworthy Jon had always been, from the moment she met him their first day of college?

Rey's eyes were soft with empathy, and his face caressed by the shadows and muted light was a picture of sincerity and openness. Somehow, she knew he wouldn't judge her with a critical heart. But even if he did, so what? His opinion didn't matter to her. Well, not much.

"He said what he wanted was to experience sex with a man."

Rey's raised eyebrows weighed on her like boulders.

"Had he ever had those inclinations before?" he asked with only curiosity in his voice, not judgment. It annoyed her how relieved she felt.

"Not that he'd mentioned. But a few months earlier, I'd bought a certain toy for us. He enjoyed it. So much so that he said he wanted to try it with the *real thing*. He all but blamed his new desire on me, because I'm the one who brought that activity into our lives."

"Hmm." Rey grunted, his winged eyebrows furrowing.

The sound and the look reeked of disapproval. But of what? The toy? Jon's desire or blame? Her?

"What did you say?" he asked.

"I told him I'd be open to it if he did it with me there, participating—a threesome."

"That's mighty accommodating of you."

"Yeah, well, like I said, we'd always been willing to experiment, and we didn't judge each other for our desires." Suddenly feeling defensive, of her and Jon and their lifestyle, her tone was a little sharper than she'd intended.

"Did you do it?"

"He said—" She swallowed, her throat almost too tight to continue this conversation. "He said he didn't want me there. That it was just for him. Not us."

"Is that when you told him to go to hell?"

What the fuck, Jon, had been her first response. "After I got over the shock and calmed down, I told him that although I understood his desire for something new, his having sex outside our marriage like that was more than I was comfortable with. I said if he did it, I'd leave the marriage. He was disappointed, but he agreed to drop it, saying that our marriage was more important to him."

"But that wasn't the end of it," Rey said.

She held his gaze tight as she shook her head, hoping he could see right through her to her broken heart so her most raw emotions could remain unspoken.

"A week after that conversation, he went out of town on business. That first night he was gone, I got a call from him. That wasn't unusual, because he always called me once he'd gotten settled at the hotel and after dinner. I picked up, but before I could speak, I heard heavy breathing. Groaning. Shuffling, like clothes being removed. I heard my husband call out a man's name—a guy he worked with—and give him explicit instructions on what he wanted him to do to him. I should have said something or hung up, but I couldn't. I was stunned. Frozen in place. I heard…everything…before I finally hung up."

Time hadn't muted the sounds of that night or the feelings of betrayal. She drew in a breath and released it to steady herself and start the next part of the story.

"Sometime later, he realized he'd inadvertently dialed my number during… He called me, but I didn't answer. He left message after message, profusely apologizing and begging me to call him and talk about it. I ignored them all. Didn't call him back. His last call was to tell me he was headed home early to fix the *horrendous mistake*—his words—he'd made, that he loved me, wanted our marriage, and would do anything to keep it and make it up to me for his betrayal."

"Did you believe him?" Rey asked.

"Wouldn't you have believed the person you loved?"

"It wouldn't have mattered whether I believed her, I'd have let her go. An action like that says she'll always put her desires ahead of what's best for our relationship." Rey said the words with such conviction, she knew it was something he'd told himself repeatedly until it became true.

"That was the direction of my thinking, too, but I wanted to make sure, wanted to make a rational decision, not an emotional one. I stayed up all night, thinking about whether all the good in our marriage we'd enjoyed to that point could push me past the betrayal and restore my ability to trust him again. But also whether the good I *thought* we'd enjoyed had actually existed or whether it was all lies."

"He made you doubt your entire life together."

She nodded, relieved that, once again, he understood. "I received a call at three-seventeen that morning. Thinking it was him again, I was going to ignore it. Then I saw the number."

He scooted closer to her, sliding his arm firmly around her, because she'd already told him this part. "It was the airline, telling you the plane had crashed."

"The thing is," she said and cleared her throat to eliminate the knot forming in her throat. "I didn't listen to any of his messages until I got the call he was dead. If I had only answered his calls, talked to him, he wouldn't have gotten on that plane. He wouldn't have died. He died because of me. I'll never forgive myself that I didn't talk to him. Not only have I lost him forever, I have to live with the guilt that he died begging for a chance to save our marriage, begging for my forgiveness. And I wouldn't give it to him. The man who meant everything to me and I wouldn't give it to him. And I am so angry at myself!"

Rey shook his head. "I understand what you're saying, but what happened is not your fault."

"It was because of my inflexibility that he died. He died thinking I hated him. To be honest, at that moment, I did hate him. I don't now, but I am still angry. Angry that he died and left me. That he wanted another person, that I wasn't enough for him, that he lied, cheated, and broke our vows when he swore he never would. Angry at myself for not doing more to ensure our marriage was solid. Angry that I didn't even try to resolve the issue. Angry that now I've lost not only him but myself."

The words crackled with emotion, compelling Rey to hug her tighter. Even Panza, from his spot at the end of the bed, lifted his head and let out a soft whine as if to show his concern for her.

"That's why you came here," Rey said. "To figure things out."

She nodded. "I came here to examine everything objectively, decide what the truth was, have it out with the guilt consuming me from the inside out, and let it all go."

Rey cupped her head, his fingers tangling in her hair, and drew her close, and she buried her face in his hoodie—Jon's hoodie. She clung, but she didn't cry. It was still odd to her that she hadn't been able to cry at Jon's death. It was as if all the emotion—the anger and guilt—were blocking the tears. She felt Panza's paw on her leg.

Rey eased out of their embrace but kept his hands and eyes on her. "That's a huge weight you've been carrying around. It's only gotten bigger and heavier because you kept it to yourself."

"I couldn't tell anyone."

"Why? Because you didn't want his last action in life to replace everyone's opinion of him?"

"Yes, but mostly, I couldn't handle them knowing it was my fault he died."

"*Farolita*, his death is not your—"

"Yes, it is," she insisted. "If I'd only answered his calls, talked to him, he wouldn't have been so determined to get home to me. He was worried I'd leave him. I finally listened to his messages, so I know what he was feeling."

Panza whined again and looked agitated, as if the angst swirling in the room was piercing his flesh.

"You can't know what might have happened, even if you had talked to him," Rey said. "If he hadn't died on the plane, he might have died some other way that night. If it's your time to go, the universe finds a way. But it wasn't your fault. You need to cut that thought out of your head, or you'll never be able to move on. He made his choice. You didn't force him to do it."

"I could have forgiven him, said the words, so even if he did end up dying that night, he could go into the next life, whatever it is, without that weight on his soul. Oh God, I was such a horrible wife!"

"I don't believe that."

"Remember when you asked whether my husband and I did activities together, and I said something about schedules not meshing?"

"Yes."

"He asked to do those things with me, but I said no. You wanna know why? Because I was more concerned with improving my run time or getting the workout done so I could move on to the next thing on my list. Schedules and goals and work. That's what my actions said I cared about most. Somewhere along the line, I forgot that my husband and my marriage were my most important goal. Now, I don't have a husband or a marriage, and everything else in my life is crumbling, too. I screwed up. I didn't love him the way he deserved, and now it's too late to fix anything."

He pulled her into his arms again and caressed her head. "My grandmother told me that our loved ones don't leave us right away when they die. They hang around, watching over us, until they're sure we're ready to let them go. They hear our outpourings of love and regret, our apologies, all the things we didn't say to them when they were alive. You said it all. Right here. Out loud. He heard."

For a long moment, they held each other in quiet, she considering Rey's comforting words that Jon had heard her confession and was somehow still looking out for her. At the thought, a lightness lifted from her shoulders, like effervescent bubbles rising from a glass of champagne.

"I admire you, Alicia," Rey said minutes later. "So many people let situations and emotions paralyze them to making the changes that'll move them forward. You faced it head on, identified solutions, and took actions to help you create a new life. That took real strength and courage. You should be proud of yourself."

Hearing his words did more than comfort her. They made her realize he was right. It had taken courage and strength to come here and try to climb out of her grief and guilt and make changes. True, her forced vacation spurred the trip, but she had chosen this place and committed to doing the work that would get her back to who she was. And she had talked through her feelings with someone, like Dan advised her to do.

As Rey held her, and she him, she marveled that a stranger was giving her the comfort she'd so desperately needed since Jon dropped his confession on her. Comfort she hadn't been able to ask for from the people in her life. Rey was a stranger and a criminal, but at that moment, he was also part of the miracle she'd hoped would manifest on this mountain.

She pulled back just enough to see his eyes.

"Thank you," she whispered, her mouth mere inches from his. "For listening and understanding and not judging. I needed that more than you know…more than I knew."

"I know how hard it was to share something so personal and painful," he whispered, too.

She licked her lips to pull his whisper into her body. It vibrated through her and toppled her remaining barriers, one by one, like lines of falling dominoes. Need rushed in over the downed barriers like a mighty river and swelled inside her, demanding a bigger, deeper closeness with this man. Demanding his kisses. His touches. His body.

In some purely feminine corner of her mind, she wanted him because he was a man and she was a woman who needed a man. But she knew in her heart that there was more to it than base need. But right now, she didn't want to explore the difference. Right now, all she wanted to explore was his mouth.

Before she could reason her way out of it, she leaned in and kissed him. Then, with a needy moan, she took it deeper.

Or tried to.

Rey pulled back and left her arms.

His rebuff stung, but she deserved it after the many times she'd done it to him. "Sorry," she said, rolled onto her side, and faced away from him.

"Alicia, let's talk about that kiss," Rey said.

"It's been an emotionally draining night, and I'd rather just go to sleep," she said.

She felt his eyes on her and felt every cell in him wanting to force her into a conversation about it. Instead, he lay behind her, curled against her, and settled his hand on the curve of her hip. Panza laid in front of her, watching her, then cut his eyes to Rey, then back to her, almost like he was telling her to talk this out with Rey.

Fine. Why not? She turned toward Rey. "I'm confused. You've been trying to have sex with me since you got here. The second I initiate it, you lose interest."

"I'm pretty confused myself," he said. "I've been clear from the start that I want you, and you've been just as clear that the answer is no."

"Fine. Let's forget it."

She turned away again, but he caught her and rolled her over to face him. "No, I don't want to forget it. I want to know whether you're serious about wanting to fuck me."

"God, you're always so crude."

She tried to roll away again, but he stopped her, then mounted her, grabbed her wrists, trapping her arms above her head, and stared down into her face with an intenseness in his dark eyes that rushed fear and excitement throughout her body. Panza scrambled to his feet, as if on alert in case Rey did something to harm her.

"Answer me, Alicia."

"Yes, I want to," she said. "Or I wouldn't have kissed you."

After a few beats, he responded. "Knowing the kind of man I am, knowing that I have secrets I'll never tell you, knowing that I can never commit to you when I leave here, you still want it?"

"Get over yourself. I'm not asking for forever. Just this moment. Yes, I want it. I want you."

He leaned down to kiss her but then pulled back

again. Was the man trying to torture her?

"Are you on birth control?" he asked.

"No. Jon had a vasectomy, so..." Without her knowledge.

"I don't suppose you packed any condoms in your suitcases."

"Condoms were the last thing I thought I'd need on this trip," she said.

He released her and sat up. Sighed.

"Alicia, you have absolutely no reason to believe me, but I don't do drugs, and I've never had unprotected sex, even my first time at age sixteen, so I'm clean. And just because it's out there, I've never fucked a guy—never wanted to, never will. I have nothing against that lifestyle. It's just not *my* lifestyle."

That he was trying so hard to ensure her that he was a good risk made her glow from the inside.

"I'm clean too," she said. "Jon was my first and only sexual partner. I got tested several times after he died in case that wasn't his only indiscretion. And I don't do drugs."

"Where are you in your cycle?" he asked.

A chuckle bubbled up from her throat at the absurdity of their conversation and by the fact that this man had taken it upon himself to understand the complexities of a woman's cycle as it related to safe sex.

His brows furrowed as if annoyed she wasn't taking this as seriously as he was. "I don't want to leave you with a baby bomb that goes off in nine months. For many, many reasons, I'm not daddy material."

"I've entered the post-ovulation stage of my cycle, so it's safe to engage in sexual intercourse," she said in her most authoritative voice, then laughed. "God, how sexy is that?"

"Every fucking thing about you is sexy."

Having sex with a stranger was crazy enough, but having sex with a stranger without protection was the most irresponsible thing she'd ever thought about doing. She'd come here to change, and boy had she! Despite the many reasons not to make love with Rey Cruz, she was going to. Because she—the woman she was at this very moment—needed it. Wanted it. Wanted him. Whoever or whatever he was.

"I want you, Rey. Even if that's not your real name." She hadn't planned to tack on that last sentence, voicing her ongoing doubts about his identity, but she was glad she did when she saw a twitch in his eyes that told her doubts were valid. Then, to prove it didn't matter, she added, "I'm willing if you are."

In response, he dove into her, his mouth caressing her face, her neck, her shoulders, her chest, relishing every taste, showing her how very willing he was. His big hands roamed over her tight nipples straining up to him, massaging her through her clothes.

She ran her hands over him, wanting to touch and caress every inch of the body she'd drooled over from the second she'd seen him.

His hands left her body just long enough to yank off her clothes and then his. Then his hand delved between her legs to her wetness, stroking her tunnel and rubbing her clit.

At the same time, she took his hardness in her hand and stroked him, pinching the thick head, swirling her thumb around the wetness at the slit. She wallowed in all the delicious evidence that he wanted her as much as she wanted him.

While they touched, he kissed her face, her neck, her breasts. He sucked her nipple into his mouth, rolling his tongue over it, then moved to the other, making them swell with every wet movement of his tongue, building layer upon layer of pleasure inside her.

He kissed and licked down her stomach, teased the tip of his tongue in her bellybutton, and left her shivering in pleasure. Running his tongue lower, he made his way down between her legs. Then he stopped and stared at the tattoo of the three-inch curved red devil's tail, golden halo hooked on one forked tip, rising from the top of her tamed auburn bush.

He grinned. "I knew you were lying about having another tattoo."

"A girl's gotta have some secrets."

"You'll have to tell me that story. Later," he said, lathed her tattoo, sucked it between his teeth, and bit it.

She moaned. "Oh God, do that again," she said, wantonly spreading her legs for him and arching up into his mouth.

"I plan to," he said and did it again. Then he went beyond the tattoo and licked the length of her slit.

"*Ahh, Rey,*" she moaned, drawing out his name through her clenched teeth. Her hips and groans rose higher at the touch of his mouth, his tongue, on her most intimate parts.

Her hands went to his head, her fingers in his hair, to hold him closer to the flutters of pleasure layering one on the other at her core, and she watched in delight as he pressed his mouth deeper into her wetness and devoured her like he was coming off a months-long fast. Her breath shuddered out of her mouth, erratic and shallow, at the desire he'd brought to life in her, not just in this moment, but the second he'd staggered into her life.

As if he knew she was about to reach the top, he kissed and licked his way back up to her breasts, his hand taking up the job his mouth had relinquished to make sure she didn't lose one thread of desire he'd woven together inside her.

He plunged a finger inside her wetness, rocking it in and out, his thumb brushing across her sensitive clit in a steady pattern. To build her pleasure even more, he sucked her nipples again, first one, then the other, licking them, nipping them.

She was close to the leaping edge, but she wanted to come with him inside her. And she wanted it now. As if he had read her mind and body, he rose over her.

Keeping her hazy gaze locked on his, she guided the head of his cock into place at her slick opening. "I want this," she whispered.

With one quick motion, he slid full hilt into her needy pussy.

She gasped at the deep, tight feel of him, at the connection, and trembled at the pleasure already rippling through her.

He held still as if wanting to give her a moment to enjoy the feeling, the fullness. But she was ready for more. So ready. Past ready. She clenched his ass and thrust her hips up against him. He smiled at her actions, as if he were happy she wanted him so urgently.

****

Nick linked his body with Alicia's in a rush, then slowed down, letting them absorb each other. It was like he could read her body and her mind, knew what she wanted. And the way she touched him and moved against him, it was clear she understood him too and was eager to deliver. He locked his gaze on hers, wanting to see inside her, and he rocked deeper into her, slowly, fully, wanting to touch every inch of her. He dragged out slowly, then did it all again, his thrusts quickening to match the hard rhythm of her breathing.

She trembled beneath him, her core gripping and squeezing his cock. He rubbed his thumb across her swollen mouth, and she took it inside, eagerly sucking it and swirling it with her tongue. The fallatory action sent her over, and her head dropped back, her mouth open, her throat arched in a silent cry before a wild groan broke through.

At the height of her pleasure, he found his. He clenched her, thrusting, hitting the top of her again and again, and let go, filling her tunnel with his hard release. After one last deep push, then another, and one more for good measure, he stilled, his breath ragged in his heaving chest, his body spent from the power of their union.

"Ah, *farolita*. I knew it would be this explosive with you," he whispered into her hair.

"Then why did you wait so long to do it," she said, smiling when a scoff left his throat.

"Just waiting for your damn yes," he said.

She laughed. "I've wanted to do this since you showed up on my porch."

"I know," he said.

"Oh, don't tell me you didn't," she said.

"Hell, even half dead, I wanted you."

"I know," she whispered and lifted her face to his and kissed him.

He kissed her back. Tenderly. Lovingly. Claiming her mouth. Her eyes. Her forehead. Her neck. It made her feel like he was trying to show her that what they'd done was more than a need to satisfy his lust and her loneliness. Tomorrow was soon enough for her to start regretting this decision. Tonight, she was applauding it as the best wrong thing she'd ever done.

Chapter Fourteen

Sleep loosened its grip on Nick's body, and a smile stretched across his mouth as memories of his out-of-this-world night with Alicia returned. Memories that were still as real and heady as the scent of the sex woven in the blankets that covered him. He'd had his fill last night, and then some, but damned if he wasn't ready for more of her.

He stretched out his arm to find her, pull her close, and rock her world again. Feeling only the cold empty spot next to him, he eased his eyes open. Except for Panza curled up at the foot of the bed on her side, he had the mattress to himself.

The soft gray light painting the room said it was morning, and the heat from the crackling fire already doing its job to warm the room said Alicia was up. Muted sounds coming from the kitchen met his ears, and he knew it was her, making coffee for them.

He found his boxer briefs and sweats balled up under the coffee table and pulled them on, then padded into the kitchen to entice his little fire back to bed.

Wrapping his arms around her from behind, he growled, "Good morning," into her neck, then kissed it. He slid his hand inside her oversized blue flannel shirt to caress her breast and was disappointed she'd already put on her bra and T-shirt. Nevertheless, her nipple pearled up under his palm, greeting him fondly, and he pinched it with his knuckles.

The rest of her body stiffened just as hard, and she turned in his arms to face him, breaking the intimate embrace. "Rey, I enjoyed last night, but I think it best if we keep it to a one-time thing."

The unrelenting firmness in her eyes and tone said she was serious. Ah, dammit. She'd thrown up her walls again.

"*Farolita*," he said with a sigh. "Don't do this."

"Do what?"

"Act like we're strangers."

"We *are* strangers," she said.

"Not after last night."

"Last night never should have happened."

Refusing to accept that, he set his hands on her hips and drew her in, pressing his morning wood into her mound. "But it did happen. Numerous times." He gripped her ass and held her tight against him. "It's what we both wanted and needed."

He leaned in to kiss her mouth, and she turned away.

"It was a mistake," she said.

"Is that what you really think?"

When she remained silent, he let his hands drop to his sides.

"Good to know." His voice was sharp with disappointment he couldn't hide. He left her, then grabbed his clothes and headed to the bathroom to wash up and dress warmly against the chill in the cabin.

****

They were quiet during breakfast. Even Panza didn't pester them for food after he'd eaten. Rey kept trying to catch Alicia's eye, likely in an attempt to figure out what had caused her abrupt about-face and to show his desire to talk about it. But she refused to meet his eyes.

She felt the second his supply of patience clicked to empty. He took the mostly full bowl of oatmeal from her and set it on the coffee table beside his, then faced her and took her hands in his, linking their fingers.

"Alicia." He dipped his head to meet her eyes, insisting she face him. She finally let her eyes settle on his.

"I don't regret what we did," he said. "Do you?"

Alicia couldn't see the heat flaring in her face that likely was as red as the glow of the embers in the fireplace, but she could feel it. How did she explain to Rey what she was feeling without hurting his feelings even more or making her sound like a psycho?

"Tell me what you're feeling," he asked almost as if he could read her mind and knew she was struggling to understand and explain the impact of last night on her mind, body, and soul.

Too many feelings vied for attention so she went with the top one. "Appalled."

His hand left her hair. "Appalled that you fucked me?"

"Yes," she said.

Her simple, harsh response had hurt him. She saw it in his eyes. His tense lips. His rigid body. His armor was back in place.

"I've been called a lot of things in my life, but I gotta say, appalling mistake is a new one for me."

He released her hand, but she grabbed it. "Hear me out."

He looked at her but didn't respond. The sharp hurt

she'd seen in those dark depths had dulled to ragged edges.

She scooted in front of him and settled her hands on his knees.

"You show up at my door, bleeding from a near-fatal gunshot wound, brandishing a gun in my face, and threatening to kill me. Against my better judgment, I take you in, treat your wound, care for you. You tell me next to nothing about yourself, and what you do tell me, I don't trust. The only thing I know about you with hundred percent certainty is that you live a dangerous, violent, covert life. Despite all of the evidence that you're a risk to my safety, I brought that life into mine."

"Alicia, regardless of what I implied when I first got here, I'm not going to hurt you. You believe me, don't you?"

Evidence so far had proved that he wouldn't. Until she had evidence to the contrary, she'd continue to believe that what he said was fact.

"I've had plenty of chances to get away from you and the danger I'm in, yet I stayed. And now… Now I've had sex with you—a stranger, a patient—and without protection." She met his gaze. "Since you came into my life, I've been making risky and dangerous decisions. And that's not me, it's not who I am. I evaluate the pros and cons, thoroughly, before I make decisions. I do the math. Twice. I measure three times before I cut. And I don't gamble or take uncalculated risks."

Throughout her speech, he held her gaze with his and seemed to listen intently to every word she said. Although she knew how she *should* end this conversation, how he probably thought it would go, she already knew she wasn't going to take that path. What she wanted most was to soothe the hurt in his eyes, soothe his soul, and only the truth could do that.

"Rey, I'm not appalled by *you*. I'm appalled by *me*. By my complete lack of control and ability to think rationally where you're concerned. It scares me because it's so outside the boundaries of the person I thought I was."

"So, you're saying, it's not me, it's you."

"What I'm saying is that I came here, to this cabin, to learn to be someone else. Who I was, who I'd become after Jon's death, wasn't working for me anymore. That woman was so angry and rigid and unpleasant that it almost cost me the job and friendships I value." She shook her head to dislodge the spikey thistles prickling her mind from thinking about her behavior. "Getting to know you—or at least the person you're presenting yourself to be—and making love with you have helped me see that I can't become a different kind of person if I'm holding on to old behaviors and thoughts."

His hands settled at her waist, and his eyes were shining as if he had read her mind, her heart, and knew the words that were coming. "So…what you're saying is—"

"I don't regret last night. Not one bit."

The satisfaction that flared in his eyes at her confession made her heart swell in joy.

"And I might have to kick your ass out in the snow if you hold me to my stupid idea that it was a one-time thing."

"Just so we're clear," he said through a grin, "you

want to have sex with me again."

"I think that's what I just said."

"I want to hear you say those actual words."

"I bared my heart and soul to you, and you try to embarrass me?" she said.

"A guy likes to hear his woman say she wants him."

She grinned. "Your woman?"

"At this moment, and the next, and the next, until we leave here, you are my woman and I'm your man."

She shrugged. "I can live with that."

He drew her into his arms and wrapped them tight around her. "Now, woman, say what I want to hear."

She stared into his deep, dark, sexy, hooded eyes and bathed in the sweet and spicy flame of love and lust that was making them sparkle. Chills of anticipation radiated over her, urging her response to leave her throat. "I definitely want to have sex with you again."

"*Farolita*, last night was not a one-time thing. I promise you that."

She grinned. "You can stay."

Laughing, he lowered her back onto their bed, and oh God, kept his promise.

Chapter Fifteen

Watching Rey at the window where he stood, again, staring outside, reminded Alicia of a caged lion she'd once seen at the zoo that kept pacing back and forth, trying to figure out how to escape the comfortable and controlled environment he was in. She set her book down, left their warm bed, and joined him. It was still snowing out but not as hard as in previous days.

She slid her arms around him from behind. "What are you looking for when you stare out into the storm?"

"Signs of blue skies and bright sunshine."

"And melting snow?" She read the yes in his silence. "Sounds like you're ready to leave here."

He turned, drew her in his arms, and kissed her forehead. "But not because I'm ready to leave you."

"Hmm." She ran her hands over his shoulders and cupped the back of his head. "We need to keep your mind occupied with something other than what you can't have."

"Something?" Gripping her ass, he pressed into her, showing her what his suggestion was.

"I was thinking more along the lines of mental stimulation," she said with a grin.

"I like my idea better," he whispered, then nuzzled her neck, then her ear, then rounded the corner to her mouth and took her lips.

It would be so easy to give in to the feeling pulling

her in, but they'd been having sex several times a day, the last time an hour ago, and while she was more than eager to make up for the seven-month dry spell, her woman parts needed a break.

With a chuckle, she moved back. "My idea first, then yours," she said and pulled him to their bed.

He sat while she dug into the coffee table drawer.

"How about poker?" she said, holding up a faded deck of cards. She sat across from him on their bed and shuffled the deck. "We'll play for answers."

"What?"

"There's still a lot we don't know about each other. If I win the hand, I get to ask you any question I want. If you win, you can ask me anything you want."

"I know there are other games in there." He slid over to the table to check out its other contents and was about to haul out the checkers set when she stopped him.

"C'mon. It'll be fun. If you're any good at poker, you have nothing to worry about," she added the challenge.

"Oh, I'm good."

She grinned. "Here's your opportunity to prove it," she said, then shuffled the deck and dealt the cards. "Five card stud, nothing wild."

She dealt the cards and picked hers up.

He left his between them untouched. "Let's agree that the game is over after five hands," he said.

"Five? We're barely getting started at five. How about nine," she said.

He held up his hand, showing five fingers.

"Seven, and you get a kiss afterward," she countered. "In that place you like."

"Seven it is." He picked up his cards.

He won the first hand.

"What's your favorite sex position?" he asked her.

She laughed. "Depends on my mood, but for the most part, I'd say cowgirl."

"Ah…you on top."

"Mmmhmm," she murmured and licked her lower lip.

"We'll do that position first if you win any of the five hands."

"Seven," she said, then shuffled the cards, dealt again. This time she won.

"Doggy style," he said before she'd had a chance to ask her question.

"Excuse me?" she said.

"My favorite position."

"Yes, well, I'm very glad to know that, but that wasn't my question."

"What's your question?" he asked, a tinge of caution in his voice.

"What's the best vacation you've ever had?"

The look in his eyes warned her that his response would be about sex. "I spent weeks in a mountain cabin with this hot nurse, having the most mind-blowing sex of my life."

She laughed. "You better be talking about me."

"You know I am." He leaned in and kissed her, trying to ease her back down on the bed, but she stopped him.

"C'mon, five more hands to go," she said and dealt the cards.

He won. Twice in a row. Both of his questions were banal, one asking about her favorite holiday—

Christmas—and her favorite color—purple.

Then she won again. The smile on his face said he expected an equally banal question from her. But she wasn't going to give him banal.

"Who are you, really, Rey Cruz?" she asked.

The smile left his face, and his eyes went dead.

"I know that's not your name."

He reached out and pulled her onto his lap, trapping her there with his muscular arms. "Now, why would you think that?" he whispered into her shoulder, then bit it, spreading goosebumps across her body.

He was really good at deflection—and distraction—but she was really good at getting answers. And she was tired of this cloak-and-dagger game they were playing.

"It doesn't fit you." She pulled back and cupped his face. "I don't know what you're hiding. But you don't have to. You can trust me. I think I've proven that."

His eyes met hers, stared deeply, unbreakingly, like he was opening himself core deep, letting her see him without having to say a word. "I'm a man who's on a course he can't get off of right now."

His tone and expression suggested the words were truthful. And final. But they didn't tell her anything. Disappointment dropped her hands to her lap.

"I fought against my very foundation to trust you, Rey. Surely you can do the same."

"That was your choice."

"Tell me one truth about yourself right now," she said, her voice insistent.

"I want to make love to you so bad my whole body hurts," he said, his voice raspy with desire, and she felt the proof of his desire growing beneath her.

"I'm very well aware you want to fuck me, so that doesn't count. It doesn't tell me anything I don't already know. Try again."

"You're the sweetest thing in my life," he said, nibbling her lips.

She jerked back. "Why do you always do that?"

With an annoyed sigh, he loosened his hold on her and let his arms drop to his sides. "Do what?"

"Try to distract me with sex and sweet words. I really need you to be honest with me. I need to be able to trust you. If I can't trust you, I can't do this."

"This?"

"This! Us. Fucking like we matter to each other."

"It didn't bother you all the other times we fucked with unanswered questions between us."

Fury pushed her to leave his lap, but he wrapped his arms around her to stop her and held her tight.

"Let me go," she said, anger seething in the words.

He gripped her hair to hold her head still, making her look at him. "I'm fucking crazy about you, Alicia. I'm happier and more comfortable with you than any woman I've ever been with. That's as honest as I can be right now, and it'll have to be enough." His frustration for her line of questioning came through loud and clear in his sharp and insistent tone. "You're going to have to trust me on faith alone. If you can't, then you're right. We shouldn't do this."

He released his hold on her. She could go. Surprisingly, she stayed put.

"I don't want to care about a man who's going to be taken by a bullet, either the law's or another criminal's."

A mask of disappointment hardened over his face at her words. "So you've decided I'm a criminal. No hard evidence. That's so unlike you."

"Then what are you?" she asked, ignoring his sarcasm. "*Who* are you? Tell me."

She could see his jaw gripping, showing he was gritting his teeth to hold back the answers she needed and he didn't want to give.

"Fine," she said when it was clear he wasn't going to budge. "I don't want you to be crazy about me, I don't want to be crazy about you, and I certainly don't want to fuck you anymore."

Before she could get up, he tossed her onto her back and hovered over her in a dominant position. Frustration and anger driving her, she tried to hit and kick and push him away, but he grabbed her wrists and pinned her arms up by her head and trapped her legs under him.

"As long as we're in this cabin, let's be who we are, not who the world wants us to be. And who we are, at the core, is two people who want and need each other." He released her wrists and used his big, strong hands to rip open her shirt, sending buttons popping off and flying across the room and making her gasp.

He didn't ravage her, like she thought he'd do. Hoped he'd do. Instead, he just stared at her heaving breasts. That alone tightened her nipples and pulled a groan from her mouth. He lowered his head as if to suck them but then didn't. The agony of his hot breath on her trembling skin triggered her desire and exploded it into a burning need that flashed through her body. Then he locked his gaze with hers and her fall into desire was complete.

"Sometimes the greatest risks return the greatest rewards, Alicia. But you have to be brave enough to give them a try despite not having all the answers. You told me that's why you came here, to try a different way. You were succeeding. Don't slip back into your old ways because you're scared."

Yeah, he was right. The old her required answers to every question, and any unanswered question was a blockade to moving forward. But this situation was different. It could be life-threatening. "At the very least, I deserve to know who you really are, so I have the facts I need to—"

He leaned over and licked her nipple, making her arch up into a ragged groan. He repeated the move on her other nipple, and the action earned the same response.

"I'm your lover. The man you love to fuck. The man who loves to fuck you. Those are the facts."

Because bad judgment was all she possessed while with him, she closed her eyes and writhed, groaning his name, giving him silent permission to continue licking her, like flames to her body.

But he didn't.

Disappointment popped open her eyes. He stared down at her. He had her submission and knew it. Why was he torturing her?

"Are you brave enough to go all the way, blind?" he said, his voice quiet but commanding.

"Yes," she sighed her answer.

"Prove it to me."

She cupped his head and tried to draw him down to her breasts. "Don't stop," she murmured.

"Don't stop what?"

The needy sound that gurgled from her mouth said everything she felt but couldn't say. But he demanded words.

"Tell me."

"Don't stop making me feel alive."

As if he'd heard the magic words, he lowered his head and fully possessed her breast with his mouth, sucking her nipple deep into his mouth, swirling his tongue over it, biting it. With a gasp she arched up into his touch. She dug her fingers into his long hair and held his mouth to her nipple.

"Bastard," she moaned.

He smiled against her breast, then bit and licked down her stomach to her pussy with an urgency that took her breath away. He yanked her flannel pj bottoms and panties down her hips and legs, then settled between her thighs, urging her with his arms to open wider, pushing her bent legs, up higher, giving him full access to the feast before him.

"I'll never get tired of your taste," he murmured and then feasted on her, lathing her clit in long slow laps that had her insides going crazy, followed by purposeful licks and sucks and bites that had her body writhing in an urgent, needy movement. He dipped a finger into her, then two, stroking her wet tunnel while his tongue stroked and flicked her throbbing clit.

Her moans grew bolder and louder, and her body quaked as pleasure erupted inside her. Unable to hold back the swirling, pounding orgasm any longer, she let go and came hard against his tongue, his lips, his mouth, her pussy clenching his plunging fingers.

It was so easy with him…finding her pleasure. She'd never been this turned on by anyone. Just watching him, seeing his eyes go black when his body possessed hers, was enough to send her over that high peak screaming in joy.

He rose to his knees and stripped off his clothes. The firelight licked his hard, naked body, and it called out to her to claw and pull him to her, eagerly, desperately, with both hands, both arms, both legs, and consume him like an addict consuming her drug of choice.

Before he could lower himself to her, she rose to her knees and gripped his arms. She kissed him hard and deep, tasting her pleasure on his tongue and lips. Then she planted a hand in the center of his chest and urged him down to the floor. She straddled his hips and kissed and lathed her way over his chest, her tongue savoring the masculine taste and feel of his body.

As he'd done with her, she licked, tasted, and bit him as his body jerked in pleasure and his breath went shallow. Meeting his eyes, she slid farther down him and took his engorged cock head into her mouth, sucking deep. He growled low in his throat and gathered her hair in one tight fist as if to better see everything she was doing to him.

"Ah, fuck, Alicia. Your mouth is magic."

Wrapping a hand around the lower half of his dick, she took the upper half deeper into her mouth and worked her mouth up and down his shaft, faster, harder, deeper, the motion and his desire reigniting the need between her legs.

His hips arched up, as if he was ready to come, but his grip tightened in her hair, and he pulled her away.

"Come here," he said, his voice husky with need. He pulled her toward him, up to face him, his expression so full of hunger it terrified and thrilled her at the same time. "Ride me."

Wasting not even a second, she connected them in her favorite position and rocked on him, deep and slow, trying to prolong this feeling so she could commit everything about it to memory. She would love him as if she were going to lose him, because she knew in her heart she would. As soon as the storm passed and the roads were passible, maybe as soon as the next couple of days, he would leave.

Until then, she would make every moment with him count. She would give herself permission to race heart and headfirst into this thing between them and get lost, not asking why or what happens next, and definitely not querying the rule book at every step. This man, this stranger, had created a dark, erotic, and dangerous place for her, and she'd never felt safer, stronger, more confident, more desired, and more satisfied, and all she knew was that she wanted more.

She opened her thighs wider and sank deeper onto his dick. She rocked her hips, filling herself fully with his hardness. She was close. As if he could feel it, he flipped them so he was on top. Staring down into her eyes, he plunged hard into her, thrusting wildly but hitting the mark every time.

"I'm risking everything to be with you like this, and it's totally worth it," he said seconds before her world tilted again at the pleasure surging through her from the spell this man had spun around and inside her.

Chapter Sixteen

The storm passed that night, and the morning greeted them with the blue skies, bright sun, and melting snow Rey had been looking for. In another two days, all but a few inches of snow was gone. What was left served as a reminder of the snowstorm that had raged outside the cabin and made possible the firestorm that had raged inside it.

From the fireplace, where she was starting the coffee, Alicia studied her lover. Her man. He again was standing sentinel at the window, arms crossed over his chest, staring into the world of dazzling blue. His posture, his body stance, told her he was leaving. She could feel it. The tension and angst running through him radiated into the room, pricking her with its needlelike sharpness.

There was no doubt in her mind that he enjoyed her, was crazy about her as he'd said, but there was something—something stronger than his proclaimed feelings for her—that was driving him to leave, to reenter his world. The world that had nearly taken his life. His work, whatever it was, was fierce competition for his affection. It was a competition she knew she'd lose.

She thought back to a few days earlier when he'd said he was risking everything to be with her. She hadn't asked him to clarify, not then, nor in the days after. In fact, she'd stopped the interrogation and focused on living consciously with the man as she knew him. The feeling of giving up control was nerve-wracking, exhilarating, and freeing, but with him it was an adventure of a lifetime and she was hooked.

The belief that he was in danger never left her mind, which meant accepting that he might get shot again. That he might die. That there would be nothing she could do to save him. And that hurt worse than the idea of his leaving her.

Longing to be close to him, touching him, she joined him. "Even with the sun out, it looks cold and brittle."

He slid his arm around her shoulders, drew her into his side, and kissed her forehead. It was surprising how quickly she had gotten used to how demonstrative he was, always touching her or kissing her to express his affection. She'd always been someone who liked her space. Most surprising to her was how easily she was becoming like him, always wanting to touch him. She liked it. A lot.

He stared outside while she stared at him, watched him explore with his keen hawk's vision the sparkling sight outside the window, like he was peering behind trees, under the snow, beyond the yard to see what was out there. While he was probably wishing for the sun to melt all the snow fast so he could get the hell out of here, she was wishing for more snow, enough to cover the doors and windows so she could keep him here.

As if he had felt her eyes on her and sensed her thoughts, he turned to look at her, then pulled her in for a long, slow, deep kiss. When he eased back and stared deep into her eyes, she steadied herself. *Here it comes.*

His goodbye.

"Let's cut down a Christmas tree today."

His words lifted a surprised grin to her face. Christmas was next week. She hadn't given a lot of thought to the holiday, much less about celebrating it or decorating for it. Then she realized what he was doing, and her smile faded. The snow was mostly gone. His wound was mostly healed. He was leaving. But he wanted to give her a Christmas—her favorite holiday—before he did.

"Will you be here to celebrate the holiday with me?"

His eyes cut to the landscape outside, held for a moment or two, then returned to her. "I will if I can."

"That's not exactly a promise."

"Is it enough?"

Her kiss was her yes. "I'll get dressed."

She left his embrace, but he caught her arm and drew her back in.

"You've changed, Nurse Alicia," he said.

"How so?"

"You've stopped the probing questions. Are you no longer interested in the answers?"

"I'm interested in all your answers, but I no longer need them."

"What changed?"

"The words you said a few days ago."

"What were those wise words?"

"The greatest risks return the greatest rewards," she said, "but you have to be brave enough to give them a try despite not having all the answers."

"You've changed me, too. In ways I can't begin to explain."

"Try."

****

The truth was bubbling in Nick's heart, pushing through the line of lies like a linebacker, trying to find a way out, and it triggered an alarm that buzzed throughout his body, a warning to add defenses to hold the line. But before he knew it, one truth was tumbling from his mouth like a rockslide.

"You made me…good again." He stared into her eyes, wanting to show her that his words though weak on exuberance were brawny on truth.

The loving smile that curved her soft lips and brightened her eyes to an emerald green was his reward for taking the risk and sharing his feelings.

She cupped his face. "You were already good. I could see it, despite the bravado you wear like armor. I have a feeling it's something you don't reveal to many people."

He could count on one hand the number of people he trusted enough to let close and see him without his armor—his mother and sisters and a couple of friends at the Bureau. But those he trusted enough to reveal his deep dark secrets, doubts, and desires to? The only one on that short list was God. With time and testing, he could see Alicia's name appearing next to the Almighty's. The thought of it shot a bolt of energy through his body that delivered a mega dose of something akin to joy.

Because he couldn't find the words to tell her all that, he wrapped his arms around her and buried his face into her hair, breathing in her scent. Then he kissed her deep, showing his love, his appreciation, his passion, hoping she'd interpret it the right way. Her kissing him back with equal enthusiasm told him that maybe she had.

"Should we go get the tree *now*?" she said as his mouth shifted to ravage her neck. "Or *later*?"

The suggestion in her final word zinged hot and fast through him, flashing brightly enough to reveal another truth—with her, he was happy. Something he hadn't been in a long time.

He tried to ignore the voice spewing from the depths of his logical mind, reminding him that the bliss he was feeling was nothing more than a sweet pause from his brutal and demanding life. That's all it could ever be. She looked at him with such love, as if she thought he deserved this kind of love.

Too bad she was wrong.

He could protect her from others, but he couldn't protect her from him. When Alicia found out who he really was and the things he'd done—and that he'd been mostly lying to her this whole time—she would become blind to his carefully cloaked goodness and see what everyone else saw. A ruthless and hardened son of a bitch.

But while he had her, while she wanted him, he'd be selfish and enjoy this slice of paradise where he was the man he always wanted to be.

He swung her up in his arms, carried her to their bed, and showed her how good he was and, more importantly, how good they were together.

****

"How are we decorating this ginormous tree?" Nick asked Alicia as they headed home, him pulling *ginormous* behind them while she gathered sticks and pinecones.

"I have some paper we can fold and cut to make snowflakes. Do you remember doing that in school?"

"Vaguely," he said, enjoying listening to her. Seeing her this happy did something to his heart, made it feel like fireworks were exploding inside it. He could live like this forever with her. "What are the sticks for?"

"We'll glue them together in the shape of stars. I think I have glue. I hope I do. If not, we'll make stars out of foil."

Just feet from the cabin, Panza stopped in the middle of the yard, tensed, and growled toward the wide-open front door.

Before Nick could grab Alicia's hand and run back into the woods with her, Henry Duggar walked out of the cabin, a gun in his hand.

Panza went crazy, barking, growling, and baring his teeth, eager to attack the obvious threat. Nick called to the dog, who joined him and Alicia, and tried to settle him.

"*Hola*, Rey. Long time no see." Henry pointed the gun toward Alicia. "And you must be the sexy redhead Johnson has a hard-on for." Henry walked down the steps toward them. Waved his gun toward the cabin. "Go on in. We need to have a little talk."

Alicia looked at Nick, and he winced at the fear in her eyes. "It's okay," he whispered and put his arm around her. Keeping himself between her and Henry's gun, he guided her up the steps and into the cabin. He kept his other hand on Panza in case the dog decided to attack.

When they were all inside, Henry closed the door. "First things first. Red, take the dog into the bedroom and close the door. I'm an animal lover, but I won't hesitate to shoot him if he attacks me. You understand?"

Alicia nodded and did as he asked, then rejoined Nick.

"Rey, you sit on the couch, there." When Alicia moved to sit beside him, Henry redirected her. "No, no, little Red, I want you over here by me."

She stared at Nick, obviously not wanting to leave his side.

"Now," Henry yelled.

She moved over to stand by Henry, and Nick sat on the edge of the couch, facing her, ready to spring up and toward Henry when the right moment presented itself.

Henry grabbed Alicia's arm to position her in front of him, like a shield.

She jerked away. "Don't touch me."

He shoved her down to the floor in front of him. She fell on her butt, legs splayed out. Nick jumped up from the couch, but Henry pointed his gun at her head. "Sit the fuck down, Rey, and stay there, or I swear I'll fucking shoot her in the head, right now."

Nick sat. "So, you found me. What now?"

"What do you think? I'm going to shoot you in your cold black heart, then cut out what's left of it and take it to Johnson as a gift."

"You've grown some big ass cojones since I last saw you," Nick said. "Saying fuck it to Johnson's rule about getting his approval before making a hit, particularly on the woman he's got the hots for. Good for you, man. I didn't think you had it in you."

"I didn't say I was going to kill her."

Nick heard the doubt in Henry's voice about whether his plan could get him into trouble. And it confirmed that Johnson didn't know Henry was here.

"How did you find me?"

"Johnson's been babbling about the hot redhead who's staying in the old Anaya cabin with her husband. It triggered the memory of that day I followed you here, watched you snooping around this cabin, checking it out. I connected the points into a line that I thought would lead me straight to you. And it did." He laughed at his brilliance.

"I knew you were following me. What I didn't know was why."

"I didn't trust you from the minute you showed up. So, I trailed you every time you left the compound, kept record of where you went, what you did, who you talked to. I wanted evidence to get Johnson and the other leaders to believe me that something wasn't right about you."

"Well, now, that hurts my feelings, Henry. I thought we were friends."

"We've never been friends, you cocky, sarcastic, Hollywood pretty boy, know-it-all bastard."

"Hollywood pretty boy?" Nick laughed. "Henry. Man. You flatter me, but I'm not into dudes. I like the women. Full-sized, juicy women you can bury yourself in balls deep. Women like *Yolanda*." Henry had been panting after Yolanda since before Rey Cruz arrived at the compound. The woman had just as long been making it known she considered all Duggars, Henry in particular, on par with roaches.

Henry stepped forward a couple of steps toward Nick. "Don't you say her name! You're not good enough to say her name. You're not even good enough to lick her boots."

"It was never her boots she wanted me to lick." Nick punctuated the lie by flitting the tip of his tongue back and forth.

Henry roared and rushed toward him. As he did, he tripped over Alicia's foot and fell forward, banging his head on the coffee table on the way down.

Nick was on his feet in a flash, grabbing the gun and pointing it at Henry.

Who wasn't moving.

Blood poured from his head and pooled on the floor.

Alicia rushed to the man, knelt, and rolled him onto his back. He stared up at them with dead black eyes, but she felt for a pulse.

"Rey," she said, her eyes meeting his. "He's dead." She stood. "He's dead, and I killed him."

Nick pulled her into his arms and hugged her tight. "No. You didn't. He tripped. He fell. You had nothing to do with that. If he hadn't fallen, he would have shot me, then you. Because he fell, we're alive. But it's no one's fault."

She clung to him, tight, and her body shook. He laid her down on their bed and curled around her, holding her, whispering soft words of comfort, soft nonsensical sounds, anything to soothe her. She never spoke.

Nick's anger and hatred for this gang member bubbled over. Not just because Henry had helped torture Cowboy, one of his informants who wanted to get out of the gang. Not just because he had ritual-raped every single one of the women gang members. Not just because he made drugs that killed the kids who took them. Or that he'd stolen, lied, and cheated his way through life, contributing nothing. Nick's anger was mostly because of how the scumbag died. He'd cheated Nick out of the pleasure of taking his life, either through a bullet or prison. Most of all, his anger was because Alicia's accidental involvement in ridding the earth of the pestilent disease that was Henry Duggar would scar her soul forever, and he couldn't fix that.

Sometime later, she stopped shaking.

Nick whispered, "Baby, I need to clean this up. I'll be back as soon as I can."

He rose from the bed.

She did, too. "I'll help."

"No. Stay here."

Nick let Panza out of the bedroom. The dog raced out of the room and over to Alicia, nudging her as if asking whether she was okay. Only after she pet him to reassure him she was fine did he leave her side to inspect the body. He sniffed it, snorted, then returned to Alicia on the bed, his head in her lap.

As Nick banked the fire, he rehearsed his plan to dispose of the garbage.

Luckily, Henry had fallen on the rug. Nick rolled him up in it like a burrito, dragged it across the floor and down the porch steps, and left it in the yard. Henry hadn't walked here, and there was no vehicle in the yard other than Alicia's, so Nick figured Henry had ridden one of the snowmobiles and had likely left it down the road.

Nick went back in the cabin, bundled up, and headed out to search for the vehicle, leaving Alicia and Panza with her gun. He found the snowmobile under a grouping of trees at the side of the road near the entrance to Alicia's property. He drove it back to the cabin and loaded the body onto it. He headed toward the main road, stopping at the place where he'd pushed the truck over the edge.

He crawled into a coat of numbness to push aside the idea that this dead thing had once been a human being, a baby, a child, with needs and wants that had never been met. He couldn't change things, couldn't bring him back to life. Wouldn't even if he could.

Blocking all but the most critical thoughts from his mind, he shoved the rug off the snowmobile. Holding onto the end of the rug, he flipped it. It unfurled, the body rolling out and then over the edge of the ravine. He heard it breaking branches on the way down, heard the dull thuds of it hitting rocks, and he felt every break, every thud, in his own body.

The snowmobile was still running. He gave it a jolt of power and it shot forward, following Henry's path over the edge.

Nick rerolled the bloody rug, picked it up, and rushed back to the cabin on foot. He stuffed the rug into the metal trash can and set it ablaze, watching until it was nothing but ash. Only then did he go inside, planning to start the process of methodically wiping down every surface, wanting to destroy all evidence that Henry Duggar had been in this cabin. Destroying evidence would get him fired, fined, and jailed, but he'd promised to do everything he could to protect Alicia. It was worth the risk.

She was already cleaning when he went in. He didn't suggest she sit this one out because he knew that doing something was better than doing nothing to help occupy her mind and hopefully blur the nightmare starting to build a home there. They moved the bedroom rug into the living room to cover anything they might have missed.

Later, while Alicia washed up and changed clothes, Nick made a stand for the seven-foot tree and set it up in the living room so she could see it from the bed. Although he knew she was not in a festive mood, tonight he'd encourage her to make those decorations she had been so excited about and decorate the tree with him. Their first.

She came out of the bathroom and headed straight to him. She wrapped her arms around him, kissed him, and pulled him down with her to the bed. Their bed. She kissed him and caressed him, told him with her body and her eyes that the thing she wanted most right now was the same thing he wanted forever—to lie with each other, hold each other, and connect spiritually, emotionally, and physically like only they could. And for him, he also wanted to pour his love so deep into her it would be the only thing she felt.

Afterward, Alicia finally fell asleep, but Nick stayed awake. No way would he be sleeping tonight, or ever, until she was safe.

The pungent scent of pinon wafting in the air drew his attention to the bare tree. It was as perfect a Christmas tree as he'd ever seen. He'd give anything if he could also give Alicia a perfect Christmas, with sparkly tree decorations and nicely wrapped gifts under it. He wished he had a gift for her. But maybe, like him, she would be content with the gifts they had given each other already. Gifts that were piled not under the tree but inside their hearts.

Before Henry's death had put a decided damper on things, Nick had been marveling at the fact that, because of Alicia, he'd never been this happy. The thought lifted a contented smile to his face until the truth cut in with a snide, *Don't get used to it. You have to leave. They'll be coming. To look for Henry. To look for you.*

He would leave. Tomorrow. But for the rest of tonight, he'd pretend this was his life and enjoy the hell out of every priceless second.

Leaving Alicia's side, he rose and went into the kitchen to find some paper, scissors, glue, and foil.

Chapter Seventeen

Rey was cleaning up from breakfast and Alicia was airing out their bedding when Panza ran to the door, growling and barking. Alicia peeked out the window and saw the sheriff's vehicle sloshing up the muddy road.

"Oh God. Do you think he knows?" she said as the SUV pulled to a stop in the yard.

Rey joined her at the window as the sheriff exited his vehicle and looked around the premises, then headed to the porch.

Rey shifted away from the window, and his eyes cut to hers. "I don't think so."

"I'll handle it. Get out of sight," she said.

He rushed to the bedroom, closing the door all but an inch as if he wanted to be able to hear the conversation. She grabbed Panza, who was about to scratch the door down, and opened the door when the sheriff's knock sounded.

"Mrs. Stone," the sheriff said, touching his thumb and forefinger to the brim of his hat.

"Sheriff," she said over the barking. Hopefully, the irritating noise would cut the sheriff's visit short.

"Mind if I step inside for a moment?"

She hesitated, but not wanting to spur any suspicions he might be harboring, she opened the door wider to allow him in. She did, however, leave it open, even though it let in the cold, and she kept Panza between them, a firm hand on him.

The sheriff removed his shades and slid them into his shirt pocket, and his gaze zeroed in on the mattress and the tree.

"Nice tree," he said. "A little rustic but charming."

She glanced back at the tree Rey had decorated for her while she slept. It was the most beautiful, memorable, and heartwarming tree she'd ever had, and that he'd done it for her was the absolute best gift anyone had ever given her. No matter what happened between her and Rey, she would never forget how special he made her feel.

"It's perfect," she said and flushed in the warmth of her thoughts of the man who made it so.

"Is your husband here?" he said, his gaze slowly circling the entire space.

"He hiked up to make a call."

"Funny how he's never here when I come around."

"We've been cooped up for days with the storm, so he's suffering from a little cabin fever. Thinks of reasons to get out of the cabin. I'm sure you know how it is."

He pointed at her. "I'm going to meet that husband of yours before you two leave here."

"Is that why you're here?"

"I came to tell you that the road into town is passible. In case you two have had enough of mountain life."

"We'll be staying through New Year's, but thanks for the update," she said. "I'll come in for more supplies in a day or two."

The way the sheriff's mouth tightened and his

eyebrows furrowed told her that either her stubbornness to stay or Panza's barrage of barking was getting to him. "Bring your hubby along when you do."

"We'll see. He doesn't like shopping."

The sheriff eyed her for a long minute before responding. "Well, I won't keep you. I've got others to check on."

He stepped out the door, onto the porch, her behind him. He walked down the steps, stood on the last one and let his eyes search the area, looking for what she didn't know. From day one, she sensed that he carried some heavy suspicions where she was concerned. Today, her guilt was probably as loud and evident as a foghorn.

"Is there something else, Sheriff?"

He turned back, his narrowed gaze pinning her in place. "Have any strangers come around lately? Before the storm, I mean."

It was almost like he knew she was hiding something—other than her husband being dead, her shacking up with a gang member, and Henry Duggar dying on her cabin floor—and trying to catch her in lie. "No."

"No one's showed up, asking for directions, food, water…medical attention."

She ignored the flutter in her stomach and the dare in his eyes when he said the last item. Technically, Rey hadn't asked for anything—except the keys to her SUV. She'd freely offered medical care, food, water, shelter. Her body. Her heart. And Henry hadn't asked for anything. He had been here to take—her life and Rey's. These half-truths allowed her to answer the Sheriff's question straight on, without hesitation. "No."

He stared at her a little longer, trying to use the prolonged glare and silence tactic to put her on edge, scare her, flaunt his power. The tactic often worked to get people to say more than they wanted to, just to fill the uncomfortable silence. She'd used it herself when talking to patients about their medical histories and about what substances they'd taken before arriving in the ER. So, it wouldn't work on her.

As if finally realizing that, he pulled a folded sheet of paper from his jacket pocket and held it out to her.

"If you see this man, it's important you let me know immediately."

She took the paper and unfolded it, then willed her body not to react to the image of her lover scowling at her from the sheet.

The photocopied image was grainy, and the black sunglasses hid his eyes, but there was no mistaking Rey Cruz. No mistaking that delicious mouth she'd kissed hundreds of times, the long hair she'd gripped as ecstasy bloomed inside her. But there was something else she saw in that picture, something she had never seen in him. Hardness. Ruthlessness. Deadly malice.

Pulsing tingles danced underneath her chilled skin, and she couldn't stop the escaped shiver that zipped up her spine. "Who is he?"

"A dangerous Los Matos gang member and cold-blooded killer. No one's safe until we capture him."

A killer. The damning words echoed in her head. This is what he'd been hiding from her. Not just that he was a gang member, but that he was a killer. While she might be able to forgive the former, the latter was unforgivable. But the longer she stared at the image, the more she struggled to reconcile the man she knew with the man the sheriff was calling a killer. Her heart refuted the statement, saying that Rey wasn't the cold-blooded-murderer type. Her head pointed out that she'd misjudged a loved one before. Her gut reminded her that she didn't trust the sheriff and therefore any information he peddled.

"Are you sure?" she asked. "I mean, are you sure he's in this area?"

"I'm sure. He murdered one of your neighbors—Harvey Duggar—up the road days before the storm hit."

Harvey Duggar. Relation to Henry? The man she'd— Oh God.

Her stomach spun at the image of Henry's blood flowing out his head onto her rug, the rug she and Jon had bought their first trip to the cabin, the rug that was now ashes in her burn bin. Like her life. And then it hit her. She had no right to judge Rey for an act she herself had committed. She swallowed against the nausea that was threatening to bring up her breakfast.

"You seem awfully disturbed by that image, Mrs. Stone. Is there something you want to tell me?"

So lost in thought, she had almost forgotten the sheriff was there and waiting for a response to some question. What was it he'd asked her? "Uh, no, I…well, to be honest, this seems like such a quiet, safe little place. I guess I'm just shocked that such a heinous crime would occur here." That much was true.

"Now, don't worry your pretty little head. I'm going to catch that scumbag before he can kill again." He reached out and settled his hand on her shoulder, then slowly ran it down her arm. "Count on it."

Panza growled and shot forward toward the sheriff.

She caught him before he took a hunk out of the man's flesh.

"I appreciate your dedication," she said, holding tight to Panza and speaking loudly over his barks.

"Well, I'll let you go." The sheriff touched the brim of his hat and nodded. "Merry Christmas." He put his sunglasses back on, then turned.

"Sheriff. This man…" She held out the paper. "What's his name?"

"Rey Cruz. Out of LA."

She nodded and watched him stroll across the yard to his vehicle. It felt like he was moving in slow motion just to freak her out. As soon as he drove away, Panza stopped barking and grumbled all the way to the fireplace before plopping down on the bed in a disgusted huff.

Alicia closed the door, shutting out the frigid weather, but her body remained ice cold.

Oh, Rey. How can we get past something like this?
****

Nick exited the bedroom and went to the window, peering out to make sure the sheriff had gone and no one else had stayed. That was too fucking close.

"I need to go," he said. "I'm putting you in danger by being here."

"You mean putting yourself in danger," Alicia said.

He turned toward her, eyes questioning her words and tone.

She handed him the paper.

He didn't know who'd taken the image, but it was him all right. "I need a fucking haircut," he mumbled.

"He said you're a cold-blooded killer," Alicia said, and his gaze rose to her.

Face pale, eyes heavy with despair, the woman he'd come to care about stood in front of him, shell-shocked and waiting for him to explain, to refute the sheriff's claim. He said nothing. Because, honestly, what could he say? He had killed. More times than he liked to admit. All in the line of duty, first in the military and then the FBI, but still… Yes, he had taken life. He couldn't deny it. Wouldn't deny it. Even to strip that stabbed-in-the-heart look from Alicia's face.

She licked her trembling lips. "Now would be a good time to tell me he's wrong, that you're not a killer. That this is a mistake. Or a lie. Or…something other than the truth."

"*Farolita*," he said, but the other words he wanted to say shattered when they hit the wall of mistrust that had arisen between them.

"This is what you meant when you said you were risking everything to be with me. Risking getting caught."

Instead of trying to explain things he couldn't, he turned away and grabbed his jacket from the coatrack, pulled it on, then pulled on his boots.

It was time to go. Past time. He never should have stayed this long. At the very least, he should have hiked up to that spot Alicia had talked about as soon as he'd been able to walk, made a call, and instructed his team to come for him and the evidence he had nearly gotten killed over. He had been well enough weeks ago to do it. Before the storm hit. And the snow had mostly been gone for twenty-four hours. But he'd wanted to stay in this cabin with Alicia because he was happy. He'd put his desires ahead of his responsibilities. That negligence and greediness had compromised his assignment and endangered her life. His dad was right. He was a fuckup.

He grabbed her key fob, then stood before her, a feeling of regret covering him head to toe. Not once had she tried to stop him, with words or actions. Another reason leaving was for the best. He could see the fear, mistrust, and disgust in her eyes. And nothing—not even the truth—would scour it from her body, mind, and soul.

But the empty, burning feeling in his chest surprised him. He didn't want to leave her, but even more, he didn't want her to want him to leave. He wanted her to pull him to her, kiss him, ask him to stay, assure him that whatever it was he was mixed up with, it wouldn't change how she felt about him.

And, God, he wanted to hold her one last time. Kiss her one last time. Breathe her into his lungs and skin to tattoo her essence on his soul. It was doubtful she'd even let him touch her now that this new information had exploded muck and mistrust all over them, opening a chasm between them. But it didn't matter. For her sake, her safety, he would leave.

"I'll get someone to bring your vehicle back." Then he headed for the door and opened it.

"Rey," she called out.

He stopped and looked back at her.

She inhaled and released a slow breath, as if she needed time to evaluate her next words and determine whether it was wise to say them.

"I have absolutely no proof other than how I feel, but I know—somehow, I just know—that you're a good man, and I know he's not," she said, pointing the way the sheriff had gone. "If you did kill the man he says you did, I'm going to believe that it was because you had no other choice. I know you need to leave, but I want you to know that I wish you could stay."

Her words were fierce enough to both pierce and inflate his heart. The emotion that radiated from her as she spoke infiltrated him, filled him, blocking every sensibility, every sliver of logic, every bit of training he possessed, blocking everything but the desire to please her and in turn enjoy with her what might be his last minutes of life.

Growling her name in a desperate whisper, he rushed to her, pulled her into him, and lifted her, his arms wrapped so tight around her that nothing could pry her away from him. She wrapped her arms and legs around him, and her hands gripped him as if she was hoping for the same thing.

"*Farolita*," he said and eased back, letting his fierce gaze cling to hers. "You're right. The sheriff is a bad guy. He's the leader of Los Matos gang. I shot Harvey because he shot me and would have continued to shoot until I was dead. That's all true, I swear it. But if you believe only one thing I've said to you, make it this. If I had a choice, I'd choose to stay with you." He swallowed hard to get the final word out. "Forever."

He kissed her then. Deep. Hard. Letting it confirm the feelings he couldn't speak.

At that moment, the electricity came on, the lights, the hum of power buzzing through the wires, and the heater. They paid it no mind.

****

Rey carried her to their bed. The fireplace logs popped and crackled as he lay her down.

"I'll never forget you," she said, her gaze

penetrating deep into his dark eyes. "You made me feel again."

"Everything about you—your taste, your scent, your touch—is a part of me, imbedded so deep it can never be erased," he said.

He kissed her, claiming her mouth with his lips and his tongue and breath, then rose up to inch off her shirt. He kissed a path from her neck to her breasts, one then the other, then lower, across her stomach, toward the liquid heat pooling between her legs.

She ran a hand over his head, the silky feel of his hair now so familiar and erotic against her palm, while her other hand caressed his back, wanting to imbed the feel of his skin, his scars, his muscles, his heat into her cells.

"I want you," she whispered, her voice raspy with yearning. "All of you."

"I give you all I am," he said, his gaze dark with passion. He hooked his fingers into the waistband of her sweats and panties and stripped them over her hips, down her legs, leaving her bare. In seconds, his clothes were off, too.

Then he took his time, his mouth sweet and giving on hers, his hands slow and gentle on her body, making sure every kiss, every touch was meaningful and filled with so much love she could feel it, smell it, and taste it. It was as if he wanted to make sure there'd be no doubt in her mind that she meant something to him.

When she was writhing beneath him, her body begging for a deeper union, he turned her so that he was behind her. She lifted her knee, opening herself to him. He slid his cock inside her and worked his body closer to hers to unite them fully.

She twisted at the waist and wrapped an arm around his neck, pulling him down into a kiss, and he began to thrust into her in a slow, steady rhythm, stroking that sweet spot deep inside her that always triggered her euphoria. As he loved her, he kissed her, caressed her, making her entire body feel his love.

Soon, the speed of his thrusts increased, ramping up the pleasure that had been growing inside her, and she gave herself over to it. As if he knew she was poised at the edge, mere steps from the leap, he caught her gaze and held his tight to hers, as if he wanted to watch the moment play out across her face so he could implant the vision in his memory.

Then the rush took her. Her breath suspended in her throat, her vision blurred, and she released a deep moan as she came in pulsing waves that started in her body and ended in his.

Her release triggered his, and he stroked her deep, again and again, groaning his pleasure, groaning her name, before finally going still. To hold on to the feeling, he held her tight, cupping her from behind, embracing her with his entire body and his love.

She laced her fingers with his as he pressed soft kisses up and down her skin. She didn't have words for what she was feeling, but whatever it was filled her lungs and her body and every molecule of oxygen in the cabin. If she had to name it, she'd say it was love.

****

"If you have to go, I'll drive you," Alicia whispered after their breath and rush had calmed. "Wherever you want to go."

That she would offer that to him was the cherry on top of this affair. But Nick couldn't let her. "I don't want you involved."

"Too late." Her lips trembled with a smile, and her low voice cracked.

His heart breaking at the tears she was valiantly holding back, he held her tight, silently vowing that when this mission was over, he'd find her so they could start something a little more permanent and a lot less risky. But for now, he had a job to do that took precedence over his personal desires.

Too soon, he once again stood before her, her fob in his hand, a goodbye on his lips, gloom in his heart. He had his hand on the doorknob when Panza's barking heralded a vehicle coming fast up the drive.

He peered out the window. An SUV from the compound. The sheriff driving, with three other men he recognized as gang members.

They'd come for him. And they'd find Alicia.

Chapter Eighteen

Nick grabbed Alicia's hand and pulled her into the bedroom, locking the door behind them. He grabbed her phone from the nightstand, tapped in a number, and pressed it into her hands, then guided her to the window and opened it.

"Climb to that spot where you get cell service and call the number I put in your phone. It's for an agent named Castillo. Tell him hibernation is over. And tell him where we are. Say it."

"Are you an informant?"

"Just say it, Alicia."

"Hibernation is over. Agent Castillo."

"Right. Now go. And baby, don't come back. No matter what you hear or see."

She started through, then stopped, turned back. "I don't want to leave you here alone."

He bracketed her face with his hands and kissed her. "*Farolita*, if this goes bad, I want you to know that I lo—"

She kissed him to stop his confession. "Tell me when this is over."

He nodded. "Go. Run!"

She went out the window, Panza behind her. The two were sprinting up the path when Nick heard the front door being kicked open.

He grabbed his gun from the closet, checked it, and

stood ready to face his fate.

He took out the first guy that came through the bedroom door, but the next one came through, gun firing. The spray of bullets missed him, and he got in a couple of shots that took the guy out. The third guy—some big-bodied, small-brained dullard everyone called Zeus—and the sheriff both appeared in the doorway, their guns pointed firmly on him.

"Drop it, asshole," Zeus said.

Having no choice, Nick tossed the gun onto the floor.

Zeus rushed in, grabbed him, and pushed him out the bedroom door and into the living room. "Henry said this bastard was here, Johnson. Guess I owe him fifty bucks," he said and shoved Nick down onto the couch.

The sheriff joined them. "I knew it the second I saw the look of recognition in Mrs. Stone's eyes when I showed her that picture of you, Cruz. Where is she, by the way?"

Nick scoffed. "When you told her I was a killer, she freaked out and threatened to turn me in. So, I killed her and her husband and put their bodies in her SUV. I was going to dump them when you showed up."

"You couldn't have killed her husband because he died seven months ago, and you were having such a good time fucking her, I know you didn't kill her either. Do you think I'm stupid?"

"Well, that's the rumor."

The sheriff's face hardened at the insult. "Where is she?"

"Fuck if I know. She freaked out and ran off. I just wanted to get the fuck out of here before she called you."

"We'll find her. And take care of her like we're going to take care of you. But first"—he perched on the arm of the couch—"you stole some things that belong to me, and I want them back."

"Things? My memory's a little fuzzy, seeing as how Harvey's lucky shot almost killed me."

"He shoulda shot you in your fucking black heart," Zeus said.

"Yeah, he shoulda, but he was always a shitty shot, like his idiot brother."

Zeus roared closer to punch him in the face, and Nick used the opportunity to kick him in the knee. The quick motion toppled him, making him fall, and his gun clanged to the floor. Nick dove for it, but the sheriff kicked it out of his reach and pointed his gun at his head.

"Jesus, pick up your gun, Zeus."

He did, then punched Nick in the face. "Keep your fucking mouth shut about my cousins."

Laughing, Nick wiped the blood from his mouth.

"Now, where did you say you put my stuff?" the sheriff repeated.

"I didn't," Nick said.

The sheriff whopped him upside the head with his gun. The hit pulled a low, groaned curse from Nick but nothing else.

"Listen you son of a bitch," the sheriff said. "Tell me where it is, right now, or I'll take that little redhead back to the compound and pass her around 'til she begs me to put a bullet in that pretty little head of hers."

"Touch her, and I'll fucking slit your throat," Nick said and lunged at the sheriff, getting in one good punch to the jaw.

Zeus yanked him away from the sheriff, who punched him in the gut. Nick fell to the floor, and the sheriff kicked him in the stomach and the side.

"Where. Is. My. Fucking. Stuff."

A blow accompanied each word, and Nick felt his wounds split, felt blood wet his shirt, maybe a rib crack. Despite the pain gripping him in a crushing fist, the beating had been worth it. With any luck, the stall had given Alicia time to make the call that might save their lives and this mission.

"Outside," Nick said, finding it hard to breathe from the pain. "It's outside."

"Get up," the sheriff said.

The pain made it difficult to comply. When he didn't move, the sheriff motioned to Zeus, who yanked Nick up off the floor and onto his feet.

"Show me," the sheriff said and shoved Nick toward the door.

Outside, Nick headed slowly toward the shed but stopped when he heard a noise and movement in the woods in the direction Alicia had gone. Panza burst from the trees and rushed toward them.

"I should have killed that mutt the first time I saw him," the sheriff said, sounding serious and pissed but also scared.

"No, don't," Nick said when the sheriff pointed his gun at the dog. He called to Panza. When the dog ran to him, Nick gingerly bent over and grabbed hold of him as he continued to snarl and bark at the sheriff.

"Mrs. Stone," the sheriff called out toward the woods. "Come on out and join us."

Nick wasn't a praying man, but he was praying now, praying that Alicia wouldn't come out, that she'd stay hidden like he'd told her.

"*Now*. Or I'll kill your mutt. And your lover."
****

Alicia had made the call, then hurried back to the cabin. She crawled in through the bedroom window in time to see the sheriff and another man push Rey out through the front door and follow him.

Her stomach turned at the sight of the dead bodies and blood on the floor, but she held it together. She had to. Rey's life depended on it.

His gun lay on the floor. Because she wasn't familiar with how to use it, she got hers from the closet. Knowing she might need to use it soon, she released the safety and slid the gun into the back of her jeans, hoping she wouldn't shoot her ass off.

She pulled on Jon's blue flannel shirt, rolled up the sleeves, and pulled it down in the back to hide the gun. All she needed was one quick opportunity to pull it out and use it. Hopefully, without killing anyone in the process.

Panza barked from outside, and she realized he'd jumped out the window and run to Rey. When she heard the sheriff call her name, she climbed out the bedroom window and walked out to them like she was coming from the trail and not the cabin. She didn't want them to know she'd been in the cabin and decide they needed to search her.

At meeting Rey's gaze, her heart clenched at the disappointment in his eyes that she hadn't stayed away like he'd instructed…and at the blood on him.

"There she is," the sheriff said as she headed toward them. "Come on over, honey. Join the party."

She headed toward Rey, but the sheriff grabbed her

arm and pulled her to him. Rey and Panza started forward but stopped with Zeus' gun in Rey's back.

"Now, isn't this nicer that we're all together?" the sheriff said, loudly to be heard over the barking. "Except for that damn dog. He's got to go." He pointed his gun at him.

"No, no, no," Alicia said. "I'll put him in the cabin. He won't bother you. Please."

"Zeus, go with her. Then bring her back to me."

Alicia locked eyes with Rey as she took the dog from him, and she could tell he was worried for her. She was worried for him. They'd beat him. His face had bleeding cuts and red splotches that would soon bruise, and blood stained his shirt. The beating had probably opened his wounds and caused new ones.

She smiled to show him she was okay, then turned and led Panza to the cabin. She shooed the dog inside and closed the door. Panza's face appeared in the window, and she heard him barking as Zeus' gun escorted her back to the sheriff, who grabbed her with one arm and pointed his gun to her head.

"I'm done being patient, Cruz," he said. "Where's my stuff?"

"She has nothing to do with this. Let her go."

"She's a beautiful, sexy woman. I can see how you'd fall for her. Hell, I'm half in love with her myself…all these red curls and luscious curves." He smelled her hair. "Turns a man's head to mush and his dick to stone just thinking about diving into all that creamy flesh."

His touch turned her stomach and made her skin crawl, and she flinched, trying to get away. He only gripped her tighter.

A sarcastic scoff came from Zeus. "Didn't realize you were a fucking poet, Johnson. Can we get on with it, already?"

The sheriff glared at the man. "Some men are inspired by beauty."

"I'm inspired by getting our shit, killing this motherfucking traitor, and getting the hell out of here," Zeus responded. "Something about this place don't feel right."

"For once, we agree," the sheriff said and turned back to Rey. "Tell me where my stuff is, and I'll consider letting her live."

Rey said nothing, his teeth gritting.

"Or I could go with my first plan." The sheriff pointed the gun at her head again.

As if knowing he had no choice, Rey answered. "In the woodshed."

"Get it," the sheriff said and held back, holding onto Alicia, gun barrel glued to her temple. "Zeus, go with him."

Rey led the way to the shed, Zeus behind with his gun trained on him.

"No hero moves, or she'll be the first to suffer for your stupidity," the sheriff called out.

****

Nick entered the woodshed alone. He shifted the pile of logs until he saw the duffel. In it were several loaded guns. He had planned to pull one out, but Zeus and his gun appeared in the doorway before he could.

"Hurry up," he said.

Nick came out with the duffel, and Zeus grabbed it, then backed up away from him.

"Check it," the sheriff said.

He set it on the ground, unzipped it, and rifled through it. "It's all here."

"Including the laptop?"

Nodding, he held up the laptop, grinned, then returned it to the bag. The man was in mid-zip when the sheriff shot him in the head. The bullet propelled him backward, and he hit the ground, blood pooling in the mud puddle where his head lay, his dead eyes open to the heavens.

"Oh God," Alicia groaned, recoiling at the brutality.

"His constant whining was getting on my nerves," the sheriff said. Using Alicia as a shield, he shuffled over to the bag and grabbed it, then shoved her to Nick, who pulled her into his arms and shifted her behind him, protecting her body with his.

Nick had been dodging bullets most of his adult life. The thought that he'd meet the same fate as Zeus wasn't a new one. But his heart galloped in his throat at the thought of Alicia going that way. He'd never felt more useless in his life. For all his training, all his experience, all his barbed-wire bravado, there was nothing he could do to protect her or get them out of this. Only a miracle would do it, and he didn't believe in them.

"Mrs. Stone. I've grown fond of you, so I'm going to give you the option of going first to get it over with or last to watch your lover die."

"You said you'd let her live, you son of a bitch," Nick yelled.

"I said I'd consider it. I decided against it. It would be bad for my health."

Alicia stepped out from behind Nick. "Sheriff,

would you give us a moment to say goodbye? Please?"

The sheriff stared at her, a wistful grin on his fleshy lips. "That's love in her voice, Cruz. Did you hear it?" He laughed. "I knew you were a ladies' man, but this is hilarious. The captive falling for her captor."

Nick looked at Alicia, and she met his eyes. He'd heard the love in her voice, too. Either that, or she was playing the sheriff.

"If you love her, too, now's the time to tell her."

If they were going to die, Nick would give Alicia the truth and let her go to the grave knowing that he really had cared about her.

"Come on, Cruz," the sheriff said. "Do you love her or not? It's a simple yes or no. Don't leave the lady hanging."

Nick cupped Alicia's face with both hands, looked into her eyes, and nodded.

The sheriff laughed. "Blame it on my romantic side, but I'll give you two your moment. Make it count."

Alicia put her arms around Nick, and he drew her in, kissing her deep, making it the hottest, most honest, most love-filled kiss he'd ever given any woman. The last kiss he'd give or get. At least he'd go to the grave with the taste of her on his lips. It was better than he deserved for getting her into this mess.

Fierce growling and cries of pain thundered through the air, severing their kiss, and they spun toward the sound. Panza had the sheriff by the back of the leg, teeth deep. The sheriff screamed, twisting at the waist, gun aimed at Panza.

"Drop the gun," Alicia yelled.

Nick looked back at her. She had a gun pointed at

the sheriff. It was the gun she kept in her closet. She must have gone back into the cabin.

The sheriff, focused only on getting away from the dog, fired his weapon.

Alicia fired, too, the bullet hitting the sheriff in the upper arm, knocking him back several steps, and making him drop his gun.

Nick rushed in and grabbed the sheriff's weapon just as Panza released his hold and pranced over to Nick to accept his accolades for a job well done.

"Good boy," Nick said and petted him.

Panza trotted over to Alicia for some praise, too, but her hands were busy, gripping the gun trained on the sheriff.

"On the fucking ground, asshole," she yelled.

Nick grinned at her, surprised by her rough tone and words.

Blood flowing from the wounds in his leg and arm, the sheriff stood still, hunched over, cradling his wounded arm.

Nick turned to the sheriff. "You heard the woman. On the fucking ground, asshole."

The sheriff gingerly lowered himself to the ground, moaning and bleeding the whole way.

Nick joined Alicia, hugged her to his side, and kissed the top of her head. "You're fucking amazing, Nurse Alicia."

She released an abrupt chortle. "I'm also fucking pissed, so take the gun before I shoot the bastard again," she said loudly enough for the sheriff to hear.

Nick took the gun from her, set the safety, and stuck it in his waistband, keeping the sheriff's own gun pointed at him.

"If you're smart, Cruz, you'll use that gun to kill her. Beautiful women will betray you, every time."

Nick drew her close. "I trust this one. With my life."

She eyed the cuts and blood on his face from where he'd taken a beating. "You're bleeding again? Why do I keep fixing you up?"

"I'm your favorite patient, remember? Did you get through to Castillo?"

"He said he's on his way." As if on cue, the sound of vehicles racing up her road, slinging mud and snow and gravel, filled the air.

"Rey, go. I can handle this."

He shook his head. "I'm not leaving you."

"But—"

"Alicia, when they get here, just stand still and put your hands up. You'll be fine. I promise. And when they question you, don't say a word about Henry showing up at the cabin, threatening us, or about what happened to him. The *only* things you say are these," he said and counted on his fingers. "I showed up with a gunshot wound, you treated me, a snowstorm trapped us here, and the sheriff and his thugs showed up and started shooting. Got it?"

She nodded just as four black unmarked SUVs slid to a stop in front of the cabin. A dozen or so agents—his team—poured out, guns drawn, and converged on them.

"Hands where we can see them," one of the agents yelled.

Johnson stretched his uninjured arm out and Alicia put her hands up. Nick dropped the guns and put his hands out to the side.

Two agents helped the sheriff up, took him to one of the vehicles, and began treating his wounds. Another grabbed the duffel and set it inside another vehicle.

Castillo climbed out of one of the SUVs and joined Alicia and Nick, his serious, stonewall face firmly in place.

"Alicia Stone?" he growled, eyeing her.

"Yes."

"Appreciate the call. We've been after this scumbag for quite a while."

She put her hands down and moved in front of Nick, as if to protect him. "Rey saved my life from the sheriff and that other man," she said, nodding toward Zeus. "They would have killed me if not for him."

"Ma'am, you can get all that into your statement, but right now, you need to step aside."

She wrapped her arms around Nick's waist. "No."

"What do you mean, no?" Castillo asked.

"I mean no. I'm not letting you take him."

"I'm afraid I have to insist."

"I'm afraid I have to insist more," she countered.

"You do know I can arrest you?"

"That's the only way I'll let go of him."

Castillo's eyes bugged out, and it looked like his head was going to pop off his neck and release a geyser of steam.

Nick wanted to laugh because that behavior was so Alicia. Instead, he'd help her see that everything was not as dire as it seemed.

"Alicia," he said, and she met his gaze. He caressed her cheek and ran his thumb across her bottom lip. "Do as he says," he whispered. "I'll be fine."

She shook her head. He nodded. After a few beats,

she let him go but stayed at his side and took his hand.

Castillo glared at Nick, and the glint in his eyes wasn't happiness to see him alive.

"You look like shit, Special Agent Navarro." From his coat pocket, he pulled out a badge on a chain and tossed it to Nick. "Thought we'd lost you."

Alicia's eyes flew to Nick as he caught his badge and slipped it around his neck. The shock and betrayal in her eyes felt like a punch to his gut and the worst pain he'd felt all year. Dammit. He should have told her the truth.

His eyes left hers and cut to Castillo's. "Good to see you, too, sir."

Chapter Nineteen

Agent? Navarro? Alicia glared at Rey, tightened her lips into a thin, angry line, and winced at the betrayal coursing through her veins like broken glass. He was the law. He was the law and hadn't told her. He let her believe he was a criminal. Put her through needless worry and fear about who she'd let into her life. Betrayal and anger feasted on her heart. Before she could call him on it and demand the truth, another agent joined them.

"Mrs. Stone," Castillo said, getting her attention. "Agent Zehr will take your statement." He nodded toward the agent.

"This way, ma'am." Agent Zehr pointed toward one of the vehicles, intending for Alicia for follow her.

Alicia took a few shaky steps toward the agent, then spun around, marched back to Rey, and slapped his face so hard it made her hand sting. Although it had to hurt him, too, he didn't even flinch, as if he had expected it and knew he deserved it.

"I would rather you had told me nothing than lie to me about everything."

They stared at each other for a long, few seconds, and even though he didn't apologize or try to explain away his betrayal or even speak at all, she swore she could see remorse softening the dark depths of his eyes. But she refused to allow herself to believe even one more of his lies.

She left him and went to the porch, the agent and Panza following her. They sat on the bench, Panza between them, and she answered the agent's questions, minus anything that related to her intimate moments with Rey, and stuck as closely as possible to the four things Rey had advised her to say. The interview concluded, and the agent joined the others inside the cabin to gather evidence and bag the dead.

Alicia and Panza stayed put, watching the activity. Watching Agent Navarro. Seeing him in a whole new light.

Thinking back on all the little clues that had floated like bubbles around him, she felt stupid for not putting it together that he was the law. The cockiness in the way he carried himself. His laser focus on every move she made, every word she said. His razor-sharp interrogation techniques. The semper fi tattoo.

He had played his part well. He was probably congratulating himself on how well he'd fooled her and made her believe he cared about her. Probably already bragging to his FBI buddies about how gullible the redhead was.

Over an hour later, he came and sat next to her. She could feel his heat enticing her to curl up in his arms and get warm like she'd done over the past few weeks. And she wanted to. Desperately. Despite his gross betrayal.

Panza dropped his head on Rey's leg with a whine, as if saying he didn't understand the betrayal either. Rey absently scratched the dog's ears but kept his gaze on her.

"I couldn't tell you, Alicia."

"Yeah, you could have."

"If you were connected to Los Matos, telling you I was FBI could have destroyed my mission and gotten me killed."

"Seriously? You thought I was a gang member? A criminal?"

"I see everyone as a criminal until I know they're not."

"I brought you into my home. I treated your wounds. I cared for you. I called the FBI to come save you. What part of those behaviors made you think you couldn't trust me?"

"You're at the cabin alone and in the dead of winter. You're skilled at identifying and treating gunshot wounds. You were reluctant to answer my questions. Johnson was coming around too often for you two to be strangers. Insignificant things individually but together added up to a significant reason to be suspicious."

"I was open with you about everything but my husband, and you know why. You're the one who refused to answer even the simplest question. Despite that, I allowed myself to trust you. If you have so little trust in me, why did you ask me to call the FBI to save your ass?"

"It was a risk I had to take."

"More like, I was your only option." She shook her head at his silence and looked down at the tips of her muddy boots. "And here we are. Alive. Because I made the call. Because I shot the bad guy. And somehow, I bet you still don't trust me."

"I trust you. Completely."

"Oh really? What? Did your team confirm my

identity or something?"

"They did, but that's not what decided it for me."

"Oh?"

"If your intent was to kill me, you had many chances. But instead, you saved me. You could have let me die, but you didn't. You could have left the cabin at any time to call the law about me, but you didn't. You didn't rat me out, even when Johnson told you I was a killer. You saved me—twice—when someone tried to kill me. You tried to protect me by telling Castillo I saved you. Those actions showed me that I could trust you. But Bureau protocols forbid me from doing or saying anything that might break my cover. They're in place for my safety as well as for the innocent others I come in contact with. I've never been tempted to break those rules. Until you."

The sincerity in his intense stare and tone told her he was probably telling the truth. She'd never know for sure, but what did it matter. Their time together was over.

"So, what's your real name?" she said, breaking the jagged silence.

He lifted his badge from around his neck and slid it across the bench.

She picked it up, ran her fingers across the weighty leather case, and opened it. Her gaze first went to his name—Nick Navarro—then to his picture. Short dark hair, not long like it was now. Clean-shaven, not a scruffy beard and moustache like now. A hint of a cocky smile on that same delicious full mouth. The same devilish bronze sparkle in his dark eyes. The same determined look on his face. And a name that fit him.

"Did you tell Agent Zehr about us?" he asked.

"No," she said and slid the badge back to him.

He put it back around his neck. "Why not?"

"Anything you said or did was a part of your cover and not relevant to the case."

He took her hand and caressed the back of it with his thumb. "What we said and did was relevant to me."

"I was a means to an end. Don't insult me further by pretending it was anything else." She tried to pull back her hand, but he held tight to it.

"My feelings for you are real."

Before she could respond, Agent Castillo joined them, and Nick released her hand.

"Mrs. Stone, our forensics team will be here another hour or so, collecting evidence. After they're gone, you're welcome to pack up and head back to Seattle. We'll contact you if we have more questions."

"Are you ordering me to leave?"

"Well, no. But I assumed—"

"I'm staying."

"Very well," he said after a few beats, then nodded at Nick. "Wrap it up."

"I'll be right there," Nick said.

Castillo headed toward a vehicle where Agent Zehr waited, and they both climbed inside.

"Come with me to Albuquerque," Nick said. "I'll get you a hotel room if you don't want to stay with me, but we need to talk about—"

"I'm staying here."

"*Farolita…*"

Hearing his pet name for her sent chills up her spine. She closed her eyes and shook her head. "Don't call me that."

The driver's side window of the vehicle rolled

down and Agent Zehr called out, "*Vaminos*, Navarro!"

"One. Fucking. Minute," he yelled.

"Just go," Alicia said in a harsh whisper.

"I'll be putting in some long hours, debriefing, writing my report," he said, "but I'll come see you as soon as I can. A couple days."

"I'd rather you didn't."

"You don't mean that."

"Yes, I do mean that. I don't want to see you again."

After a long moment, he stood and headed down the steps toward the vehicle. Panza whined when he opened the door.

Nick turned back to Alicia, held her eyes in a final goodbye, then climbed in and shut the door. As if that were the signal, all the vehicles, except the one the forensics team arrived in, drove away, single file, as quickly and efficiently as they'd arrived.

"No, I don't mean that," she whispered.

She stayed on the porch while the team inside collected evidence and photographed the scene. An hour later, they and the bodies were gone. She and Panza stayed put, him whining as if he didn't understand why Nick was gone, and the pieces of her broken heart grinding against each other because she knew why. But no matter how much she was hurting or how sincere Nick seemed about having feelings for her, she wouldn't be with a man who lied to her and betrayed her. Not again.

With a resolute sigh, she went inside and cleaned up the mess left behind.

When the sun dawned the next day, Alicia threw herself into the chore that had sent her on the journey to the cabin. Endowed with innumerable amounts of energy and determination—and no sentimental fog in her eyes—she went through the closet and the bags of clothes like a whirlwind, tossing them into a keep, donate, or toss pile. She did the same thing with the clothes Nick had worn.

With the same vigor, she attacked the living room, bathroom, and kitchen until she'd sorted and packed everything but the things she'd need for the duration of her stay. She piled each item into its respective bag or box and lined them up by the front door. That the "keep" bag was the smallest was a visual reminder that she was ready to break the past's grip on her present. Stripped of their memories, they were just things, things she no longer needed. That included her ring, which she'd keep but no longer wear, and the cabin.

In the keep pile, too, were her memories of Jon and her marriage. The good and the bad ones. She recognized the importance they'd played in shaping her past, which overall had been pretty awesome, but she had stripped them of their power to shape her future.

Her memories of Rey Cruz/Nick Navarro also were in the keep pile, in a box with his name on it. During the long day and night after his departure, she'd decided that, despite his betrayal, the memories she had of him didn't make her sad. Quite the opposite. The joy he'd lighted inside her would go with her into her new life as a reminder of what was possible.

At the end of the day of purging, she was physically and emotionally exhausted. She took a shower, shared dinner with Panza, then the two of them sat on the porch, staring out into the growing darkness and absorbing the visible, audible, palpable quiet that she'd come here for.

As she'd hoped, being in this magical place had awakened a greater awareness of herself and allowed her to start rebuilding her edges that had become sanded down over time in order to more freely knit with Jon's. She had forgiven him, forgiven herself, and had achieved what she'd come here to do.

And so had Nick.

She didn't know whether he was the man she'd known these many weeks or someone else completely. He'd had a role to play, and he'd played it well. The man she knew as Rey Cruz was the man she'd fallen for. Who was Nick Navarro? She'd never know. She'd never have either man. But as far as rebound lovers went, she was lucky to have enjoyed one so satisfying.

In such a short time, he'd permeated her cells and skin and every fiber of her being. He felt so much a part of her, she expected to be able to conjure him into being and watch him strut out of the darkness toward her, that sexy grin directed at her. He'd take her by the hand, pull her to their bed, and make her come apart before putting her back together again. The ache she felt knowing that would never happen again surprised her.

As if picking up on her swirling emotions, Panza lifted his head, looked at her, and whined.

"I miss him, too," she said and scratched his ears. "But we'll get over him."

Her companion's snorted response sounded more like "doubtful" than "totally."

****

The next day, Alicia went to Doc's and bought food for a Christmas feast along with enough food and supplies to last until the new year when she'd go home.

As the cashier bagged her items, Alicia saw the Albuquerque newspaper in a stand near the counter. The headline above the fold caught her attention. *FBI Takes Down Virulent New Mexico Gang.* She bought a copy and read it in the car.

Wednesday morning, the FBI raided several dozen mountain homes and a multiresident compound in Sandia Hills belonging to members of the violent drug trafficking gang, Los Matos.

The takedown was part of an ongoing investigation and effort to eliminate New Mexico's largest east mountain gang. Operation Hibernation resulted in three hundred and eighty-seven arrests and solved a dozen cold case murders in the state. Of those arrests, most were drug and gun related.

"That's nearly four hundred suspected killers and drug traffickers who might still be on the streets were it not for Operation Hibernation and our courageous agents," said Jose Castillo, operation lead and captain of the FBI Gangs and Violent Crimes Division, at a news conference in Albuquerque.

Captain Castillo would not comment on the full scope of evidence his undercover agents had confiscated over the year-long investigation but did say that it included the gang's "green light" hit list — informants, witnesses, federal agents, and prosecutors that gang leaders had instructed their members to target.

It also confirmed that local Sheriff Lionel Johnson, who sustained non-life-threatening injuries during the takedown, was the primary leader in the faction and had used his official office to benefit the criminal organization. He is suspected of orchestrating or carrying out numerous hits as well as funneling law enforcement data to gang members, warning them when raids were planned or arrest warrants had been issued.

One alleged gang member, who refused to give his name, said as he was being arrested that the undercover agents involved in the takedown "better watch their [expletive] backs." When asked for comment on the safety of his agents, Castillo said, "We've crippled the gang, and my team won't rest until every single member of this terrorist group is behind bars or dead."

The article didn't mention names, except Castillo's and Johnson's, but Nick had been one of the undercover agents involved in getting the evidence on the gang he'd infiltrated. He had a critical job. Had almost paid for it with his life.

As angry as she'd been at him for not trusting her with the truth, she understood now why he hadn't. His job demanded secrecy and caution. As an ER nurse, it was the same for her. She too was forbidden to share certain information.

Another reason her anger had diminished was that she was leaving this place with newfound clarity. Specifically, she no longer believed that she was responsible for Jon's choices or his death. She had forgiven him, and herself, and realized that she could continue to believe in and cherish the good memories she had of their life together.

She also believed that what Nick said was true. The greatest risks can return the greatest pleasure. She had taken risks and enjoyed a lot of pleasure and was now convinced that she was capable of feeling joy and love again.

That abundance of clarity wasn't all Nick's doing, but it was he who had presented the new plan, challenged her to stick to it, encouraged her to get back on track when she fell off, and held her hand as she entered the dark unknown.

Chapter Twenty

Christmas Eve arrived bright and sunny, the entire area around the cabin clear and dry. The tree Nick had decorated cheered her, so she left it up. This was her first year ever with no presents under the tree, but she didn't feel shortchanged, not with the miracles that had shown up in her life—finding herself again, resolving her past, mapping a new path forward, and meeting Panza and Nick. She had come out of the madness, and nothing was holding her back.

Panza started whining and scratching at the door seconds before she heard rumbling coming up the drive. A black motorcycle pulled into the yard and stopped next to her SUV. A tall, sexy, clean-shaven man, with short dark hair, black shades, and a black leather jacket climbed off the bike. He slowly scanned the area, then set his sights on the cabin.

She opened the door as he approached the porch, and he stopped when Panza bounded out to him and set his front paws on him in a warm greeting.

"Hey, boy," the man said, petting Panza enthusiastically like they were old friends. "Good to see you, too."

Panza trotted back to her and had the audacity to look at her with an I-knew-he'd-come-back smile.

Special Agent Nick Navarro pushed his shades onto the back of his head and settled his sinful gaze on her, then unzipped his jacket, revealing the FBI badge dangling around his neck.

Seeing him again ratcheted up her heartbeat and heated her from the inside, like his essence had raced ahead of his body and infiltrated hers like a possessing spirit glad to be home again and eager to get settled in. Then he moved toward her, across the yard, up the steps, across the porch, giving her the chance to take in every movement. And take it all in she did, just in case it was the last sight she'd be privileged to see before going blind forever.

His faded jeans hugged his body in an intimate caress. His long-sleeved white T-shirt fit like a second skin, outlining the muscular chest and stomach she had licked, kissed, bit, and caressed. Her gaze dropped to his waist, and she wondered whether he'd seen a doctor for his wounds. Her gaze purposefully avoided the hefty bulge in his jeans and returned to his eyes when he at last stood before her. The sight of him made her knees weak…made her body forget she had knees.

"Hello, Alicia." The silky, spicy, sexy rumble that was his voice forced her to brace her shoulder on the doorframe to bolster her liquid legs and calm her pounding heart.

"Special Agent Navarro. I'm surprised to see you. I thought our business was settled." She swallowed to dispel the warmth in her voice and, for good measure, crossed her arms to hide her rising nipples.

"There's a few loose ends we need to wrap up before your part in this case is officially closed," he said.

"I didn't know I had a part in it," she said.

"Mind if I come in?" he said as he stepped forward

into her space. He settled his hand on the doorframe near her head, and a tiny, winged creature trilled in her throat.

"I'd like to see some identification."

He started to lift his badge to show her, but she stopped him. "Something other than that."

With a grin, he reached into his back pocket, pulled out the wallet that Rey had used and removed his license.

"I commend your caution," he said. "You can never be too careful about letting someone in." He handed it over, gaze on her.

"It's important to be careful even when you think you know someone," she said as she took it. "They lie."

She scanned his license. The picture was of the man who stood before her. The name matched the one she'd seen on his badge, Nicolas Navarro, but with a first initial of R, and an Albuquerque address. The birthdate listed was November 18, which made him thirty-four—and a Scorpio, not a Cancer. If *this* license could be believed.

She met his eyes. "What does R stand for?"

He grinned. "My first name is Rey—Reynaldo—after my dad, but I've always gone by my middle name."

"Why?"

"Never thought the name Rey fit me."

She handed the license to him and restrained her desire to say, I told you so.

"Satisfied?" he asked.

"Not by half," she said.

"I thought you might say that." He pulled a folded paper from his inside jacket pocket and handed it to her.

"What's this?"

"Open it."

She did and was surprised to see his birth certificate. She read every line, slowly and carefully, until the realization sank in that he was who he claimed to be. Unless this document was fake, too. But that was a lot of trouble to go through at this point in the game, when it didn't matter who he was or whether she believed him.

She handed it back.

"Can I come in?" he asked, folding the paper and tucking it back into place.

She shifted away from the door and let him walk through. As he passed her, she inhaled him and her eyes fluttered closed. He had a different name and a different look, but he smelled the same, like this place—fresh, clean, spicy, rugged—how she wanted her man to smell.

After closing the door, she settled her back against it, needing to keep some distance between them. She didn't trust her traitorous body to behave.

"Mind if we sit?" He pointed to the bed, which she'd left where he put it because it comforted her.

She pointed to the kitchen table.

He sat in his chair, and she sat in hers after grabbing the cup of coffee she'd been drinking when he showed up. She cupped it in her cold hands to still them, warm them.

"Coffee smells good," he said as his gaze flit to her cup, then back to her face.

"This is the last cup in the pot." She had continued making coffee by fireplace even though the power was back on. She could make him a cup from the coffee machine, but she didn't want to be that accommodating.

He reached out and settled his fingers on hers that cupped the mug. "I don't mind sharing."

She pulled away from his touch, and he took her cup, sipping from it like he'd done dozens of times over the past weeks.

"Ahh. I've missed that taste. You've ruined me for all other coffee."

He slid the cup back to her. She wanted to bring it to her lips, taste him on the rim and in the brew, but she left it untouched between them.

"You're not wearing your ring," he said.

She laced her fingers. "How about we get to those loose ends you're here to tie up?"

He pulled a small notebook from his pocket and flipped through it. Stopping on a page, he glanced at it, as if reading something, then cut his gaze back to her.

"You told Special Agent Zehr that Rey Cruz pushed you out the window and instructed you to go up the mountain and call the FBI."

What game was he playing? "Yes."

"Did he say anything else before you went through the window?"

He'd started to say I love you. Maybe. She wasn't sure. But she wouldn't fall into that trap. "Nothing of importance," she said with a shrug.

"Let me be the judge of that. What did he say?"

"I don't really know. I interrupted him and climbed out the window to make the call."

"What do you think he was going to say?"

"You'd have to ask him."

"I did." He closed the notebook and set it on the table. "Would you like to know his answer?"

"No." She got up from her chair, wrapped her sweater tighter around her body in a protective hug, and stepped away from the table, from Nick, from his scent and heat and body and the sweet memory of him almost saying he loved her.

He stood, too, and walked to her, making her back up to keep from letting her body touch his. "What he was saying before you stopped him by kissing him was, 'I love you, Alicia.'"

She bumped into the counter and could retreat no further. "I'm sure he was lying. He was really good at it."

Nick stopped right in front of her, so close she could feel his body, taste his breath on her lips, see the amber flecks in his eyes that appeared when he was excited. "He passed the polygraph."

"Polygraphs aren't reliable," she said without stammering even though her body was trembling. "As a law enforcement officer, surely you know that."

Better question— Why was she playing this stupid game with him?

He reached out and cupped her face with his hand, and her lungs inhaled a sharp needy breath. *Ah, this is why she played. For a chance to win his touch.* Her eyes fluttered closed, and her breath flickered in her lungs.

"*I* love you, *farolita*. Me. Nick Navarro."

She shook her head. "Don't do that." The plea rode her shuddering breath.

He leaned in and brushed his lips across her forehead, softly, sweetly. Not a kiss. More of a scout caress to test the waters, prime the pump, drive her crazy, weaken her resolve. "Do what?"

She swallowed the rising joy tickling the back of her throat at his touch. "Continue to lie to me. You accomplished your mission. You got what you wanted. Why are you torturing me?"

His gaze met hers and held her captive as effectively as handcuffs. "I'm not lying."

"You can't love me. You don't even know me."

"I know you, *farolita*."

"Well, I don't know you."

"Yes, you do. You saw the real me during the time we spent together."

"The *real* you?" she scoffed. "That's a laugh. The man who was here didn't exist. The man who's standing before me wasn't here. Rey Cruz avoided my questions and lied to me at every turn. Of the two of you, I know him better, which isn't saying much. I don't know you at all."

He took her hand in his, linked their fingers. "Get to know me now. I'll tell you anything you want to know."

"How can I trust it would be the truth?"

"You'll have to have faith."

She shook her head. "Not sure I have any left when it comes to you."

"I want us to be together, Alicia," he said firmly.

He was lying. She was sure of it. But oh if he was telling the truth… Her heart soared like a balloon at the possibilities filling it, but she would pull out every pin she could to pop it before she'd invest her heart again.

"I don't want to be with a man who lies and kills as easy as he breathes."

"Like you, my main goal is to save lives. I only lie or kill if I absolutely have to."

"Your work is dangerous. I don't want to be with a man I'd worry about all the time when he's undercover."

He took her other hand and linked their fingers, then traced her tattoo with his tongue, making the line, and other things, pulse. "Be with me and the only covers I'll go under are yours."

"You'd give up your job?" she asked, surprise and skepticism coloring the question. Was he serious? Or was this just another lie?

"I can get out of deep undercover work. And I will to be with you."

"You'd still be called in on a moment's notice…nights, weekends, holidays. I'd never see you," she said, even though it was a weak argument because her job demanded similar obligations from her.

"You work ER, which means you also could be called in at any time, day or night," he countered. "But I promise, we'll always find time to be together."

"I live in Seattle. You live in Albuquerque."

"I could move. Or you could."

"You have an answer for everything, don't you?" she said.

"I never let a few fixable obstacles prevent me from getting what I want."

"What do you want?" she asked, nearly breathless from their exchange. The tone of her voice had changed—even she could hear it—and it clearly said his words were one by one demolishing her pitted pillars of objections.

Drawing her arms behind her back, he wrapped his around her and pulled her closer, pressing against her. His body molded against her breasts, her belly, her thighs, and her traitorous body started down the slippery slide into nirvana with him.

"Glad you asked," he said with a grin, that same grin he used when he was undressing her so he could blow her mind. She could almost feel her jeans unzipping on their own out of habit.

"I *want* to spend Christmas with you," he began. "I *want* to spend the rest of this year with you and welcome the new year together. I *want* a chance to prove to you that the man you fell in love with is the man I am. I *want* to make love to you several times a day in every position I know to show you how much I love you. When we're not making love, I want to tell you everything about me until you're bored to tears and begging me to shut up. And I want to learn everything about you. I want us to know each other inside and out, all the good, the bad, the ugly, the weird, and the embarrassing. If, by the first of the year, you never want to see me again, I'll abide by that decision. I'll be pissed as hell, but I'll abide by it. But if it turns out you love me as much as I love you, I want to move to something more permanent."

"More permanent? Like what?"

"We'll discuss that when you tell me you love me," he said and kissed her. And she let him. Then she let herself kiss him back, showing she was on board with his plan.

****

On the third day of the new year, Nick loaded the last of Alicia's things—the box of books going to the literacy center—into the back of her SUV. But before he could push the box deeper into the cargo area, it slipped off the edge. He caught it before it fell, but one book toppled out, spilling three photos onto the ground. After shoving the box deeper inside, he picked up the thin tome and tossed it back into the box. Before he could get the photos, Panza picked up the closest one with his mouth and held it out. Nick knelt on one knee and took it from him.

It was a blond man, blue eyes, blue plaid shirt tied around his waist, an axe in his hand. He'd guess the picture was of Jon. It was how Alicia had described him. And he recognized that shirt.

The dog picked up a second photo and brought it to Nick.

It was Alicia, wearing the same shirt, fully unbuttoned to show a generous swath of her beautiful naked body beneath.

Nick swore he saw sadness in the dog's eyes as he handed over the last picture, which showed the embracing and smiling couple in front of the cabin.

He set his hand on the dog's head, looked into his eyes, and nodded. "I'll take care of her. I promise."

Panza lifted one paw and set it on Nick's knee, as if in a thank you. Chills raced over Nick's skin at the eerie moment.

The screen door squeaked open, and Alicia came out. After locking the wooden door, she opened the passenger side door of the SUV and set her purse and a bottle of water in the seat. "You guys ready?"

Nick tucked the photos into his jacket pocket and shut the back of the SUV, then joined her. He pulled her into his arms. "Are you sad to leave the cabin?"

She let her gaze scan the area before coming back to him. "I love it here, but I feel excited about my life again, and I'm ready to get started. To take some of those risks you keep raving about."

"Who knew you'd be so good at them."

"I had a good mentor."

"We both did," he said, looking deep into her eyes. She'd shown him that he could be the man he was, warts and all, and still be loved.

"We did." She pressed into him. "Let's get on the road. I can't wait to see your home."

"Just to warn you, it's a mess. I left in a hurry to come up here to be with you."

"Is the mess going to keep us from getting to the bed?"

"No."

"Then it won't bother me."

He laughed. "You really have changed."

"Getting you into bed has been a priority since I met you. That hasn't changed."

His hands gripped her ass and yanked her against the bulge hardening in his jeans. "I'll make sure it never does."

She kissed him, and when he would have taken it deeper, she eased back. "Let's go so you can prove it to me." Leaving his arms, she opened the back door of the SUV. "Panza! Let's go!"

The dog stood several feet from her, looking at her, but not moving.

She bent over and patted her thighs. "C'mon, bud. Get in the car." When he wouldn't, she knelt and held out her arms to him. He walked slowly over to her.

She scratched the caramel spot on his head. "You're going to have a new home. And you're going to love it. But you gotta get in the car."

The dog moved in closer and licked her face. She

laughed, hugging him, then stood and again tried to get him to jump in, but he backed up.

She looked at Nick, confusion on her face. "Why won't he get in?"

Nick slipped his arm around her. "His job here is done."

"His job?"

Panza woofed, whined, then trotted off into the woods.

She rushed after him. "Panza!"

He stopped, turned back to her, smiled the way he did, his tongue lolling out the side, then ran off.

Nick joined her, taking her hand. "C'mon, baby. Let's go."

"I'm not going to leave him."

"It's what he wants."

"How do you know what he wants?"

He told her about the photos and the dog's actions.

"Let me get this straight," she said. "You think that dog is Jon, and he came to me to what, make sure I find my happy again?"

"I know it sounds—" Nick laughed and shook his head. "—completely ridiculous. But maybe it was Jon's way of making things right with you and telling you that he's okay. And that you're okay."

"You're right. It's ridiculous."

"Think about it. He showed up out of nowhere when you needed him. He protected you—and me— from the sheriff. He stayed long enough to make sure you and I were safe and together. His job's done. He can move on. And so can you."

"Well, *I* think he's just out doing his business or chasing a squirrel and will be back any minute." She walked back to the SUV and leaned against it. "And I'm going to wait for him."

"Okay. We'll wait. What? Five minutes? Ten?"

"He's usually done in five minutes, but let's say ten to be sure."

"All right." Nick leaned against the SUV beside her.

Fifteen minutes passed. No dog.

"Maybe he's hurt," she said. "We should go look for him."

To appease her, Nick walked with her, going the way Panza had gone. They had walked for at least fifteen minutes, calling out his name, before she stopped in her tracks.

"He's really gone," she said, her eyes flooding with tears.

Nick didn't know whether she meant the dog or Jon, but it didn't matter. They both were gone. He drew her against him, held her tight, and kissed her wet eyes. "But I'm here."

Nodding, she sank deeper into his embrace and wept, deep, noisy sobs that made her body shake.

To Nick, it felt as if this was Alicia's final goodbye to Jon that she hadn't had before. Now, she really could move on, with him, and, when the time was right, become his wife.

Chapter Twenty-One

Alicia clocked out and headed for the hospital parking structure at a brisk clip. Nick's flight was due soon, and she was headed home to shower and change before picking him up.

They'd talked every night since she left Albuquerque and, for the past three months, had taken turns visiting each other every other weekend. It was great, but she wanted more. She'd lay out her plan tonight, after dinner, after they'd made love and reconnected to remind him how perfect they were together.

She made it to the airport with minutes to spare. As soon as he was through security, she flew into his arms. Their long, deep, wet kiss made it clear to anyone watching that they'd soon be tearing up the sheets.

After grabbing his bag from baggage claim, they rushed to the parking garage, and she led him to the spot where she'd parked, not up front, close to the door, but farther back in the lot where fewer cars were.

"Is there a reason you chose such a dark, deserted spot?" He eyed her, his sexy knowing gaze making her pulse throb between her legs.

"You're so suspicious, Agent Navarro," she said with a grin.

After stowing his bag in the trunk, they climbed into the front and closed the doors. Their gaze held tight to each other, and the roaring intimacy swallowed them.

He reached out and touched her hair. "I've missed you, *farolita*."

Pleasure shivered inside her at his low words, the thirsty note of his voice, his gentle touch, and the hungry look in his eyes. "I've missed you, too."

His hand slid to her thigh and squeezed. "I can't wait to touch you."

She swallowed the moan racing up and down inside her body. "Then don't wait."

Her fingers crawled in the silky fabric of her dress, making it bunch and rise, higher and higher, exposing her skin to his eyes. She spread her thighs, inviting him to explore the inferno barely contained behind the silky strip of her tiny thong.

His breath caught in his throat, but with no hesitation, he ran his hand up her bare thigh, slid it between her legs, and rubbed the already damp material covering her pussy. She watched as his fingers slid underneath, followed by his hand, and he cupped all of her, squeezing and tugging and pinching the wet lips against each other at her clit.

The moan that had been building inside left her throat as a slow rush.

"You like that," he whispered.

"You know I do," she whispered back. Her head dropped against the seat, but she kept her gaze glued to his. She wanted him to see how good he was making her feel. She wanted him to see how much she wanted him.

Her clever man got the hint. He dragged a finger into her seam, parting the turgid flesh with his fingers, and burying one, long digit into her needy emptiness.

She gasped, arched against his hand, the need-choked sound zinging from her body, begging him to fill her fully. He didn't disappoint. He added another finger to the first, and they glided in and out of her slickness, opening her, readying her to accept the thick hardness tenting his pants.

Her breathing was labored, her breasts falling and rising as if she were out of breath. She bent one knee to open wider and covered his hand with hers to help him pleasure her.

"Nick," she groaned. The one word, his name, was powerful enough to express everything she wanted and needed from him, and she gloried in the knowledge that he could read her body, her mind, so effortlessly.

"Get over here," he growled and hauled her over the gearshift onto his lap, where she straddled him.

He thrust his hands up inside her dress and lifted it, then ripped the side string of her thong and pushed it aside, giving him full access to her wetness. His fingers went back inside her, stroking her. His other hand grabbed her ass and held her close.

The second she unzipped her sleeveless front-zip dress and unhooked her front-clasp bra, his mouth went to her breasts like he was starving for the taste of them. He sucked them, first one, then the other, full mouth, then lips only, then tongue, while she fumbled between their bodies at his pants.

She unbuckled him. Unbuttoned him. Unzipped him. His hips rose so she could shift his pants down. Her hands dove into his boxer briefs and pulled out his cock. It was stiff, wet at the tip, throbbing, and eager to pleasure her.

If there'd been room in her car, if she didn't need

his cock filling her so desperately, she'd have pulled his hardness deep into her mouth and sucked him fast and hard to fill her hungry belly with his cum. Instead, she wrapped her hand around him and stroked, running her thumb over his wet slit.

"Did you miss me?" she asked, her voice husky.

"Fuck, yeah," he said.

"I was talking to him," she said and yanked his cock.

"Here's his answer."

His fingers left her pussy, and with both hands, he grabbed her hips, fingers digging into her flesh to hold her firm. He centered her over him and pulled her down at the same time he thrust up. He went all the way inside her, filling her to the top with his long, thick cock.

The connection ripped her breath away like it always did, and her name slid from his mouth on a long, quiet exhale.

He held still, not moving, his eyes closed. She tried to move, but he held her immobile.

"Wait," he said, his breath rough and shaky, as if the connection had stripped him of his breath, his control, and his senses. Then he released a short, soft sigh, opened his eyes to hers, and moved…slowly. As if he wanted to make each stroke count.

He grinned. "Did you miss me?"

"Every day."

"I was talking to *her*," he said and plunged into her core at the word *her*, his hips leaving the seat to drive deeper.

She snorted a hybrid sigh/laugh. "She says 'less talking, more fucking.'"

At his chuckle, she gripped the seat so she could take more, give more. Her breasts bounced in his face to the rhythm of her rough riding. He moved one hand to her clit and circled it with the tips of his fingers. It thrilled her that he always knew exactly what to do to put out the fire that twisted and burned inside her.

The sounds of their slick skin slapping together, the sounds of their grunts and groans, the scent of their steamy juices, the feel of him so deep and tight inside her sent her over. Her core opened wide, and she let go, grunting like an animal at the release he drew from her.

This! Him. She wanted it. Every day. Every night. Forever.

His rhythm became rough and urgent, demanding. His fingers dug into her ass cheeks. She felt him swelling and tightening with every thrust, and she rocked harder and faster and focused on him, helping him find his release.

"Ahh, baby," he said, a split second before a deep guttural noise exploded from his mouth and he jabbed hard up into her, releasing everything that was him into her body. He plowed into her again and again, giving her even more than she'd asked for, taking what he needed.

Seconds later, they collapsed against each other, their hearts racing, breathing ragged and noisy as their lungs fought to function in the thick, sex-filled air they had created. She melted against his chest, tucked her nose into his neck to pull his scent into her lungs.

This euphoria surrounded them and infused them whenever they were together. It was proof they belonged together.

"That was so good," she murmured into his neck

and nipped it, sucked it, remarking him as hers.

"Just good?" he teased.

She smiled into his satiated eyes and ran her hand across his shirt at his chest, wishing it was his skin. "How would you rate it?"

He sighed deeply. "Fucking awesome."

She laughed. "Fucking awesome it is."

He wrapped his arms around her, holding her close, as if he never wanted to let her go, and kissed her. Her hands raked his hair, holding him close, kissing him back like she didn't want to let him go either. Ever.

Then he pulled back, let his gaze tangle with hers, telling her things she hoped he would say to her later, like, *You're all I want, forever, and I want forever to start now.* He brushed back her hair from her face with his knuckles and kissed her forehead. Her eyes. Her cheeks. Her lips. His tenderness spoke of the deep affection between them.

"I love you, *farolita*," he said.

She released a deep sigh. "Almost as much as I love you."

"More."

She chuckled. "I hate to let you win this argument, but if we don't clean up in another couple of seconds, you're going to have to walk into the restaurant with a big wet spot. And they do have a dress code."

He grabbed a handful of paper napkins from the door pocket. She rose, letting his spent rod slip out of her. He put the napkins between her legs to catch their mingled fluids, and she sat back down on him.

He tasted her nipples again, gently, softly, then hooked her bra. He buried his face in the swells of her breasts, covering them in kisses, licking her freckles, before zipping them away behind her dress. He pulled her close for another few kisses, then helped her clean up, wrapping the wet napkins in another napkin and putting them in the little trash bag in the floorboard. She had changed, had relaxed, but the need for cleanliness was something that would never be exorcised.

She climbed off him, sat back in her seat, and adjusted her dress. Feeling her ripped thong hanging around one thigh, she reached up and pulled it off, then added it to the bag with the napkins.

"Are panties optional at that fancy restaurant you're taking me to?"

"Let's not ask."

He laughed. "Guess I'm going to be buying you another pair of panties this weekend," he said as he tucked his well-spent cock into his underwear.

"Yeah, we're not going to have time to shop this weekend."

"Sounds like you have some interesting things planned for us."

"Don't I always?"

"Always," he said and kissed her.

She started the engine and blasted the heater to smother the chill that had invaded her. Their quickie had been awesome, like he said. Like every single time they made love. But it wasn't enough. And if he couldn't give her more, what would she do? The thought of giving him up ripped the fire from her body and replaced it with ice. She would get answers tonight. If they weren't the answers she needed, she might have to make an unpleasant decision.

Somewhere between the first and second bites of

her salad, she'd realized she couldn't wait any longer to know whether the first day of the rest of her life would start now.

"Nick, last month I applied for a nursing position at the Albuquerque-Downtown Hospital. Two days ago, they offered me the job. I can start as soon as the first of next month. I just have to officially accept it and give my notice here."

Other than a slight rise of one eyebrow, Nick didn't move. Worse, he didn't speak.

Needing to fill the thick silence with anything but his coming words of refusal, she continued her speech. "I need to know whether you're serious about us and are ready to take the next step."

"Serious," he said under his breath, laughed, and shook his head.

"Nick?" she asked, not at all sure what his reaction meant.

He looked at her, the grin still in place that reached his dark eyes, making them sparkle. "Two months ago, I asked a buddy of mine in the Seattle FBI office to keep me in mind if they ever had an opening. Earlier this week he called, saying there was an opening and that he'd put me at the top of the list if I wanted it."

Her heart flipped in her chest that he'd been doing what she'd been doing, planning a path toward a more permanent togetherness.

"Did you want it?" she asked, happiness spreading her mouth into a soft smile.

"I wanted to make sure you wanted me to."

"Do you have a preference?" they said at the same time, drawing a laugh from each other.

"I'm open to discussing it," she said, "but to be

honest, I'm ready to try someplace else, build a life that doesn't include so much of the old one."

"You wouldn't miss your friends? Your job? Your city?"

"I gave it a lot of thought before I applied for the new job."

"I'm sure you did. So, you wouldn't mind if we lived in Albuquerque?" he asked.

"Not if that's where you are," she said. "But there's something I need to know first."

"What's that?"

"Where you see our relationship going."

"Are you asking about commitment?"

"If I move, the main reason is to be with you. So, if I do, I want an exclusive relationship with you. We date only each other. No one else."

He let her words and his impending response hang in the air for so long that each passing second without an answer tied her stomach into a tighter knot.

"That won't work for me, *farolita*," he said finally. "I don't want a girlfriend."

Her stomach dropped to her ankles. She swallowed hard, hoping it would help keep her calm. How had she misread him and the situation so completely? From everything he'd said and done, she'd been convinced he was ready to have something serious with her. So much for taking risks.

"Oh." She eased back, away from him.

He leaned forward, caught her hand, and linked their fingers. "I want a *wife*."

"A wi… What?" The words nearly didn't make it out of her suddenly tight throat.

He took a sip of water and licked his lips. "I was

going to wait until we got to your place to do this, but it seems important that I make my intensions clear, right here, right now."

He stood, stuck his hand into his pocket, and pulled out a diamond ring. Then he dropped to one knee in front of her.

"I love you, Alicia. Join your life with mine. Be my *farolita*, my wife, my only love for the rest of our lives."

Tears welled in her eyes and euphoria filled her body, blocking the many words she wanted to say. So, she answered his question with a simple and heartfelt, "Yes. Yes!"

"You don't need to think about it first?" he teased. "Weigh the pros and cons?"

She chuckled. "Oh, I did that months ago."

"You decided I'm a good risk then?"

Alicia cupped Nick's face in her hands, stared deep into his eyes, all the way to his soul. "The best I've ever had."

He took her left hand, kissed her palm, then slid the ring into place on her finger. To the applause of the diners seated near them, he stood, drew her up into his arms, and kissed her to seal their union.

Epilogue

Nick pulled the SUV to a stop in front of the cabin and killed the engine. Alicia stared out the windshield at the place that held so many good memories—old and new.

The good times of the old life she had lived with Jon remained untouched, preserved. The new life she'd started here with Nick was changing, growing, strengthening every day. She smiled, thinking about all the memories they were going to make over the next two weeks.

Nick took her hand. "Are you glad to be back at your cabin?"

She turned toward him. "Our cabin."

"Our cabin," he said and kissed her. "Let's get our things in."

"Or we could leave our things here and unpack later," she said. "Right now, there's only one thing on my mind."

He grinned. "Mine, too."

They jumped out of the SUV and raced for the cabin. He pulled open the squeaky screen door, and Alicia unlocked the wooden one. Before she could walk in, Nick scooped her up into his arms, stepped through the doorway with her, and carried her to the bedroom.

He set her down on their new bed, then collapsed beside her with a deep sigh. She curled against his side, arm and leg around him, and with a matching sigh, closed her eyes.

They had stayed up until the wee hours of the morning at the wedding reception and gotten up after a couple of hours of sleep to pack for their honeymoon, so they were exhausted. What they needed most was a nap.

But then a terrifying thought came to her, stealing her bliss and popping her eyes open. "Oh, no."

"Hmm?" he mumbled against her hair.

"In our rush to get away, I forgot to pick up my birth control pills from the pharmacy." She tried to get out of bed, but he stopped her and rolled onto her.

"Whoa, where do you think you're going?"

"Nick, we need those pills. I only have enough in my purse for a few days." If the situation weren't so dire, she could laugh at the panic in her voice. "We have to go back to Albuquerque."

"No, we don't." He kissed her again. "We don't need the pills."

"We do unless we're not having sex for the entire time we're here, or you've packed a jumbo-sized box of condoms, or you've changed your mind about arming a baby bomb."

"Oh, we are having sex, Mrs. Navarro. Lots of sex. Lots and lots and lots of sex." He followed each utterance of "sex" with a kiss, to her neck, her face, her mouth. "There's not a single condom anywhere in this cabin. And I'm ready to arm that bomb."

"Whoa." Her hands shifted to his chest to stop his kisses. "I remember you clearly stating, in this very cabin, barely seven months ago, that you aren't daddy material…for many reasons. With a huge emphasis on many."

He grinned. "You must have me confused with some other guy."

She knew he meant Rey Cruz, but the teasing statement didn't negate what Rey had said to her then or what Nick said later when they'd had the official children talk. During the latter conversation, they had agreed to set the decision on the shelf and later bring it down to analyze. So, it was more than surprising, during the first couple of hours of their honeymoon, to hear Nick say he was ready for a child. And now.

She stared at him, trying to translate his words and the emotions on his face, thinking about what this step would mean for them, and wondering what had changed his mind.

"Are you sure about this?" she said. "I thought we'd decided to hold off on discussing it for a few years."

He kissed her forehead. "I want babies with you, *farolita*. And I'm ready to get started."

She raised her eyebrows. "Babies? Plural? What's going on, Navarro? Why are you suddenly so eager to have kids? Don't tell me your mom finally got to you."

"Nope. Yours."

"Liar. My mom would be the last person advising us to have children."

"No lie," he said with a chuckle. "Remember her comment at the reception about not wanting to be called *grandma* if we had kids?"

"Yeah."

"Later that night, she told me she hoped we'd have kids because—and I quote—life conceived in love, born into love, and raised in love are gifts not just to the couple and their families, but to the world. That they bring fresh hope that will make it a better place. As proof, she talked about how much you and I had done to make humanity better and how proud she was of you."

Obviously, her mother had enjoyed one too many refills from the open bar last night. Those sentiments were so unlike her. "So, you're saying my mom made you want kids?"

"She got me thinking. And what I realized is that I want kids, and as soon as possible."

"Why?"

"Because I love you."

"I need more than that."

His face went pensive, like he was searching for the right words to describe how he felt about the subject.

"I didn't want kids before because I hadn't found a woman I loved enough to want to have kids with. I've found that woman. I married that woman. Having kids is…" He ran his hand up her side where the dandelion seeds flew. "Well, it's like this tattoo. We're spreading love into the world through our kids. And God knows the world needs more love."

She'd fallen in love with Rey, then deeper in love with Nick, and now they were a committed, married couple. And if a child wasn't in the picture, she could still be blissfully, completely happy. But the fact that he wanted a child with her was game-changing, she realized as joy suffused her body. Only…she didn't want it right now.

"But I'll love you just as much without kids," he added when she didn't respond. "You know, if you don't want any."

"Nick, I love that you want children with me."

"But…"

"I don't want to share you right now. I want to be greedy. I want to spend our every spare moment together, just the two of us."

"So, are you saying you don't want kids?"

She rolled him off her and immediately rolled onto him, straddling him, assuming her favorite position.

"What I'm saying is that you are and always will be my most important relationship, and I want to devote as much of myself as I can to making it as strong as possible before we decide to share it with a child who will demand our full attention. I don't ever want to take you or what we have for granted."

She slowly rotated her hips on him, the enticing moves intending to excite and expand the bulge in his jeans. "Do you understand?"

His eyes were already going hazy at her targeted movements on him, but he responded with grunt that sounded a lot like, "Yeah."

She pulled her sundress off. Before it hit the floor, Nick had unhooked her bra and pulled it off. She took his hands and put them on her breasts, her hands over his.

"How about we wait until next year to start trying," she said.

"Next year," he repeated, strumming her nipples with his thumbs and arching his hips up against her.

"And we'll go back to Albuquerque to get the pills."

"Tomorrow," he said.

"Or the next day," she said.

"Yeah," he grunted.

"Do you know what this position is?" she said.

"Yes, ma'am," he said in a low drawl. "I'm mighty familiar with it. Your favorite, as I recollect."

"Yes, well, it's also one of the *least* effective positions for baby-making. So, if you're serious about wanting to make a baby, we're going to have to choose another position. And practice. A lot. But it's a sacrifice I'm willing to make."

Knowing him as she did now, the light in his eyes and grin on his face told her that he, too, was willing, but what he said was, "How do you know it's the least effective?"

She scoffed. "I'm a nurse." She scooted back and put her hands to work undoing his jeans, then pulled them and his boxer briefs down far enough to release his growing hardness. "We know things. Lots of things. Especially about anatomy." She wrapped her hands around that hardness, stroking. "And how it works."

"I appreciate your sacrifice, Nurse Alicia," he said, his voice low and husky.

"Show me how much you appreciate it," she said.

He ripped the sides of her thong and sent the pieces flying across the room.

Positioning her body over his rigid cock, she slid down onto it, taking him deep inside her, gasping at the pleasure she had enjoyed from day one with this man—her patient, her lover, her husband, and potentially the father of her children.

"You didn't say what the *best* baby-making position is," he said, gripping her hips with his hands and increasing his speed to match her need.

She grinned. "*Your* favorite position."

He laughed, and the rumbling vibrations rippled through her, adding to her pleasure. He cupped her face, fingers in her hair, and pulled her down for another kiss.

"With you, *farolita*, they're all my favorite," he whispered against her mouth.

"Same here," she whispered before doubling down on the highly practiced movements that reminded her how lucky she was that fate had sent this man to her cabin, giving them both a life-changing miracle on the mountain to help them accomplish their most important mission—finding love again.

A word about the author…

Sophia Ryan is the author of a more than a dozen steamy contemporary romance novels and short stories. She writes the kind of romances she likes to read, where heat sizzles off the page and the characters always get their happy ending. When she's not writing about passion, she's indulging in it—yoga, hiking, laughing with friends over hot chile and cold beer, and being lazy and crazy with the family. A corporate writer by training and a storyteller at heart, Sophia makes her home in the American Southwest.

~*~

Visit Sophia at
http://sophiaryan.webs.com